MISCONCEPTIONS

By

Blu Daniels

MISCONCEPTIONS

Copyright © 2014 by Blu Daniels

All Rights Reserved

Dedication

"This one right here goes out to all the baby's mamas, mamas...Mamas, mamas, baby mamas, mamas..."

Ms. Jackson, OutKast

Preface

Dear Me,

    According to the undeniably accurate resource that is Wikipedia, 54% of all pregnancies are unplanned and unexpected. A whopping 15% of those pregnancies arise despite the "proper" use of preventative measures, such as condoms and other forms of birth control. Condoms have a 95% effective rate against pregnancy; the patch a 98% effective rate. If used together a less than 5% chance of conceiving.

    Further, there have only been twenty-two accounted cases of quadruplet births in North America. Only four of those were conceived without the use of fertility treatments, a probability of 1 out of 800,000 plus pregnancies. Thus, the probability of conceiving minus the unlikelihood of multiples equals my chances of becoming pregnant with quadruplets with the world's biggest asshole falling into the 0.000001 percentile, a one in one trillion gazillion chance.

    Congratulations! You are now a statistic! You win your very own Wikipedia page as your pregnancy rates second to the Immaculate Conception.

    Love,
    The Virgin Mary

Conception

I am the world's biggest punk.

"No!"

I moaned, forcing my way out of a kiss that could make any woman soak right through her jeans. But nothing stopped him, as his thick lips made their way down my neck.

"No... I can't. We shouldn't," I begged and sat up on my elbows at the end of the unmade bed he pinned me on. He stood up, straddling my dangling legs, and adjusted himself.

"Ok," he said with a patronizing devilish smirk. He knew he had me. We stared at each other; the room infused with his scent and my mouth watered.

"I only invited you over here to say goodbye. Not for all...this."

Frantic, I stood up trying to gain better control of the situation and caught my pants just before they fell to my ankles. I didn't even realize he unbuttoned them.

Damn, he's good.

"You act like I'm never gonna see you again or something," he said, kicking one of the storage boxes by his feet that contained my well used MBA books. His seductive voice echoed in the emptiness of the master bedroom of my once much lived in apartment.

I can't fall for this, not today. And he knows good and damn well he has no intentions on visiting me in New York.

"Don't do that. Don't give me hope like that. This is for the best. A clean break."

He shrugged with a smug smile.

"If that's how you feel."

Damn, he's gorgeous.

"Well, I guess that's it then," I said with a forced grin, my tone hinting it was time to wrap up our cryptic conversation before the situation spiraled out of control.

Really, before I lose control.

"I guess so."

"I'll...I'll walk you downstairs."

I gulped and slid by his unmoving body, stumbling over my own feet. His sultry eyes following my every step.

"Okay."

Zipping up his hoodie, cooler than frost, he sauntered toward the bedroom door, with me only a few steps behind him.

"Oh wait...my keys!"

It would be just my luck to get locked out on my last night in Washington D.C. My back was only turned for a moment to reach for the keychain on my nightstand when the room went black.

Uh oh.

I spun around to protest but his hands cupped my face, lips locking their place on mine like a muzzle. He engulfed me as I mercilessly tried to push him towards the door. He humored my feeble defenses, knowing he was much stronger. His hungry hands kept their place around my back while my hands yoked at his shirt, pulling him closer.

"No, we can't—"

"You know you want to," he breathed into my ear and my body quivered.

Alert! Alert! Abort mission. Retreat!

He stopped short, kicking the bedroom door closed behind him without skipping a beat, trapping us. More like trapping me. I gripped the back of his neck as he pinned me to the adjacent wall.

"We...shouldn't...do this."

I tried to pry myself away, but he tasted so good I couldn't let go. I hit my fist against his chest but he ignored my weak attempts to fight him off and held me tighter.

"Just one last time," he whispered in my ear as his lips sucked on my collarbone just as his hands made their way up my shirt. Tickling...grabbing...

WHY can't I resist him?

"Come on...just one more time."

And just like that, I was hypnotized.

My hands reached for his waist and tore at his zipper. He unfastened my jeans and had them at my ankles before I could blink. Then he lifted me up, slammed me on the wall, and wrapped my limp legs around his waist. Unnecessarily rough, just the way I hated to admit I liked it.

And there goes my will.

I cupped his face as we kissed like we were starved for each other. In one single movement, he slammed me on to the unmade bed and we fought with our remaining clothes. The sound of the condom wrapper tearing was my last chance to escape but I only gulped.

Yup, world's biggest punk right here.

He slid in hastily and my once unwilling mouth dropped at the sensation.

"I'm gonna make you wish you never decided to move back to New York," he warned as he plunged deeper into me. I gripped the mattress pad to keep myself from screaming and waking the neighbors, though my steady pants were loud enough.

I cried out as he flipped me on my stomach and laid on top of me. My back arched as he slid in from behind, at first slowly but then quickened. I bit into the pad and pushed at his thigh. The poor bed wailed beneath our scrimmage. Sex with us was like a street brawl.

He grabbed a fist full of my hair, tugging it as his lips moved closer to my ear. The winded chuckle from his lips was menacing. It was hot. He was hot.

"Say it...you know you want to. Just say it," he breathed.

No, I won't let him win. Not this time.

"Say my name. Go on, say it!"

I groaned as he lifted me off of the bed, holding me mid-air as my legs locked around his slim waist. His thrusts forced my cries out, I could barely breathe, insane lust suffocating me.

"Why...are...you...fighting...me Alex?"

Oh, is that my name? 'Cause I definitely forgot it.

Feeling myself about to fall, I gripped his shoulders and he dropped us back onto the bed, never skipping a beat.

"Oh God," I heard myself moan. My leg started that uncontrollable twitch from the sensation building inside me.

His eyes locked with mine, his mouth twisted into an evil grin. He knew what was coming next. The harsh pants spat out of my mouth and echoed in the empty room.

"I'm...I...I'm cumming!" I screamed, throwing my head back in release. He held his position, letting me pulsate around him.

God I love him... NO, I hate him. Wait, no I—

"Whose is it?" he asked with that cocky smile I hated yet loved.

"Yours," I mumbled, feeling lightheaded.

"You gonna mess with any other dudes up there?"

My head snapped up.

Weird. He's never asked THAT before.

"No!"

The words he wanted to hear were spewing out of me like water from an open fire hydrant. He gave me a sharp look.

Why did he say that? Does that mean he wants to be with me? Like exclusively?

I closed my eyes and painted a memory. Listened to the sound of his heavy breathing, smelled the sweat off our bodies, savored the taste of his tongue. The one thing I would miss about D.C was the one thing I hated the most.

He was my Bad Habit, my only vice. The one thing I couldn't shake no matter how many times I tried. My need for him took over my common sense and logical reasoning. He was an addiction. Cigarettes, alcohol, even crack had nothing on him.

And even as he cums inside me, and the corner of his mouth slips into a satisfied smirk, I knew one thing for sure.

Bad habits never go away easily.

One Month

I jolted up from my X-rated dream, covered in my own post-copulate sweat. Tangled in sheets, I whipped around in search of the knocking interrupting my porn in the making.

"Hey dork, you up yet?" Chris's voice called from the other side.

I took a quick panic-stricken survey of the room. No, I was not in a fuck contest with Bad Habit. I was alone in my childhood bedroom, two hundred and thirty eight miles from him, and my teenaged brother was about to walk in on me and my soaking wet sheets.

Aren't I too old to be having wet dreams?

"Yeah, I'm up!" I shouted, hoping it would deter him from busting into my room like the little know-it-all usually did.

"You left the TV on again. You know there's support groups for your type of addiction!"

I grabbed the remote and turned off *The Notebook* DVD that was still playing.

"Shut up punk!"

Did I mention I love my brother?

When I was fully back to reality, I raced around the house in a superwoman blur, attacking the shower and gulping down two bowls of Honey Nut Cheerios. I threw on my new crème power suit with a white button down oxford to match my new Christian

Louboutins and stared into the full-length mirror. I looked hot, in the professional-not-trying-to-be way. Just like Michelle Obama, my shero, the archetype of style and grace, definition of fierce, and my best friend (well, in my head).

It was day one at the ultimate dream gig. It took my entire final semester to land the New Media Manager position at Cloverstein Media Group. It's the type of job that you give up your first-born child for. I'm a giver. I'm also a Queen's girl. Girl spelled with an "i" not a "u". That hood gurl left back in high school with my Jordans, tight jeans, and hair gel. Although my attitude had miraculously survived my transformation, now I was a girl with a degree, a briefcase, and a blowout.

Since moving back to New York, I was camping out at my folk's place until I found a suitable apartment closer to work, preferably one with a deep walk-in closet and stainless steel appliances I would never use. Well, I guess I shouldn't be too hard on myself. I'm an expert at boiling water for Velveeta shells and cheese.

My insanely over-protective mother was in her favorite room in the house, pulling out a tray of fresh buttermilk biscuits. Never the canned stuff since she believed those give you cancer. She wished me luck before I ran out of the front door of our cramped two-story townhouse, one of a dozen on our block.

"Hey baby! Two sugars and cream?"

Ricky's was the Grand Central Station of the hood. The stereotypical always-crowded bodega was a block away from the subway and had the best coffee drug money could buy. Ricky knew how I liked mine without me uttering a word.

"Make that four sugars today. And you got any dollar glaze?"

"Careful Mama," Ricky teased in his thick Puerto Rican accent. "Your ass getting a little thick."

I smiled and stuck my butt out. "More cushion for the pushing! How's the wife?"

"Oy, a pain! I blame you for making me marry her."

"What can I say? I'm in love with love!"

He laughed. "Aye! I see your girl's on the cover again."

Michelle was front page of the New York Times, on stage with her hubby, Barack. She was wearing a tangerine long sleeved number and caramel kitten heels, sophisticated yet classy. My God, I've wanted to raid her closet since junior year of undergrad. I'd wear her tube socks if I had the chance. I turned to grab another paper for my collection and tripped over a doublewide stroller, splashing coffee on my suede pumps. The joyriding toddler looked at me as if I was Medusa. I grabbed a stack of napkins and began to blot the stain.

Jeez! Chicks seriously need a license to drive those contraptions.

As I struggled frantically to save my shoes, I was suffocated by the overpowering smell of Blue Magic hair grease. The local corner staple, Larry, stepped way deep in my personal space.

"Hey sexy! Looking fine in those red bottoms."

Larry was about fifty with graying cornrows, a gold tooth, dressed in baggy jeans and a squirrel fur vest.

Swoon.

"So Ma, when you gonna let me take you out?"

"Hmm...I don't know. Why don't you wait on this exact corner and see? You seem pretty good at that."

His glare was classic. I shrugged since there was no other appropriate response and I didn't believe in disrespecting my elders.

"Fucking bitch," he grumbled.

"What was that Charlie Wilson? I didn't quite hear you."

Ricky cackled. If Larry wasn't so dark, he would've turned red.

"It's why bitches like you are single now! Don't know a good…"

"Larry, really? Come on. You've been hitting on me since I was fourteen. Statutory rape aside, you and me…ain't gonna happen."

Larry fixed his mouth to reply but nothing came out.

"Don't think too hard on a clever response. Let's just call this a win-win situation."

I slipped Ricky a tip, leaving Larry speechless before heading to the subway.

It was great being back in New York, close to my batty family and the insanity of the alphanumeric train system. I didn't even mind sitting next to the sleeping homeless man carrying a fully trimmed plastic Christmas tree on the express train in the middle of May. I was home.

Bad Habit clung to my brain like a day old migraine. He was exactly his namesake, an ugly habit, like nail biting or nose picking. Funny how I was headstrong about nail polish and facials but weak when it came to him. Why? Because he was like sex on a platter. A toffee complexion and thick horse-like hair groomed with meticulous precision, just like he dressed. He was slender, strong, brilliant, articulate, in short, damn near perfect. Two inches short of being Greek Godlike, otherwise known as "not my type." I was never into guys that were too attractive for their own good.

Don't get me wrong, I'm pretty. At least that's what Mom has spent the last twenty-five years trying to convince me. Two shades lighter than a manila envelope with brownies for eyes, I have my mother's slender curves and my father's long, kinky hair that perms and prayer have helped me maintain beautifully. But my aversion to proper upkeep (i.e. exercise) and lack of stripper booty leaves me nowhere near the video vixen type of girl you'd expect him to be with.

Bottom line, no one knew the real Bad Habit. Not like I did. Imagine being treated like a personal call girl for the one person that everyone liked. It's as if your heart was crushed by that Jesus Christ superstar quarterback the entire school body worshipped.

Yeah, I was that loser. I mean Mary Magdalene. I mean girl.

***

"Hey, Mom? What should I take for a stomach ache?"

I was blessing my new office overlooking Bryant Park with eye-watering farts. The mixture of my morning cereal and the smell of piss on the subway caught up with me and I hurled chunks in the lobby bathroom as soon as I walked in. I caught a couple of side-eyes, but they didn't know how passionate I felt about my cereal. Bulimia was not an option.

Three hours later, the cauldron in my stomach was bubbling something fierce.

I've never had gas like this before.

It took everything in me to make it through morning training without melting the paint off the walls.

"Pepto-Bismol...ginger ale I guess. Why, what's wrong, you nervous?"

"No, I don't know. Maybe the milk in my cereal was spoiled?"

"I just bought that milk yesterday!"

I giggled.

The nerve! How dare I insult her shopping techniques! I love my Mommy.

I tested the windows to see if they would open.

If someone walks in here and lights a match, this building is done for.

"Ma, I gotta go. I have a meeting in twenty minutes."

We said our goodbyes just as I heard a knock at the door.

Aw hell.

"Come in," I croaked.

Claire, the VP of my new division entered. Claire was like that aunt you had that was stuck back in some pubescent time and unaware of her inappropriateness. Her oatmeal colored mini skirt suggested thirty, but her crow's feet and spider veins suggested fifty. From the twitch on her cinnamon face, she was not immune to the Hiroshima-sized stink bomb I dropped but she held her composure.

"Hi...Alex," she struggled, like she was trying not to breathe in too deep. "I want to introduce you to the head of our ad sales team."

In walked my funk's next victim.

"This is Ralphie Saunders," she announced, as if he was the king of the seventeenth floor. From the way she eyed him, it seemed she wanted more than just a sales report out of him, but Ralphie didn't seem to notice. In fact, he ignored the blinding smell and greeted me with a caressing handshake.

"Pleasure to meet you, Alex," he said as I slipped out of his sweaty grip, hiding my hands behind my back to keep him from reaching for them again.

Yuck!

"Nice to meet you too."

"Looks like we'll be working together a lot in the next couple of months."

I winced a smile.

Cloverstein Media Group created promo packages, commercials, and trailers for entertainment networks. I was hired to oversee their new Digital Media Division. My job was simple; manage workflow, employees, and budgets all while keeping our clients happy.

"Ralphie will be working with you to create the new promos for the Raven and Specter accounts. Oh, what am I saying, you probably know nothing about that yet. Sorry Ralphie, she's a fresh MBA."

"Actually, I read the files this morning. I took a look at the Raven's budget and called down to graphics to schedule a brainstorming meeting. There's plenty of opportunity to create a new brand for them with the monies allocated. I'm also having lunch at Butter with the reps from Specter tomorrow and scheduled a focus group to identify the flaws in their ad campaign. They seemed pretty happy with my proposal and we'll certainly be on schedule for delivery by the end of this month."

Claire's eyes widened and I resisted brushing off my shoulder. Just like Michelle, always two steps ahead and fabulous.

"Well, you certainly are off to a great start!"

We laughed a polite corporate laugh, giving Ralphie an excuse to touch my shoulder.

"You know, we should meet outside the office sometime to discuss our new re-launch. I bet you have some great ideas."

The way his eyes ripped off my shirt made my stomach cough up another bubble. I feigned another laugh and checked for Claire's reaction, but she was too busy checking out the bulging package in his too tight khaki pants.

***

Three draining meetings later, I started working on my flow chart. It's a color coordinated weekly itinerary, mapping out a detailed schedule on a large dry erase board. It's something I've done since I was a kid, even on chalkboards. I never missed snack time and my toys got equal amounts of attention. Only I could find a way to micro-manage myself when insurance doesn't cover OCD.

I had just put on my finishing touches when one of the fresh picked interns from accounting stopped by with a cost report. She stood in the doorway.

"Jesus, you even scheduled potty breaks!"

Potty breaks? Who says that?

"Well, it'll keep everyone on a tight schedule," I defended. "Anyone who dares to defy it should expect water torture."

The blonde ex-cheerleader stared like I was speaking Japanese.

"Well, I think it's a tad bit over-compulsive. Don't you think?"

She chuckled and shoved the folder in my hand. I held my breath and counted backwards from ten, but I still couldn't shake the feeling that I needed to karate chop her in the throat.

I didn't know they were paying you to think, I thought they were paying you to input freaking numbers.

Her faced turned up as if she could smell my farts from earlier. *Wait, did I say that out loud?*

"Oh, wait...sorry I—"

"Whatever. People would be crazy to follow this."

She stormed out with a huff. First day and I was already making enemies. It's hard to be diplomatic as Michelle when you have a diva's temper.

Perfect time to take a lunch break and a short stroll down 5th Avenue for my favorite pastimes: ice cream and shopping.

The Bank of Alex was a bit low on funds for Saks and Louis Vuitton but that never stopped me from window shopping and daydreaming. I picked up a vanilla gelato and an *In Style* from Barnes and Nobles then strolled down the heavy populated block.

There's something magical about ice cream. The taste, the cool sensation, I even loved it when it melted into a thick soup-like milkshake. My father always said my first steps were towards the freezer. I thanked big baby Jesus every day that I'm not one of those retarded lactose intolerant people. I'd be devastated!

My Crackberry buzzed. It was a picture from my best friend, Kennedy, with her new flavor of the week, a delicious NFL player, on the beach in Miami. I sent her back a text.

Married?

Her response: **Irrelevant :-)**

Ken was my kick ass sidekick, my ace boon coon. We went through high school and college together, convinced that the world was full of idiots meant for us to laugh at together. We shared the same taste in every arena but men.

Dick size?

Her response: **Award winning :-)**

She was Hollywood glam. Petite but curvy, with perfect olive skin and hair that was always in the latest style. Probably could have any man she chose, but she preferred the fuck them and leave them approach. Dependency, on any level, was not her thing.

Another two emails with invites to sponsored liquor events. I forward them to my crew and made plans to meet for sushi. A short night with a lot of drinking and delicious food, another one of my favorite pastimes.

There was a new boutique on the corner of 5th and 47th. I notice these type of things because I've had 5th Avenue memorized since I was twelve, dreaming of days where I would drive from my house in the Hamptons in my turbo speed cherry red Mercedes Benz for weekend shopping sprees. Now that I was older, with a six-figure salary, the dream was a quarter sleeve length away.

The pink and yellow awning of the store was jarring, like Rainbow Bright threw up chunks on my favorite block, but the window display was gorgeous. The headless mannequin was fitted in the most exquisite strapless off-white mermaid wedding dress I had ever seen. Silk organza with crystal beading around the bust and waist, it flowed into a long train that wrapped around the floor like a large rose petal.

It'll be perfect with my grandmother's pearls and my Tiffany princess cut solitaire diamond engagement ring.

I imagined myself walking down the aisle in a dimly lit church adorned with white grandiflora roses. My long hair spiraling down my back as I head towards the faceless man of my dreams. Probably some well off Wall Street trader or plastic surgeon. Of course, Michelle would be there. The reception would be held under huge tents in Central Park, walls dripping with ivy and sparkling lights. We would have prime rib followed by a six-tier butter cream cake. The grand finale, fireworks over the East River. The entire event would be flawless. Marrying my perfect man, in my perfect dress, in my oh-so perfect wedding.

That'll make Bad Habit jealous.

The cup of ice cream fell from my hands, zapping me out of my daydreaming.

Shit! What in the world made me think of HIM?

I sulked at my ice cream, dead on the concrete and turned back towards the office, taking one last glimpse of my future dress.

Someday.

***

I took a quick time check as I ironed my jeans. Forty-five minutes before my date with Ralphie and I was not nearly as excited as I should've been. After four weeks of his incessant advances, Claire finally convinced me to go out with him, more so she could live her cougaresque lifestyle vicariously through me. There was nothing special about Ralphie except the fact that he was the epitome of a cheese ball. The prime example of that high school dork all grown up, living a lavish lifestyle off his computer millions, assuming it made him an instant chick magnet and no one ever told him otherwise. An indication he had no real friends in the world. I was itching to tell him that the crushed velvet blazer and faded stunner sunglasses were a tad bit much for casual Friday and that he actually needed real muscles for that tight fitting V-neck tee. But then that would require me having to hear his nasal voice as he spit out more unnatural sounding slang. He sounded like an eighty-year-old grandma saying 'word up' for the first time.

We didn't have much in common, but I welcomed the distraction. I needed a replacement, a new fantasy to take over the ones of Bad Habit. Four weeks since I left D.C. and he hadn't called once.

Am I surprised? Not at all.

He barely called when we lived a mile from each other.

The actual status of our year and a half long relationship was still under negotiation. Ok, so maybe "relationship" is the wrong word to use. Yes, we were sleeping together, but I never intended for it to be a strictly dickly fling; of course, I wanted more. But after discovering a well-hidden secret and being disrespected on multiple occasions, our relationship dwindled to nothing but jump-off status, or what I like to call, a permanent booty-call. Our arguments, epic. No matter how many times I swore him off, a week would go by, and I would be right back in his bed, screaming his name.

Though I finally put states between us, I still wanted him to want me. Nothing like an ex calling to stroke your bruised ego.

Jeez, I'm pathetic.

My Crackberry buzzed. A text from Kennedy.

Aye! What ya doing?

Getting ready for date my with the mouth breather.

Jesus be a Listerine strip!

LOL!

I threw the phone on the bed and stretched into my long navy blue tunic top to hide my rapidly developing gut. Evidently, one-month home with my mother's cooking had added at least five sagging pounds to my petite frame. I planned on wearing my dark blue skinny jeans with my chocolate suede flats and a pink chunky necklace, the one outfit I didn't feel I was wasting on Ralphie. I slid my feet in and tugged the jeans up until they came to an abrupt halt at my thighs.

Uh oh.

I gave them another tug but they only budged slightly. Not a chance in hell they would make it to my waist.

Ok, got to cut out the late night ice cream.

I tossed the jeans and pulled out the next pair.

"Ow!"

It was an unfamiliar struggle. I sucked in my gut and looked down. The button was nowhere near the intended destination.

Jeez. And those Hostess cupcakes.

Laying back on the bed, I sucked in my breath, determined.

"Mom!" I called, hearing her walk past my room.

"What's wrong?" She came in with her usual worried eyes behind her bifocals.

"Help me put my jeans on!"

She snickered. The sight of me sprawled on the bed wrestling with myself was amusing.

"Well, why don't you just put on another pair?"

"No they're gonna fit. Just help me!"

"OK! Boy, have you been cranky lately."

True, I had been a grumpy pants for the last couple of weeks but I chalked up it to PMS and told everyone to just blame Mother Nature if they their feelings had been hurt by my outbursts.

"Sorry Mom. I didn't mean it. Can you help? Please?"

She sighed the way mothers do before the event leading up to the 'I told you so' speech and hovered over me.

"Okay, what do you want me to do?"

"Hold these together and I'll zip it," I said, while holding my breath.

She chuckled again as she proceeded to struggle with the button while I pulled at the zipper.

"I don't think it's gonna—"

"Just hold it MOM!"

With brutal force, the button secured and I eased the zipper up. She stood back and quickly covered her mouth, hiding a devilish grin.

"What's wrong?" I asked, peering down to try to get a better look at my condition.

"There's no way you're gonna be able to sit up in those," she said before breaking out into a hysterical hyena-like laughter followed by a snort. I frowned and sat up in spite of her. The jeans pinched my stomach like a mean Grandma as a muffin top of flab formed over them, the button screaming in agony. I forced a fake smile.

"It's fine Mom," I croaked. Even breathing the response was painful. She struggled to compose her giggles.

Defiant as always, I reached for my shoes on the floor and the piercing sound of splitting fabric echoed in the room.

That did it for my mother.

***

I remember a time when dating was easy for me. Dudes were lining up and down the block just to take me to the corner and back. Flowers delivered to my chemistry class in high school, walks through snowstorms to bring me late night dinners in college, personal chauffeurs in grad school. It wasn't that I was using them ('use' is such a strong and nasty word). I was just giving them what they wanted, which was me. Now, one year later, I regret all the men I let slip through my fingers, blew off for the next, or was just plain bored with, stupidly believing there were plenty of fish in the sea. Because around twenty-five, the harsh reality that every black woman faces is we don't live in the sea. We live in a fish tank. Options are brutally limited.

And Ralphie was one of those malnourished goldfish you win at the street fair.

"I had a really nice time tonight," Ralphie cooed inches from my face.

We were parked in front of my house after a peculiar evening at Duvet, one of the hottest clubs in the city, where he paraded me around his pretentious and equally geeky friends. Okay, it wasn't that bad. Ralphie did treat me like a princess. I felt guilty and sorry for him all at the same time.

"God, it's hot!"

I unbuttoned the light sweater covering the only thing in the house that I could fit, a floral dress I borrowed from my mother. I was boiling the entire night, a change from my usual frigid condition. I've been known to wear wool sweaters in August. But that didn't stop Ralphie from pressing against me in the tight quarters of his BMW.

"You know, I can really see a future with us."

Yeah, I bet.

"Oh really. That's...nice."

"I'll be honest, I'm living the single life right now. But I can see myself settling down soon."

Settling with whom?

He brushed my hair back off my shoulder, exposing my neck.

"You know, I always wanted kids with good hair."

"Yeah, I don't want kids. Not for me. But good luck with that."

He was eyeing my lips like he was preparing for target practice.

"I bet I can change your mind."

Is this fool serious? I don't feel THAT guilty.

He leaned in closer, wrapping his arm around my back. I tried to figure out a way to reject him without using mace.

Oh God, he smells like teen body spray. I'm gonna be nauseous.

I regretted not moving away faster the moment his chapped lips wrapped around mine. He engulfed me, ravenously kissing me like he was afraid to stop. My head thudded against the window as he forced himself upon me. He was bad kisser. This only added to the many strikes against him.

There was a sharp pinch on my left breast, like a needle stabbing my nipple. My eyes flew open and I shoved him away. He fumbled back onto his seat, wild-eyed and confused.

"What! What happened?" he asked frantically.

I cupped my left boob.

"Why did you grab me like that?" I said, trying to catch my breath.

"Alex, I barely touched you!"

I crossed my arms over my chest then yelped. The needle was on my other boob.

"Ow!" I sucked in air between my teeth.

Oh no! Save the tay-tas!

My breasts were sore and swollen, like he had tried to twist them off in some satanic ritual.

"Sorry, I...must be getting my period or something."

"Um...oh," he mumbled. We sat in awkward silence while I caressed myself with Ralphie stealing glances.

Figures the pervert would be turned on. This confirms the likelihood of a large amount of porn saved on his computer. Watching a girl feel herself up in his obnoxious automobile, a dream come true.

His eyebrow arched up and he cautiously leaned toward me.

Is he seriously thinking of trying to kiss me? Again!

Nausea returned in full force. The two bowls of nuts I devoured by myself at the party rushed into my throat.

"I...I need some air!"

Frantic, I fumbled with the controls on the dashboard. But the moment I took a deep breath of the forced air is when the stench of his drug store cologne hit my throat.

I hurled like an inebriated college freshman, all over his German wood-grain dashboard.

Two Months

"Are you ok?"

"Yeah...I'm fine," I coughed.

"No you're not, Honey. You just puked in front of Bergdorf's. The fashion police give summons for that," Claire said as she handed me a tissue to wipe the chunks off my chin.

With one last spit, I slammed the cab door shut and looked at the driver.

"You can go now."

The African driver eyed me again, fearing I'd barf in the backseat, forcing him out of business for the day.

"Go!"

He jumped and stepped on the gas. The cab smelled like spoiled raw chicken and old wet socks. Though the stomach bug I'd had for at least two weeks left me queasy and exhausted, it did nothing to my sense of smell but enhance it. I was like a female Wolverine. The night before, I walked in and could tell exactly what my brother had for lunch from across the room.

Due to my weak stomach, Claire and I were running late to a business lunch at Ocean Grill on the Upper West Side. I had already prayed twice to the porcelain gods before even making it to work.

"Late night?" Claire smirked and turned off the taxi video.

I looked at my reflection in the rearview mirror and saw the face of a walking corpse in need of an undertaker. My wrap dress was cutting off circulation and my pumps had an excessive amount of foot cleavage. I couldn't keep down toast, yet the weight gain was a vicious demon.

"Ha, I wish. I haven't been to a party in weeks. I even missed this crucial Tory Burch sample sale this morning. I'm just...exhausted."

Claire nodded and rolled up the window, trapping us in the stuffy car. This was our fourth client lunch together and I was a little annoyed about having a babysitter. I impressed all of my prospective clients and superiors by establishing new protocols to fit each company's needs. I created detailed delivery schedules and assigned new responsibilities to my staff that made the entire team more efficient. I even saved Cloverstein thousands of dollars by catching a fatal accounting error, solving a potentially detrimental work crisis with ease. I was a rock star!

Now if I could only get rid of this fucking stomach virus.

I'd go to the doctor, but at Cloverstein all new hires were contracted under a temporary 90-day probationary period until they were cleared with Human Resources. Being on probation means no insurance. And I wasn't about to waste my shopping money on frivolous matters like health.

Clutching my weak stomach, I dug in my Marc Jacobs tote and pulled out a bottle of water, gulping it down like I had no home training. My unknown condition also left me unquenchably thirsty.

Such an embarrassment. Michelle would never let anyone see her sweat or puke. Claire stared at me with a slight flicker in her eyes, as if she recognized something. She had seen me puke on a couple of occasions after business lunches and offered to reassign some of my projects until I felt up to par, but I declined. I wasn't the type of person who asked for or accepted handouts. In fact, it was almost impossible for me to admit when I needed help. Call me prideful, but help taints my victories.

"So, why do you look so beat? What kept you up last night?" She asked with a devilish grin. I was in no mood for girl talk, especially with my boss, but with the cab in motion, there was no escape.

I opened my purse and pulled out the new beauty arsenal I picked up from Sephora. Heavy concealer, dark bronzer, jet-black eyeliner, and Vaseline for my cracking lips. My eyes looked sunken, not the ones you would expect on a person who just had ten hours of sleep.

"Well, I keep having this strange dream," I said, spreading the concealer over the potholes under my eyes while the cab cut through Central Park.

"About what?"

"Fish actually. I was having a dream about fish. It wasn't just one fish, more like a school of fish floating around me. So many that I couldn't break through them."

My eyes shifted from my mirror to the empty water bottle. Thirsty again, I dug through my bag and pulled out another two water bottles, barely stopping to breathe between my gasping chugs. I turned to Claire. She stared at me with this large, goofy smirk plastered across her face.

"I knew it."

"Knew what?" I asked after my last swallow.

"The throwing up, the water, the constant fatigue, dreams about fish...so when did you find out you were pregnant?"

I feign a laugh. The cab driver's head popped up.

This chick can't be serious.

"Claire, I'm not pregnant. Don't be ridi—"

"So when was your last period?"

The interrogator smiled while I tried to calculate, remembering the last time being right around the same time new *Grey's Anatomy* episodes started airing. Bad Habit just passed the bar and was out celebrating. I wasn't invited.

"New Year's, but that really doesn't—"

"New Year's! Honey, we're in June! How far along are you?"

I prayed the car would slow down enough for me to tuck and roll out. But, as if he read my mind, the driver double locked the doors. Trapped.

"Don't be ridiculous Claire. I'm not pregnant!"

Wait, did I just call my boss ridiculous?

"I have an extremely irregular cycle. I can go months without a period. It's sort of a gift and a curse, but no need to register at Babies-R-Us."

"Sure, sure. But have you ever gone six months without one while getting seasick in a cab and dreaming about fish? When's the last time you had sex?"

That I could remember without question. The erotic memory of Bad Habit thrusting me against the wall flashed into my head. I remembered every scorching detail of every sexual encounter with Bad Habit. The 'v' his ab muscles made towards his dick, the way he yanked back my hair and sucked on my ear, the way he'd grip my ankles together in the air...

Oh yes. I remember EVERY detail.

I shifted in my seat, wincing at the memories, controlling the need to touch myself in front of my superior.

"Three months ago, the day before I left D.C. But what do fish have to do with anything?"

She sighed, satisfied that she solved the mystery.

"Fish are a sign, honey. When women dream about fish, they are either pregnant or someone around them is. And since I had my tubes tied when I was thirty-five, I'm pretty sure it's not me. Don't believe me if that's easier for you. But I would go to the doctor, maybe just to check out your...sudden nausea."

She grinned as the cab pulled up in front of Ocean and climbed out, leaving me alone with my thoughts, my sore boobs, and the cab fare.

***

Sore boobs, puking, weight gain...last period in January.

I was pacing in my office, downing spoonfuls of Ben and Jerry's while listing my symptoms over and over again. The gift and the curse was haunting me.

No way. It's impossible!

It took a minute to realize I was scraping the bottom of an empty cup and digesting spoonfuls of air. Begrudgingly, I raced out to the corner pharmacy and picked up a home pregnancy test. It burned a hole in my purse as I walked back into the building, headed straight to the restroom, and slipped into the farthest stall. Not bothering with the directions, I ripped open the box and took out the first test. A pencil shaped piece of plastic would be responsible for determining my future. That made the test seem even more ridiculous.

Besides Bad Habit's perfect condom usage, I wore a contraceptive patch. It was far easier than the pill and less harmful than the shot. Some people are afraid of heights, spiders, and serial killers; I just don't do needles. When I was seven, my parents had to buy handcuffs for doctor's visits, which still didn't stop me. There were a several police reports of a little brown-skinned girl in a smock, running barefoot into traffic, leading me to hate doctors as much as I hate knock-off bags.

I blessed the stick, placed it on top of the toilet paper dispenser, and pulled out my cell phone to clock the three minutes needed. Two blue lines, pregnant, one blue line, not pregnant.

Having irregular periods left me downright un-dateable at times. Guys were terrified at the slightest chance of becoming a father in college, as much as I tried to convince them it was a simple fluke. Bad Habit, on the other hand, never seemed to mind or maybe never really cared. He was apathy personified.

This is ridiculous. I'm letting that old broad get to me.

I grabbed the unnecessary test to trash it until a splash of color caught my attention. Two blue lines appeared within the first minute.

Hmm...strange. Must be defective.

I tossed the test in the disposal box and took out the next one.

Best two out of three.

Two minutes later, two blue lines appeared. My heart stopped beating. I hit my chest to revive it.

It's just not possible.

I pulled out the final test.

"Don't do this to me," I ordered, not caring if anyone heard me talking to an inanimate object.

My bladder was drained and the last test was taking longer than the others, which was somewhat relieving. Then like magic, one obedient line appeared. The perfect, single cobalt blue line stood alone. Grateful, I exhaled, preparing to do the electric slide solo but just as I reached to toss it, that bastard of a second line appeared, bitch slapping my relief away.

***

It was the after lunch bathroom rush that brought me back. The click-clacking sound of heels against the tile floor woke me out of a trance.

Am I really still sitting on this toilet? How long have I been in here?

I walked out of the stall in a daze and I glanced at the mirror. I was wearing the same blue J. Crew pencil skirt and sparkly cream cardigan Michelle wore during the re-election campaign. She paired it with a gold chain embellished belt. Michelle is all about the right accessories. Belts, broaches, bold necklaces, and leather gloves.

The skirt didn't fit. Neither would the belt.

This is a mistake. I'm not pregnant. Just fat.

I reviewed the concrete facts again. I was on the patch. Bad Habit used condoms. We had sex. Multiple times. I moved back to NYC. He stayed in DC. I stopped using the patch. Not a drop of sex since the last time. Last time was with him. The day before I left. Three months ago.

Shit.

I ran back to my office and called Claire, making up something about my stomach virus and that I needed a doctor. She laughed, as if she was in on the prank that was clearly being played on me.

"Go ahead, take all the time you need. Let me know if it's a boy or girl!"

***

"Congratulations, Ms. Stone. You're pregnant!" The overweight doctor beamed.

"Is that a joke?"

He cocked his head to the side. "Excuse me?"

I checked the rudeness in my tone.

"I mean, are you sure?"

When I walked into the clinic, they handed me a piss cup and drew my blood for further testing. After thirty minutes of waiting, denial was the only defense I could muster.

"Well, yes, I'm sure."

My heart did a somersault and landed on my kidney.

Or was that the kid?

"That's impossible! There must be some mistake! I was on birth control. He used condoms. There's just no way!"

"Well, the patch is only as effective as it's used, along with condoms. This is very unusual...it could have just been an anomaly. Both contraceptives are only ninety-nine percent effective."

The glare I gave him could have burned the skin off his wrinkled forehead.

"So what you're trying to say is that I fell into the smallest possible margin of error? Ever?"

His face turned into a fat hairy tomato and he doodled on his clipboard. The smell of rubbing alcohol was making me dizzy. I couldn't think straight.

"How long do I have...I mean, how far along am I?"

"Well, we would need to see the results of the blood test to determine that. We should have them back in five days."

I nodded, my mouth going dry, unable to formulate words. The room started to spin. I caught the concerned look from the doctor, right before my body took a nosedive towards the floor.

"I need a nurse in here!"

***

The clock on the dashboard screamed ten-thirty when the cab pulled into my parent's driveway. I exhaled and hugged my knees, a technique I used to keep me from hyperventilating. I learned it from a nurse at the clinic where I spent all afternoon.

The lights on in the living room meant Dad was still up, watching television. He never slept well with me still out on the town. Most nights I'd come home and we'd watch movies till two in the morning, talking about my day. But I wasn't ready to have this conversation with anyone, let alone a parental figure. I had yet to cry. Shock wouldn't allow it and disbelief was waiting for me to wake up from this nightmare.

Every muscle, bone, and pore on my body was unstable. The world surreal, like I was caught between the land of make believe and reality.

Holy shit, I'm in the motherfucking Twilight Zone!

I peeked through the window and my dad was on the couch, watching TV and operating on what used to be an alarm clock. He owned a hardware store and knew how to fix just about anything.

My biggest life challenge, well other than being knocked up, was wearing my emotions on my face, making it impossible to lie. So I referenced my Acting 101 class from undergrad and walked on stage, ready to put on the best performance of my life.

"Hey Al, how ya doing?"

"Hi, Father!" I said, my voice peaking to a crack. His eyebrow shot up.

"Ok, what are you up to missy?"

"Nothing at all, don't be silly."

I chuckled and glanced at the television, looking for a scapegoat to change subject but my heart crashed into my rib cage.

"Oh, I'm watching *She's Having a Baby*. Come watch, we can play Six Degrees of Kevin Bacon."

Are you kidding me!

"Uhhh..." I stumbled backwards over my own feet, about to tumble on the floor before Chris caught me.

"What's with you dork?" He balanced me and passed my dad a fresh bag of popcorn. "Still haven't figured out how to use your feet yet."

"Nothing! Just tired... Busy day. Got to go. Later!"

I backed away from him and raced for the stairs but doubled back to grab a handful of popcorn, then made a beeline for my room.

***

It was the day of the Annual Spring wine tasting party at the office. There would be alcohol, people were expecting me to drink.

Company politics, like mandatory volunteering, the ridiculous unwritten laws of the corporate world. I didn't know how I was going to avoid the drinking since I was still feeling the effects of my permanent hangover called pregnancy. It had been two weeks and I hadn't told a soul.

How could I explain something I'm not ready to believe myself?

My practiced acting skills came in handy as I attempted to imitate a normal person during the day. But at night, alone in my room, my growing stomach was a terrifying tumor. Yet, to my credit card company's delight, the weight gain gave me the excuse to do some major therapeutic shopping. I maxed out on Spanx alone.

The wine tasting was held in the penthouse. The space was phenomenal with floor-to-ceiling windows and a wraparound balcony surrounded by a picturesque view of the city. I almost forgot my office was only a few levels below. I walked out onto the balcony to enjoy the summer air with my other schmoozing co-workers. Claire smirked at my all black ensemble. I was fooling everyone but her.

"Did you hear about the merger?" Ralphie almost attacked me with the question.

Lawd, he smells like oils you buy from bean pie sellers.

After our wildly fantastic date, I offered to pay to have his car detailed but he refused. He wanted another date, which I was avoiding like a heavy handed mother with a hot comb. But he was worse than Sallie Mae.

"Merger?"

"Yeah, the company is merging with Star Group Media. It hasn't been officially announced, but I have my sources."

A waitress approached us with a tray of red wine. I shook my head in disgust.

"Really, I didn't know that."

"I think there's gonna be some layoffs. There have to be," he concluded, more to himself than me. He looked frightened so I tried to remain positive.

"Well, you shouldn't worry about all that. As long as you do a good job you'll be alright."

I lied. Of course mergers were scary, especially with a company as small as ours in the middle of a recession. All of our jobs were at risk, but this was small change compared to the problems I was dealing with.

Maybe I should've waited before buying that new Bottega tote...and those Yves Saint Laurent platforms.

Bad Habit floated in my mind again and I shuddered. There was no doubt the little love child was his. The question remained whether it was worth telling him or would he even want to know.

Another waitress approached us, this time with white wine. Ralphie took two glasses and held one out for me. I sighed, accepting it.

It really shouldn't matter if I drink this since I have no intentions on having that man's baby.

It wasn't ideal but I made the executive decision to have an abortion. I was just starting to build my career and having a baby, with him of all people, was worse than a life sentence. The saying goes: first comes love, than comes marriage, than comes Alex pushing a posh baby carriage. I refused to accept one of the three. Michelle would never get preggo before she was married. Besides, children were more of a mandatory accessory to the fantasy than a desire anyway. I wanted to be married to a man that adored me first. Or at least one I could tolerate.

Hmmm...I wonder...

I glanced at Ralphie. He finished his glass of wine like it was a shot and wiped his mouth with the back of his hand.

Never mind.

"Come on Al, you're babysitting that glass. You don't get to drink on the company's dime too often you know."

I was in the middle of an adult peer pressure commercial. The entire room was waiting for me to join the party. With an uneasy deep breath, I faked a smile and took a quick sip. The guilt of the wine burned my tongue. I swished it around my mouth until an image of a decrepit baby, like the one in all those perfectly placed alcoholism subway ads, popped into my head. I gagged, spitting the wine onto the floor. The entire office turned to view my spectacle as Ralphie pulled the hair out of my face.

"What's wrong? What happened?"

I hacked up half a lung.

"Al, are you ok?" Ralphie insisted.

"I'm fine...really," I croaked, trying to laugh it off. "Still getting over that nasty bug that's all."

Ralphie didn't look convinced and removed the glass from my hand. Mumbles surfaced from the crowd.

"Thanks, Ralphie," I said and glanced over my shoulder at Claire who seemed to be having the most amusing time laughing at my humiliation.

***

When I made it home, doomed to be the topic of office gossip for at least two weeks, the worst part of my day was just starting. The results of my blood tests were in; confirming the date of conception was within two days of my last go around with Bad Habit. There was simply no denying it.

Bad Habit and I met a little over two years ago while attending a social media conference during my internship. He was law student speaking on the Judiciary Media panel, addressing the crowd like a young Barack, when we locked eyes. I didn't think much of it. No way everyone's favorite entertainment lawyer-to-be would be interested in me. But during the break, he found me.

"How do you like it?" he said from a seat behind me. I spun around and our lips almost collided, shocked to find him so close in my personal space but mesmerized by his scent. It was strong, sharp, and manly.

"What?"

"I said...how do you like it?" His voice was like a late night phone operator, lickable and intoxicating. I coughed up a nervous laugh and he smirked, nodding at the new Chris Anderson book on rising trends and niches I was reading.

"It's...umm...predictable."

"Mmmm...really? How so?"

Next thing I know, we talked through the entire break. I stuttered through my life story like a fool while he undressed me with his eyes, remaining a mystery, oozing sex effortlessly. The bell rung for the next panel and I stood, clutching my book like a shield.

"Well...better get going."

He stared up at me, but it wasn't like two students looking at each other either. It was like a man lusting after a woman, the chemistry palatable. No one has ever drank me in that way before. Then he stroked my arm, fingers gliding up my forearm, cuffing my elbow and sending shivers straight between my legs.

"Why don't you stay awhile?"

And just like that, I was hooked.

I finished Facebook stalking him around one in the morning. His photo albums featured pictures from his law school graduation and subsequent parties (none of which I was invited to) and the new house he bought in Atlanta. That was his plan, to move to Georgia, a hot bed for young professionals. I considered telling him in person but feared his actual reaction. There's enough television dramas and talk shows to know conversations about unwanted pregnancies never go well.

Besides being the new Director of Legal Affairs for a growing entertainment firm, he also owned his own real estate company and was co-owner of a new sports lounge. Bad Habit was about one thing: money. He lived and breathed for it. If something wasn't profitable, he had no time for it. Money was not a problem for him but, unlike other girls that hung off his dick, I'm not a gold digger. I have my own savings account (well, when I'm not shopping I do).

And yet here I was, a year and a half later, sitting in my childhood bedroom, pregnant with his baby.

I scrolled through my phone a couple of times, debating. Even though I swore I would never speak to him again, I still saved his number. Just another part of my vicious cycle of weakness.

You busy? It's Alex.

Pressing send on the dooming text message was like getting a manicure with tiny paper cuts on your cuticles.

Nah, what's up. Thought u weren't talking 2 me.

I imagined him snickering at the message and sighed in defeat. Yet another instance where I went back on my word.

I'm not but something came up. We need 2 talk About Us

What about us

UGH! He makes everything so damn difficult.

U need to call me. It's important.

Pride wouldn't allow me to dial his number. Pride is my homie.

Give me a sec

I clutched the phone like a lifejacket, waiting for it to light up and vibrate with his call but was losing my battle with exhaustion and in danger of falling asleep at any moment. Forty-five minutes later, still no call.

Hello?

No response.

Not this again.

You really need to call me. It's really important.

Still no response. I leaned my head back against the pillow, surrendering to the fight. Morning came faster than expected and I popped up to check my phone. No missed calls. No missed text messages.

That asshole.

***

"I could've sent a message that I had been hit by a Mack truck and only his blood could save me and he still wouldn't have called," I complained to Kennedy over the phone.

"Forget him. I can't believe you're pregnant!"

I couldn't hold it in any longer, I had to tell someone. The weekend had passed and there was still no word from Bad Habit. Even after my urgent text messages.

"You've had a gut full of human this whole time and you're just telling me now?"

"I was trying to tell the semen depositor first."

"He can go suck on a tail pipe for all I care! What are you gonna do?"

I stabbed at the chicken Pad Thai on my desk. Kennedy still lived in D.C and our daily lunchtime conferences were incredibly important to our sanity.

"I...I...I really don't know Ken."

"Wrong answer!"

"Best two out of three?"

My throat was sore from hurling in the office bathroom. I tried to keep my morning sickness at bay until I was out of sight of my mother's watchful eye.

"Wait a minute...you're not seriously thinking about keeping it...are you?"

And for the first time, I took a pregnant pause.

Am I really ready to give up living the single life? Am I really ready to be someone's mom? What reality shows would I have to give up for the mind-blowing entertainment on Sesame Street?

The thought did cross my mind. After all, I wasn't getting any younger. The job was great and in two months I would be fully on staff with entitled benefits. But the disgust in Kennedy's voice made me question my own sanity. Granted, she didn't care much for children. Some women looked at babies and see precious little angels. Kennedy sees expensive poop pushers.

"I don't know...honestly."

"You don't know? You're seriously thinking about having a baby with that asshole? Bitch, he doesn't even call you back half of the time, how would he be any help? I told you not to let him come over that night. But noooooo, you just had to say goodbye!"

"You know I'm not like you Ken."

"Damn right, cause I would've been kicked that habit a looooooooong time ago. Now look what he's done to us! I mean, you."

Out of the two of us, she despised Bad Habit the most. She hated the way he treated me and hated how I allowed it even more.

"Well, do I really need him Ken? I could do this without him. He would never have to know. He probably wouldn't believe me if I told him anyway. I could live at my parents for a while, cut back on the shopping, and save up money. Then, I could find a perfect little two-bedroom in Brooklyn and be set. I wouldn't even need Bad Habit."

Wait, did I just say cut back on shopping?

An unexpected silence came over the phone. Then she takes a deep breath.

"Alex, whatever you decide, you know I got your back. But if you do this, he has a right to know. As much as I hate that rat bastard, as the father, he does have some rights."

***

Hey. Since u refuse to call or text, I just want to let u know I'm pregnant. It's yours and I'm keeping it.

I pressed send before giving myself the chance to regret it and passed out like a drunk on the subway. The next morning, I pulled back the covers and found my phone buried in the sheets. Seven missed calls and a four text messages from Bad Habit. The first message:

Not funny

The next message:

R u serious?

The next message:

Don't play these types of games Alexandria.

And the last message:

Answer ur damn phone!

Is it worth calling him back? I'd given him all the information he really needed to know. What good would speaking to him any further about it do? I don't need him.

It's my body! He may own it in bed, but that's the only place.

But I guess he didn't get the memo on my newfound feministic philosophy as the phone buzzed in my hand.

"Why would you send that type of message?" he said, skipping straight to the point. Stupidly, my heart flutters and my cheeks burned. I hadn't heard his voice in months.

"Because you wouldn't call me back. And good morning to you, too."

"You don't joke around with something like that Alexandria."

"I wasn't joking," I said, matching his stern tone.

Silence came over the phone at first.

"That's just not possible. How is that possible?"

"I have no idea."

"And how...how could you be so sure it's mine?"

Ouch. Well, fuck you very much!

I fell back into my pillows, recovering from the blow to my head. I should've known that would be his first question.

"I had a blood test. The results gave the day of conception, two days after the last time we...you know. But that doesn't make a difference. You're the only man I've been with...I can't say the same thing about you." It was a cheap shot, but it was my only retaliation.

"So...what are you going to do?"

"I'm keeping it," I said, feigning confidence.

Wait! I am?

"Are you sure you wanna do that?" he asked in his regular condescending manor.

"Yes...and no, I don't expect anything from you–"

"I didn't say that–"

"But you were thinking it, I know you. I'm not out for you or your money. I didn't do this on purpose–"

"I thought you were on the pill?"

"On the patch, yeah. I thought you were using a condom?"

"I did! Why didn't the patch work then?"

"Well why didn't your condom work? I thought you were also using some special spermicidal–"

"I did, but that was just a precaution. I mean, you were supposed to be the main backup so this type of shit wouldn't happen!"

The accusations were enough to stir-fry my blood.

"Don't you dare try to blame this on me!"

"I'm not, I'm just saying–"

"Yeah, sure, whatever," I mumbled, trying to keep my voice down in the thin walled house.

We let our conversation die to silence that lasted for something close to eternity. Time enough to load another round of ammunition in our war of words. Then he groaned.

"So what now?"

"Nothing. You can go back to your life like I don't exist. You're good at that."

"Are you serious? You really expect me to do that?"

"Just think of it this way, you can treat me like you usually do, just ignore me, and I'll go away."

I hung up, half expecting him to call back, only to feel the pain of rejection when he didn't.

***

Dear Me,

I haven't written in a journal in years, but this seems like a good enough time to start. First, let me start with introductions:

Hi, my name is Alex, I love Thai food, Jimmy Choos, Michelle Obama is my bestie and I guess I'm pregnant.

Fanfreakintastic, right? It wasn't my intention to breed with the devil. In fact, I'm still not sure how it happened. But, my name is about to be added to the single mother's club, because I'm keeping it. I'm not worried (I'm terrified). I'll be the hottest Mom on the block though, a total MILF. I'll kick ass at PTA meetings and bake sales (well, store bought cookies count). I wonder if Gucci makes diaper bags.

Love,

Alex

***

"Good Morning Alex! How are we feeling today?"

Dr. Carroll, my new OB-GYN, opened the door to the examining room, looking like a red headed Betty White.

"Fat," I said under my breath.

I looked like I had swallowed three Goodyear tires, my boobs headed past the double 'F' category. I poked at my enlarging stomach as if it would pop like a blister; its growth was at super human speed.

Bad Habit never called back. I hated even thinking of him while on the examining table, staring up at the fluorescents. But Bad Habit was a disease called Fucktard. First, he infects your mind, then your uterus.

"People do gain weight differently," she said without skipping a beat. It was one of the reasons why I liked her. Nothing seemed to faze her. She was direct and to the point, plus she had a mean shoe game under her white lab coat. My visits to other doctors weren't as pleasant. Most often, they gave me an irritating look of pity. Nine months of that would drive me to the bottle.

"Thanks Doc! I appreciate the advice. I'm going in blind here."

"Well, let's take a look and see what we've got."

It was an expensive doctor's visit, about the price of a pair of Dior sunglasses, since my insurance wouldn't kick in until the end of the month. I decided not to tell Cloverstein until it was absolutely necessary, like right around the time my water breaks.

She scanned through my chart as a nurse prepped behind her.

"Hmm...that's odd. Your HCG levels are rather high, but it could be from the stress or possibly a miscalculation. We'll know more from the AFP."

"Uh-huh." It was the only response appropriate for her doctor mumbo jumbo and flinched as the sonographer squirted jelly that they clearly kept in a freezer on my stomach.

It would've been nice to have a man with me, elated and encouraging, holding my hand, ready to go through the process. Alleviating the feeling of regret. They say Barack was super excited and was with Michelle every step of the way for their two daughters, Sasha and Malia. But I couldn't imagine Bad Habit excited about anything other than money and I wasn't giving birth to an eight-pound bag of it.

Dr. Carroll was staring at the ultrasound monitor awkwardly. She was too close, as if she needed a pair of trifocal glasses. She seemed rather puzzled for someone who has been a doctor for over twenty years.

"Hmm...must be something wrong with this ultrasound."

She called another nurse to bring in the backup. As they set up, I once again drifted into my fantasies. My husband, rushing to the toy store to pick up a little football, in hopes for a boy. Having a boy didn't sound so bad. The less pain my child had to feel the better. I wouldn't wish the emotional pain of love, heartbreak, or morning sickness on my worst enemy.

I shifted my new big booty. My back ached from lying in the same position for what seemed like eons and I was in dire need of a piss break.

How long is this gonna take?

"Dr. Carroll, my Hi-C fruit juice levels are off and now your ultrasound time machine thingy is broken. You sure this table can support my weight—"

The look on her face made me stopped short. It was a mixture of horror and disbelief. I sat up to take a better look at the monitor. It couldn't have been that bad.

"What's wrong?" I demanded. Thoughts of Sigourney Weaver in *Aliens* raced through my head. It would be just my luck having one of those creatures growing inside me. Bad Habit was a monster after all.

"Well, it appears to be more than one heartbeat."

Aw hell, twins! You got to be kidding me.

"What does that mean, exactly?"

"I...I think...well, I'm not sure..." she stuttered, clearly petrified, trying to fake a confident smile. "Or, I've never...I mean. Well, I'd like to consult with my colleagues. Wait one moment."

Whatever it was, it was taking the words right out of her mouth. She jumped up and rushed out of the room, murmuring something I couldn't quite translate. Minutes later she returned with a small army of doctors. One stared at the monitor, another pressed lightly on my stomach, the other read over my chart. Dr. Carroll pointed to the monitor as she murmured.

"Now, look here. Then, look over here. You see that, two heart beats...but there's one over here as well..."

The doctors glared at me curiously.

"Alex, did you take any specific hormones while you were trying to conceive?"

I chuckled. "Trying to conceive? Please, I used a patch and a condom and still came out like this. I'm an after school special."

The doctors looked at each other bewildered. A room with about five hundred thousand dollars' worth of education and they were clueless.

The nurse flicked my arm, prepared to take another twenty vials of blood. I slapped her hand away at the sight of the needle and she jumped back.

"Sorry, instincts."

I wasn't sorry.

"You used nothing? No special pills or vitamins that you weren't aware of?"

Confused with the line of questioning, I only nodded. She turned to Dr. Carroll.

"No in vitro?"

Dr. Carroll was now the one nodding.

"Well...Alex, it appears that two of your eggs were fertilized...and they both split."

Damn, if I only paid attention in health class.

"O...k. So what does that mean?"

"Well, it looks like you're having two sets of twins."

"Quadruplets!" Another doctor chimed in, happily.

Dr. Carroll exhaled, letting out an uneasy chuckle. I stared, repeating the word a few times in my head.

Quadruplets? It sounds more like a pop group. Quadruplets? Hmmm...quad meaning four. As in the number four? As in FOUR BABIES!

"HELL NO! You're not serious?"

I wanted to swing, hit one of them dead in the face. Especially the one in the glasses, he seemed to be enjoying the ridiculousness.

They froze, checking with one another to see who should speak first.

"Dr. Stevens wants to run some more test, but based on the first examination..."

Her voice trailed off because I stopped listening to the life sentence being handed to me.

Shit.

Three Months

For the first time in my life, I was fully aware of my clumsiness. I stepped with extra caution on the sidewalk, assuming I would trip on a random crack, sending one of the babies flying out onto the concrete.

Babies. I actually have to refer to them in the plural.

It had been over a week and I was still pretending that everything was normal. Working late, eating a ridiculous amount of take-out food, buying every black dress I could get my hands. I simply wasn't ready to face reality so drowning myself in projects became my salvation from nine in the morning to ten at night, when the cleaning lady would force me to go home.

Being a pregnant New York pedestrian and daring to take mass transportation was like a daily football scrimmage, my stomach being mistaken for pigskin. I dodged elbows, four wheel suitcases, and messenger bikes. The jabs seemed almost deliberate as I ran away from the stench of pissy stoops, hopping over piles of dog shit and empty Heineken bottles. For once in my life, I didn't mind the slow moving, air gazing tourist.

The subway station by the office was a mob scene, more than usual for the late hour. Then I remembered a new Disney play was opening on 42nd Street. It was too late to turn around.

I swiped my metro card as my stomach made a sharp right turn away from my body. It felt as if I just got off a high-speed merry go round. I held the sides of the turnstile to keep myself from falling.

"Move!" A disgruntled man shouted behind me. I jumped to free the traffic jam and was caught in the undertow of foot traffic as the too eager crowd corralled me towards the train platform.

Why are my hands shaking?

A cold sweat formed across my forehead and nausea kicked in. I cupped my mouth to keep myself from puking on a woman in a red pea coat who was standing in my way. Morning sickness had turned into evening sickness.

May God have mercy on the poor soul I throw up on. I scarfed down four McDonald's cheeseburgers, two extra-large fries, and a strawberry shake today for lunch. It will not be pretty.

The platform seemed to be moving under my feet as we waited for the train and no one but me noticed. I could smell just about every human in the crowd, like I had grown a third nostril. The air around me was damp and funky with a touch of vomit. The ground, baked with dirt, loogies, and melted gum, seemed ten times more comfortable than standing on my own two feet. Drifting towards it, I caught myself.

Oh God, I gotta sit down!

I turned to find the nearest seat just as the cool relieving breeze of the arriving train kissed my skin. One step closer to home. But my relief was short lived. The train was as packed as a Dominican hair salon on a Saturday.

The doors opened and the crowd corralled me inside. I grasped onto the nearest pole manageable before being surrounded by a wave of coats, damp umbrellas, and briefcases. Trapped.

"Stand clear for closing doors," the conductor announced.

Oh no! My last chance to escape.

The door shut and my wheezing began. The sweat of the people surrounding me was a suffocating mix of curry-pork-fish-like funk laced with cheap perfume. My knees started to buckle, straining under my own weight. I clung to the pole as the train stuttered into motion. It was a slow moving express train. The kind that gets stuck in tunnels between every station stop.

Of course it would be, when I am only a stop away from death.

Closing my eyes, I tried to relax and block out my surroundings, but the heaving in my chest made it impossible. The train swayed and jerked through the tunnel, as my wheezing grew louder, much more pronounced over the noisy pedestrians.

"Uhhh...Ma'am...are you alright?" a voice inquired, I couldn't tell from where.

Everything was a blur. I tried to focus, cringing away from the attention. The crowd had the same look as the fat doctor in the clinic did.

"Yes...I'm..."

But I didn't finish the sentence. My eyes rolled to the back of my head and my knees finally had the chance do what they wanted to do the moment I stepped on the train.

***

"Ms. Stone? Can you hear me? Can you open your eyes for us?"

Please tell me that's Jesus...

The soft mattress that curved to my body wasn't the grimy train floor that I was expecting. There was a rush of frantic voices and beeping monitors surrounding me but I still couldn't open my eyes. Something was hovering over my nose and mouth. I tasted the forced oxygen and knew immediately where I was. The wave of embarrassment was not far behind.

"Ms. Stone...can you hear me?" A man's voice called out to me.

I shook my head, eyelids flickering.

"Ms. Stone? Can you try to open your eyes?"

A blur of light came through. The shapes in front of me started to focus and sharpened till a tall piece of gorgeous flashed a dazzling smile.

"There you are. Welcome back!"

Helllloooo.

My face flushed to his perfect smile and welcoming eyes. He smelled like warm cocoa butter, different from the stench of rubbing alcohol I was expecting. This only meant one thing.

I died on that train and he must be an angel.

"I'm Dr. Leonard. You are at the hospital," he said, pronouncing every syllable like I didn't speak English. The room grew warm, he was so close I could almost reach up and kiss him. But my tongue was like sandpaper sticking to the roof of my mouth and I thought against it.

"What happened?" I asked in a raspy voice with an uncomfortable strain on my chest.

"You had an asthma attack and fainted on the subway."

"Fainted?" I frowned and felt a sharp sting on my forehead.

"And when you fell, you hit your head on a pole and lost consciousness. Don't worry, it's only a mild concussion, although you have a bit of a bump. But first, we need to get your breathing under control and then we'll see what we could do about the pain."

He flashed another smile that made my heart skip a few necessary beats. He was literally taking my breath away.

Are doctors this good looking even allowed in hospitals? Shouldn't there be some type of special ward for people like him?

I nodded and he turned to the nurse by his side, ordering my medication.

"How did you know that?" I asked, hearing him ask for the one steroid I could take that I wasn't allergic to. It was impossible to guess.

"How did you know I had asthma?"

"Oh, it's on your medical emergency card," he said and pulled out the familiar beat up neon yellow laminated card that usually lived inside my wallet. "It also helped identify you."

I accepted his answer with an uneasy smile. The attention making me fidgety. Nothing could distract me from the fact that I was in an emergency room. I hate hospitals. Even ones that held Dr. Feel Goods like him.

"Relax Ms. Stone, you're in good hands. We'll take real good care of you and have you out of here in no time. And besides, someone as pretty as you shouldn't be cooped up in a hospital with me all night."

My face was a flame and I tried to ignore the twitch between my legs.

Was he just flirting with me? Dear God, please say yes!

He chuckled and pulled out his stethoscope, pressing it to my chest.

"I just want to check your lungs. Now, take three breaths for me."

I did as asked, ignoring the pain because Dr. Feel Good was caressing my back and touching my tay-tas, even if it was for medical purposes. I glanced at his left hand.

No ring... Yes!

He noticed and grinned.

"One more deep breath."

I inhaled again, the scent of his cologne tickling my nose. As he slid the stethoscope away, his long fingers grazed my left breast causing my nipples to harden under the thin hospital gown. I crossed my arms over my chest to cover them.

"Okay. Better. Still some wheezing but the nebulizer is helping to regulate that. I'll be right back with your CT scan." He glided out of the room as if he were on ice.

He's just that damn cool.

Once he was out of sight, I turned to the nurse.

"You wouldn't happen to have a mirror on you, would you?"

With a mischievous grin, she dug into her smock pocket, pulling out a compact.

"I always do when I'm working with Dr. Leonard."

I held back a girly shriek and took the mirror. My eye makeup had run down to my chin, my lips cracked, and the knot on my forehead was far from small, it was its own planet. I touched it slightly and pulled back at the stinging tenderness. A crack whore looked better.

"Gah! Uhhh...do you know where my purse is?"

Still grinning, she turned and placed my bag on my lap. I ripped off my oxygen mask and searched for my emergency makeup kit, the one I keep for moments such as these. Where my future husband was staring me in the face, about to perform surgery on my heart. I cleaned up the runny makeup, applied fresh blush, combed down my frazzled hair, and glossed my lips. The nurse nodded with approval.

"You did that pretty quick," she said, placing the mask back over my face. "I have to admit, you might have a chance. I've never seen the doctor flirt with a patient before. I wasn't sure if I was gonna have to leave the room."

So he WAS flirting with me. I knew it!

Dr. Leonard walked back in, taking a once over at my new appearance.

"Ah, looking even better I see."

The nurse winked at me, moving to the far corner.

"Yeah, I feel a little better too," I said, which was a lie. It felt like Dumbo was bouncing on my chest. And the small bump on my head was turning into a rather large migraine.

"Hmmm..." He checked the monitor. "Well, once you have the shot your breathing will improve and it won't feel like an elephant's sitting on your chest."

Wow! He knew what I was thinking? We're destined for each other!

I played with my hair, trying to relax as he stared at me from the foot of my bed.

"Ummm...is there anyone you need me to call for you? A friend...boyfriend...anything?"

Ekkkkk!

I covered my chest with my blanket.

"No, I'm fine, thanks. There's...no one...I mean," I said, hoping he caught the hint I was speed balling at him. He flashed a smile and rocked back on his heels.

"You know, it was a good thing you had that card on you. Otherwise, we wouldn't have known how to treat you so quickly. Or your beautiful name."

I nodded with a smile, trying to remain cool. My mother has made me carry around that card, which listed all of my various ailments, allergies, and medications, since I was a child. It was then that I gasped at the horrifying thought of my mother.

"Ummm...Doctor, you didn't happen to contact the 'in case of emergency contact', did you?"

But my mother screaming from down the hall answered that question.

"WHERE IS SHE?"

"Oh no," I murmured, ducking under my blanket.

She raced into the room, damn near knocking Dr. Leonard over.

"Alex! Are you alright? Oh my God, what happened?"

"I'm fine Mom, please, stop yelling."

She hovered over me, holding my chin to perform her own examination, believing that keeping me alive for twenty-five years has earned her an honorary medical degree.

"But look at your head...and they said you passed out on the train!"

"Her head is fine, actually. I just came to give her the good news." Dr. Leonard said, seizing his opportunity to chime in. She spun around, noticing him for the first time.

"Oh," she gasped, taken aback by his smooth sensual Barry White tone. Her eyes glazed over like a love struck teenager. "Well, thank you doctor."

"I'm Dr. Leonard, pleasure to meet you," he said, reaching a hand out. "You have a wonderful daughter."

"Well, of course. Like mother, like daughter."

"Mom," I groaned, while she tried to straighten my hair.

The nurse walked in with a vitals cart and Dr. Leonard stepped away to help, giving my mother ample opportunity to bombard me.

"He's cute," she said in a loud whisper.

"Mom, he's still in the room."

"I know, but he's still cute." She fidgeted with my hair some more. "You know, it would be nice to have a doctor in the family."

"Mom!"

My face turned a bright shade of red as Dr. Leonard turned just in time to catch her last comment.

"Ok, Alex," he said, stating my name for the first time with clear delight. "We're going to give you something to help with the wheezing, should be an instant relief to your chest."

Oh that's right. I still can't breathe.

My mother held my hand like I was on my deathbed.

"I just don't understand what could've brought this on. She's usually so careful about her asthma. Something just doesn't seem right."

Dr. Leonard picked up the chart hanging on the end of my bed, scanning it with his finger.

"Hmmm...well, all her vitals seem to be normal, though her pressure is a little high. We're just waiting for the results of her blood test," he said, caught up in his own analysis. "She's not running a fever...Alex, what were you doing before you fainted?"

Memories were a blur with the fight to breathe.

"I was on the train...it was really packed...I was dizzy..."

"Have you been dizzy like this before?"

"She is not a dizzy person, if that's what you mean. She just got her MBA!"

"No, I haven't," I replied, shooting my mother a warning glance.

"Ok. And when was the first day of your last menstrual cycle?"

Oh. Shit.

It hit me, like another elephant dropped on my chest.

How could I forget I'm pregnant?

"Um...January eleventh," I admitted, near whisper while composing the fear painted on my face. His expression morphs. My mother jumps to my rescue.

"Oh, but she has really spotty periods. When she was in high school, she went six months without one. I thought I was gonna have to kill her, making me a grandmother so young," she said with a nervous chuckle. Even she sensed the tension in the room.

Dr. Leonard gives a closed mouth smile while I remained blank faced.

"Oh, and you don't think you're pregnant...now?"

Uhhh...does he really expect me to answer that...in front of my mother?

Even though I was a grown woman, that wouldn't stop her from throwing me over her knee in a hot second. She was traditional as apple pie and wasn't too fond of babies out of wedlock.

"Of course not! What kind of girl do you think I raised? She's just gained a little weight cause of my cooking that's all! She's always a skinny little thing."

"Oh, I'm sorry ma'am. Just this type of steroid could be both harmful to her and the baby if administered. Standard procedure."

The nurse chimed in. "Doctor, her heart rate is—"

"Oh, yes, I'm sorry. Let's get you feeling better!"

He smiled with his perfect dimples and reached for the syringe as the nurse prepped my arm.

Shit, not a needle!

"By the way," he said with a playful wink. "I never doubted you."

It was the moment of truth. There was no way out of Dr. Feel Good or my mother finding out. I stared at the syringe, the impending danger looming, mind racing with options. What if I didn't say anything, what's the worst that could happen? Maybe it would induce a miscarriage and this whole crazy ordeal would be over. I'll leave and go to another hospital to treat it. Dr. Leonard would never know. Then he would take me out on a date, or two, or three.

We'd get married; live in a five-bedroom estate in Westchester...vacation in Martha's Vineyard, a second home in the Hamptons. He'd have his own practice while I would raise our two point five children and the purebred Cocker Spaniel. We would host grand dinner parties, have memberships at the country clubs, and attend lavish benefits. I would rock all the furs, shoes and bags I could ever want. It was a much brighter future than I could ever have with Bad Habit. I would be the perfect socialite, the perfect wife, and the perfect mother.

Perfect mother?

How could I be the perfect mother, knowing what I was about to do? Would a mother hurt her child, knowingly? Would my mother? She's the most selfless person I know. She would give up all her internal organs if it meant my brother and I wouldn't feel an ounce of pain.

Most importantly, what would Michelle do?

The nurse flicked my arm, inspecting it for the best vein. Suddenly, an overwhelming sensation came over me, one I had yet to feel until that very moment. The sudden urge to protect the things growing inside me eclipsed all other emotions.

"Wait…" I said, my vision blurred by the tears forming puddles in my eyes. My mother rubbed my arm.

"She's really afraid of needles."

Dr. Leonard leaned in closer and grinned.

"Relax, Alex. It's only going to hurt for a second."

I stared into his glorious brown eyes, the eyes of my potential future then glanced at the syringe, filled with a clear liquid poison.

Him or the baby? Final answer?

I closed my eyes, took a deep breath and I let it out.

"I…am pregnant."

My voice stuttered out the words and a gasp filled the room, which couldn't have come from anyone but my mother. Her hand on my arm locked stiff.

"I don't want to hurt…it."

The room was still. I kept my eyes shut tight since I didn't want to see their faces filled with harsh judgment. In fact, I was hoping I'd go blind and deaf, a virtual pregnant Helen Keller, so I would never witness the silent criticism that would be everyone's first reaction.

Dr. Leonard placed the syringe down on the cart.

"Well...ok," he said softly. "I'll...just go get your labs and then...well...we have other options."

I opened my eyes as he tried to regroup, disappointment evident.

"I'll be right back," he said, avoiding eye contact.

He glided out the room, followed by the nurse.

Well, there goes my future.

***

Dear Me,

I'm writing this on the train to work, even though I should be home. But I had to get out. My mother's eyes have been stuck in a permanent bulge since we left the hospital like she came down with a sudden case of Graves' disease. I hate disappointing her most of all.

The update: a small squad is growing inside me. Turns out Bad Habit and his super sperm did some type of karate chop on my eggs! Things could not get any worse!

Love,

The baby-making machine

***

Winded from the small walk from the train station, I plopped in the chair, three hours late. My office was muggy and humid, and my head was still pounding from my episode on the train from hell. I should have taken the day off but I needed to get out the house and away from my mother's never ending questions.

It'll be fine. I can do this. I'll just need a bigger place... Oh God, how big am I gonna get? I'll probably have to work from home. They should be ok with that, right? Right! I kick ass here, they won't want to lose me. I'll be fine. It'll be fine.

Claire rushed into my office and I cursed myself for not locking the door. She looked as frazzled as I felt, like she was looking for her missing youth.

"I came as soon as I heard. I'm so sorry Alex!"

I almost fell out my chair.

"Excuse me?"

There's no way she could've known already. I haven't told anyone! Was she on Dr. Carroll's email blast or something?

Claire cocked her head to the side with a frown and gave me a once over.

"Are you just getting in or are you leaving?"

"I just got here. I called and said I was going to be later, remember? What's going on?"

Mortified, she slapped a hand on her face and collapsed on the sofa near my desk.

"Oh no! I didn't know. They didn't tell you yet?"

What the hell is she talking about now?

Through the open door across the hall, I noticed our department coordinator packing up the trinkets on his desk. There were empty file boxes lined up in the hall. People walked by snatching them up like they were parking tickets.

Oh no.

"Tell...me what?" I managed to ask with the similar feeling of being on top of a steep rollercoaster, about to descend.

"Because of the merger...the company has decided to take the Production Division in a new direction. So they are keeping Star Group's team and...well."

My migraine returned full throttle. I glanced at the windows, remembering they didn't open. That was the only thing that stopped me from jumping.

"I see...well. So are they letting everyone go?"

She noticed my accusatory glare and quickly jumped to defend herself.

"They are keeping part of the Digital Division...to work on the website...for now I suppose."

I exhaled to keep from hyperventilating but it was too late. The utter wave of emotion I had been holding back surfaced.

"Oh God," I gasped, wrapping my arms around my stomach, hunching over to embrace the impact. Claire jumped to her feet and was by my side, stroking my back.

"Ok Alex, calm down, it's going to be ok. You don't want to stress yourself out. It's not good for you or the baby."

Baby? Ughhhhhh!

My career was my identity, my reason for living. Babies weren't even an afterthought.

"Babies," I corrected in a whisper too low for her to hear.

"Well, maybe it's a blessing, you know," she began but the daggers my eyes threw at her were enough to split her in two. She threw her hands up in defense.

"Not like that Alex. Just think about it. You really shouldn't be on your feet in your condition. You're already starting to show. You live at home, so you don't have to worry about bills and your health benefits usually extend after your unemployment. Just save your severance package..."

Severance package?

The thought of the status of my employment kicked me in the ass. I groaned louder, burying my head in my hands.

"What's wrong now?"

"I'm under contract, remember? I was supposed to start on staff next month. I don't get a severance package. I don't have benefits. I have nothing."

***

The company was laying off seventy-three employees, myself included. And the cherry on top of this already fantastic news was that I was right about the severance package. Since I was still under contract, I was not entitled to receive one. I was to leave my office immediately. Escorted out no less, meaning I couldn't take my white board with me.

Claire was kind enough to help me pack, although there wasn't much to take, being that I had only been there two months. It was a nightmare, worse than any horror movie ever made. I was waiting for the onslaught of tears that refused to come. My nerves were paralyzed.

My Crackberry vibrated on the table. Claire picked it up, chuckling.

"Hey, who's Bad Habit?"

I stiffened at the sound of his name then rushed to grab the phone from her.

"Yes?" I snapped.

Claire took a clue from my cold demeanor.

"I'll be in my office, let me know when you're ready to leave," she whispered and dashed out.

"Hey. What are you doing?" he asked in his normal dead tone.

How did he already know? Did he call to gloat? Bastard!

"I'm... I'm... well, why?"

He sighed in annoyance. "I'm in New York and I want to talk. Can you meet me?"

As usual, his timing was impeccable. Only he would call on the worst day in history next to finding out I was pregnant.

Sure, I'm not doing anything important. Just getting ready to throw myself off the Brooklyn Bridge.

"Umm... I can't. Just today... it's just not a good time." I was too mentally exhausted to deal with his bullshit. "Can we do this tomorrow?"

"I can't. I fly out in the morning."

"Well, that was a quick trip. When did you get here?"

He hesitated before responding. "A week ago."

"You've been here an entire week and you're just calling me NOW?"

"Well, I wasn't sure what your reaction was going to be. After our last conversation, you didn't seem too inclined to speak to me."

"So you were too afraid to call? Typical!"

Losing his patience, he finally snapped.

"Listen, just bring your ass over here! I'm staying at the Grace Hotel in Times Square."

***

The remnants of my career were in a Whole Foods bag by my feet. I knocked on the peach and gold trimmed door of room 501, kicking myself for being so weak. The door swung open, his back already to me as he slipped into the bathroom. Typical Bad Habit.

Of course, he wouldn't hold the door open for me and greet me properly. It's only been three months and I'm only carrying his tribe.

With a huff, I walked into the chic hotel suite and stood in the foyer, letting the door slam behind me. It was surreal being in his presence again. His aroma filled the room, smelling like rain, black soap, and lust. My nose twitched at the scent. Bad Habit popped his head out the bathroom door, brushing his teeth and stared.

"What the fuck are you doing?" he asked, the question muffled by his foaming mouth.

Charming, as usual.

His forehead wrinkled, catching a glimpse of my new stomach.

"Well, it's nice to see you too. Thanks for the warm welcome."

I waddled towards the mahogany writer's desk by the window with a view of busy traffic heading towards the depths of Times Square then sank down into the leather sofa. If he was in the bathroom, it meant he was going to be a while, as he had no concept of time. I left the Whole Foods bag by the door.

I don't know what's sadder, the bag or me?

Thirty minutes later, he emerged intoxicating all my senses. His crisp black dress shoes looked like two Mercedes under his tailored heather gray slacks. He sat on the love seat parallel from mine buttoning his baby blue dress shirt, eyeing me inquisitively, like he couldn't make up his mind what he thought.

I smirked. "You seem surprised."

It took him a moment but he tore his eyes away from my stomach and stared down at his sleeves, latching his gold cufflinks.

"I wasn't expecting you to...to look so different, I guess."

"That makes two of us."

We sat in silence, staring at everything but each other with only the deafening silence to keep us company. A part of me was disappointed. On the way to the hotel, I imagined him greeting me with open arms, begging for my forgiveness, wanting to talk about everything under the sun. Instead, it was the same old Bad Habit, silent and emotionally unavailable.

"Sooo...what's up?" I asked, trying to hide the utter annoyance in the back of my throat, his sex appeal infuriating.

He continued to play with his cufflinks for a moment then paused. He exhaled slowly, like he was building the sentences in his head, calculating his next move.

"Well, I know you said you wanted to handle this yourself, but that's unrealistic. I can't pretend that you or my...child doesn't exist. I would like to be a part of the child's life. But we need to come to a resolution on how to work together, constructively."

You know that laugh you have when it's super late and you're so deliriously tired that everything seems comical? Like, 'oh look, the traffic light changed, it's three a.m., laugh out loud'. Well, that's exactly what happened. I stared at him for a beat then broke out into hysterical laughter. He glared, repulsed by my cackle.

"What? What's so funny?"

Well doesn't this top off my already stellar day.

Weeks after he questioned whether the kid was even his in the first place, he now wanted to play the role of Daddy. It couldn't have been for my benefit. It was most likely to make himself look good, appearances being everything to him.

"Babies. You mean to say babies."

"Babies? What are you talking about?"

Sighing, I reached into my bag, pulling out a large manila envelope.

"Here," I said, tossing it at his lap.

"What's this?"

"Pictures from the ultrasound I had today."

He pulled out the black and white photo, noticing the red markings.

"What am I looking at?" he asked, oozing impatience.

"You are looking at four heart beats, none of them being mine."

It took a moment to register and then, as expected, his eyes bulged and his mouth dropped. He rose to his feet as if he was about to attack, then he sat back down. It was pure comedy seeing him so flustered, I stifled another giggle fit. He held his head shocked disbelief.

"They used the word quadruplets—"

"I...how...how did this happen?"

"Well, you did take Health 101, right?"

He glared up from the picture, not amused.

"You know what I mean."

I gave him the run down while his eyes darted from me to the picture and back again.

"This is...I just don't understand! It doesn't make logical sense."

"Welcome to my world."

He placed the pictures on the side table and stared at me through narrowed eyes.

"This isn't a joke! I'm not playing around. I really am pregnant! That's a real ultrasound. I wouldn't make this up!"

He folded his hands together, cockiness and accusations brewing.

"I'm just trying to understand exactly HOW this happened, Alexandria?"

I hated when he used my government name like I was the maid. No one else did. It was as if he refused to use a nickname, signifying we were no more than mere acquaintances.

"What are you saying?"

He shrugged. Only he would immediately conclude I was the webmaster of this epic catastrophe.

"Look, I don't need this bullshit today. Today, of all days! After you've been here for a fucking week! I'm out!"

I stood, of course not as gracefully as I would have liked, and headed towards the door. He sprung to his feet, following.

"Where the fuck do you think you're going?"

He jumped in front of me, slamming the half open door closed before I could fit through it, my escape botched. I stared at my feet, avoiding his glare and leaned back against the wall in defeat.

Why is this happening to me? I did everything right. I followed all the rules.

It just didn't seem fair. I graduated high school then college, with honors. Worked my way up the intern corporate ladder while in Business school and landed the job of a lifetime. But the one time I veer off the good girl path, I get pregnant by a guy who thought it was my intention to trap him. Now here I am standing in the bastard's hotel room, the one his company paid for, jobless, broke, partially homeless, and knocked up beyond belief.

I am no Michelle. Michelle wouldn't be caught dead with a stupid girl like me.

The tears I had been waiting weeks for finally swelled in my eyes.

"I lost my job today," I said, voice raspy with shame. He frowned.

"Did they fire you due to your pregnancy? They can't do that, that's discrimination based on your medical condition and they are liable to treat you like any other employee."

Always the lawyer, I could see the wheels spinning in his legal psyche.

"No," I explained through my sobs as the hot tears blinded me. "They had no clue. The company went through a merger, I was just one of the casualties...I was on contract, so no severance package, no health benefits, nothing. I'm living at home now, but..."

"So...what are you going to do?"

"I don't know. I...I can't afford...I...I don't know! I waited too long, and now it's too late to have an abortion! I didn't know...I can't..."

Sobbing, I refused to meet his eyes. I let my pent up emotions explode in front of the one person I swore I would never see me cry.

Bad Habit stared, seeming unmoved. When a woman breaks down crying, a normal man would console her. Bad Habit, on the other hand, seemed to hate the idea of touching me outside of the bedroom. So I wasn't surprised that he stood there with his hands in his pockets, watching my meltdown as if I was Hallmark special. It would be too much for him to even think of holding me when I needed it so desperately.

A hard knock on the door startled me and I rushed back into the bedroom, wiping my tear soaked face with my sleeve, trying to pull myself together. Bad Habit watched from the door. His eyes were heavy, weighted by stress and hopelessness, matching my own sentiments. Another impatient knock at the door made me jump. With a heavy sigh, he opened the door half way, greeting the person behind it. A woman's voice purred from the other side.

"Hey you. You ready to go?"

Of course the bastard would fit in a date but wait until the last minute to see me!

I rolled my eyes and stormed towards the door to leave. Bad Habit raised a hand to stop me without even looking.

"Can I meet you downstairs? I just have to finish something up."

"Aww...well. I can just wait for you here," she cooed like she was trying to make her way in but he didn't budge from his spot.

"Just, give me five minutes. I promise." He shut the door before she had a chance to argue. He brushed passed me, grabbing his blazer off of the bed. I caught a glimpse of myself in the adjacent wall mirror. My eyes were blood shot from the tears and my skin was ashy. He stood behind me, staring at my reflection, adjusting his jacket.

"I have to go to a dinner with a prospective client. You stay here."

"Stay for what? To talk? I'm done talking with you! And I'm not gonna sit here and wait for you to—"

"Alexandria, just sit your ass down and wait! I'll be right back!"

He took one last long look before walking towards the door. "And you better be here when I get back. Order room service or something."

Then he slammed the door behind him and I did what any other mature pregnant woman would do. I flipped him the finger.

***

In Bad Habit's world, the words 'be right back' never actually meant what they suggested. Bad Habit had his own interpretation of time. Once, when we were supposed to go on a date, he showed up at my apartment two hours late. That didn't surprise me because he was late for just about everything. What did surprise me was his sudden realization that he left his cell phone at his apartment. Since he lived only five minutes away from me at the time, he left, claiming he would be right back to pick me up and I believed him. I sat there, dressed and ready to go, for three hours. He was nowhere to be found, nor did he answer his phone. He never showed up for our date and I didn't hear from him again until he called two days later like nothing ever happened.

I tried to ensure myself this time was different. After all, I was in his hotel room, surrounded by his luggage, laptop, and favorite wave cap. He would have to come back, if not for me, for his belongings. The question that remained was exactly when he would return? I ordered the steak dinner, devoured it with little air, and watched a repeat episode of Michelle on *David Letterman*. The antics of my exhausting day took their toll around midnight, with no sign of Bad Habit. Laying in his bed, I wrapped the comforter around me and fell into a coma.

The sound of the door slamming shut woke me up. Feet shuffled in the pitch-black room. I stiffened and opened one eye to peer at the clock on the nightstand.

It was two-thirty in the morning. I had been waiting for six hours.

I shut my eye, clenching my teeth to keep the raging temper at bay as he pulled the sheets back beside me. He climbed into bed, hitting his pillow with a thud and a relaxing sigh. Moments later, he wrapped his arm around my stomach and jerked me closer. He smelled like a sponge soaked with Hennessy.

"Seriously? What the hell do you think you're doing?"

He didn't respond, just tilted his head, letting his pillow lips brush against mine.

"You're drunk. I think you should stop."

He giggled.

"Why? You afraid you're gonna get pregnant? Oops, too late for that!"

He broke into a big mouthed drunken cackle. I shoved him away but he held my wrist with one hand, keeping us locked together.

"Get off me!" I fought to break my hands free.

"Nope."

I tried to kick my legs free but they were tangled within the sheets. I was buried in a sea of hotel linens.

"Get off!"

My threatening voice made him laugh harder.

"Not until you listen," he warned. I calmed down, knowing it was the only way to get rid of him.

"You are going to come to Atlanta and live with me."

I waited for the punch line. He just stared.

"You're drunk, clearly."

"What OTHER options do you have? You're unemployed. You don't have insurance. You don't even have your own place! How do you think you're going to take care of FOUR babies by yourself?"

Disgusted, I once again tried to escape but he pinned my arms tighter.

"And it doesn't make sense for you to live with your parents when I have adequate space and resources. You have no choice. It's done."

I didn't have much, but damn him being my only option.

"First of all, I have plenty of options. Second, we would kill each other. Third, you're not going to remember any of this in the morning."

"You plan on shacking up in your room with four cribs? Don't be absurd."

Thoughts raced through my head, clouding my logic. He was right, about everything. And I hated him for it.

"And I'm not worried about your attitude. I know how to put you in your place, I've done it for this long."

His lust filled eyes softened as he licked his lips.

Uh oh.

"You're wasted. Get off me."

"I think I deserved a drink after the shit you just dropped on me."

He sucked and flicked his tongue on my neck. My body was conceding but my mind was still racing.

Is he serious? He can't be serious? Move to Atlanta? But...where would I shop?

"You're not asking me—"

"No. I'm not. I'm telling you," he warned. His eyes changed, like he wasn't completely convinced of what he was committing to. Then he tilted his head to kiss me. His lips were soft and warm as his tongue swept inside my mouth. His hands moved to my breasts, feverishly unbuttoning my shirt and tugging at my pants at the same time.

"So...is this a part of the deal?" I said in a pant, gasping for air under him. He lifted his head and stared at me.

"Are we going to...um...be together?"

It sounded ridiculous, but it was a valid question and my only real concern. If I was even going to consider the insane idea, I needed to know where we stood.

Was this all I needed to do? Get pregnant so he would want me? No wonder hood chicks pull this trick. It actually works!

"Uhhh...let's just call that part of the contract a work in progress as we have yet to agree to the terms and conditions."

Humph!

"Very funny."

"I aim to please," he said with that boyish charm that made him so irresistible.

He buried his lips into my neck, shoving the blankets off me, wrapping my legs around his waist. He cupped my breast with both hands and squeezed.

"Ah!"

"These are bigger," he mumbles, kisses gliding down my stomach.

It had been so long that it felt almost right, like I needed him more than I realized. But I couldn't escape the uneasy feeling. In usual Bad Habit form, our status remained undefined, his true feelings still unknown. It would sit there like a pink elephant in the room drinking Moscato, waiting for acknowledgement. But who had time for wine sipping elephants when he was ripping my panties? Who could think about definitions when his fingers were slipping inside me? And who wanted to think about babies when his tongue had me screaming his name?

***

A week after the insane proposal, my mind and thighs still ached from the weight of Bad Habit as I shook hands with the woman who would ultimately determine my future. Her name was Ellen Sampson, a close friend of Claire's, who owned a private adoption agency specializing in matching surrogates with eager couples. These desperate parents paid up to a hundred grand plus medical expenses. That's a six-figure tax-free yearly salary, compacted into nine months.

And let the church say Amen!

We were eating at Chez Leon on the Upper East Side, two blocks from Central Park. It was a good place to have my last meal given the budget cuts I had to make until I found a sponsor for my ridiculous mistake. I already had to return two pairs of shoes just to make the minimum payments on my student loans. I had less than four hundred dollars to my name.

Ellen was about Claire's age, except she dressed the part and had manners like she got her master's in table etiquette. We chatted for a bit, making small talk, until we found ourselves bonding like two college roomies. She was funny, sharp, even-tempered and cool, just like Michelle. Even after I told her how many children she'd be selling off of me.

"Well," she gasped, lightly setting down the fork to her garden salad. "Now, THAT is interesting."

"So as you can see, I'm in quite the precarious situation."

"Indeed. And what made you decide adoption would be the best alternative?"

I didn't want to tell her that I saw an ad for egg donors on the train and thought I'd make way more selling fetuses.

"I...just feel it is the most appropriate, most responsible thing to do. To give my children a loving home."

Her eyebrow shot up at the term "my" and she shifted forward.

"What about the father? Do you think he'd support this decision? His offer seemed legitimate. And very tempting."

Funny, I thought his offer seemed suicidal.

"He is well aware of the circumstances I'm up against and truthfully has no interest in becoming a father. He'll agree. Trust me, this is a wayyyy better option."

Ellen winced a smile, as if to say, "I see" and played with her glass of Chardonnay.

"Alex, have you ever heard of the term 'risk pyramid'?"

I had but shook my head no, not feeling the direction the conversation was headed.

"It's a finance term." She used her hands to demonstrate. "See the bottom part of the pyramid is low risk, which means a low return and the top part of the pyramid is high risk, which means a high return. The lower the risk, the lower the probability of loss, the higher the risk, the higher the probability of loss. See, one part of my job is risk management. To analyze and determine what's best for my clients who are subsequently investing into their future."

I didn't know we were talking stocks and bonds, I thought we were talking babies.

She stared for a beat to make sure her statement fully penetrated. Our waiter brought fresh rolls and I faked a laugh to break the tension.

"So you consider me a high risk investment?"

"Respectably, yes."

I scoffed with a chuckle.

"Respectably, I'm sure."

Ellen smiled and grabbed a roll while I kicked the stuff mushrooms around my plate with a fork.

"It's actually a high compliment. Most don't have your innate quality. I've met women who are as far along as six months and have never seen the inside of an OB/GYN. It's insulting to every woman struggling with infertility."

"I don't know what quality you think you see, but it's not there. I'd make a terrible mother."

She laughed.

"That's what they all say."

I sipped on lemon water and smoothed the front of my maternity tunic, naturally gliding over my new stomach. Earlier that week, I was staring at an unfamiliar naked body in my bathroom mirror, beautifully freakish and mesmerizing. In that split second, I wanted to be the illusion I saw in the mirror. Life itself was growing inside. Arms, legs, and minds were being built inside my tummy. It would be something physical that I could hold, proof that I had played a part in creating it.

A baby...

But after that moment, I walked downstairs to find my parents in the kitchen, hovering over their financials, trying to figure out how they could support me and my massive mistake. Even talking about cashing in their retirement. It was a reminder that the things growing inside me were a pain in every way to everyone. Especially me. I walked right back upstairs and called Ellen.

"Ellen, believe me. You'd be doing social services a favor."

"Okay Alex. Give me one good reason why you wouldn't be a good parent. One good example and I'll drop it."

I sighed, stared out the window, and tried to think of a non-superficial reason other than I would look terrible in Mom jeans. A couple passed by with a little girl holding a doll baby, squeezing it so tight it'd choke to death if it was alive. A memory sparked like it happened yesterday.

"So...when I was like eight or nine, I had this doll name Tabby. She was one of those 'baby alive' type dolls. You know the ones that blink, drink, and poop. She was so cool. I treated her like she was a real baby. I fed her, burped her, washed her, did her hair, I mean the whole nine yards. Anyway, one day I was on the train with Dad, we got off on our stop, and somehow I forgot Tabby on the train. My poor dad went running after the train, called lost and found, but nothing. I made signs and hung them around the train station, neighborhood, school, hoping I'd find her. Still nothing. She was gone. And I was devastated."

Ellen stared at me blank faced.

"Alex...you couldn't possibly be basing your parenting capabilities...on a doll? You were just a kid!"

"It's not just that. That's just one example. Ellen, that was my baby in every real way and I forgot her. Ever since then...I don't know. I just think I'd be terrible at it. I mean, come on, I can't be anyone's mother! I have the compassion of an ironing board."

Ellen chuckled and placed a new napkin over her lap. Our entrees arrived; baby lamb and purple potatoes. I was no longer hungry.

"Claire was right, you are charming. And hilarious."

"Thank you. I'll be here all week!"

"Can I tell you something, and you promise not to take it the wrong way?"

I finished my water and smiled politely.

"Sounds like Tabby had an amazing mom."

I swallowed that solemn thought and nodded.

"Yeah. I guess she did."

Four Months

Atlanta International Airport is just as insane as New York's LaGuardia, except with bigger assholes. It took everything in me not to kick the old lady that ran into me with her Power Scooter. My flight was about an hour late and I was sure Bad Habit was finding some way to blame the plane's tardiness on me.

When I reached baggage claim, I surveyed the crowd. No sign of him. I was accustomed to him being late, but didn't think he would be this time. Not on such an important day. The alarm on the conveyor belt screeched, and the bags began to rotate past. It would take a miracle for me to manage the four sixty-pound suitcases alone.

Although Bad Habit really didn't leave me with many options, the decision to move to Atlanta was ultimately my own. He Fed Exed a one-way ticket two days after he left. One way to a city eight hundred and eighty-two miles south of what I knew, absent of my friends, family, and the familiarity of New York. But the thought of my parents paying my all my bills as well as the five of us, four wailing babies and myself, crammed into an already crowded household, didn't make much sense either. I couldn't let my family suffer for my indiscretions.

My mother, naturally, hated my decision.

"You don't even know him!" Mom shouted over the stove while frying some chicken after I revealed my plan. She made it sound like he was a random one-night stand. In a way, she was right. I really didn't know Bad Habit. I only knew the parts he allowed me to know. Never the parts his friends were privy to. To learn the deepest levels of him was like trying to play a game of Clue without the possibility of winning.

"I know Mom, but this is strictly business. I have to try. If not for me, for the sake of my unborn seeds," I said dramatically with a smile. She didn't see anything funny.

"You don't need him, you have us!"

"What are you going to do down there?" Dad asked. He didn't attempt to change my mind knowing I inherited stubbornness from Mom's side of the family.

I had no clue, even while my pea green bags passed me twice on the conveyor belt.

This was a stupid idea. I can probably sneak back on a plane if the threat level is orange.

"Red Cap ma'am?"

I hadn't even noticed the dark skinned man with his cart parked next to me. While I was standing there daydreaming, the section had cleared out. Still no sign of Bad Habit, not even a missed call.

"Yes please, thank you."

The graying Red Cap didn't need to ask which bags were mine since I was the last man standing. He huffed as he dropped the first bag on the cart.

"Damn! You got a body in hu're or sumthin?"

He laughed and grabbed another bag. I watched him load my life onto his cart with trepidation.

"No, but I may put one in there later."

"First time in Atlanta?"

"Yes. It is," I said, checking my wallet, making sure I had enough for a tip. Or for a hotel, if it came down to it.

"Well welcome to what you out of towners call Hotlanta! A fine female like yourself will get into a lot of trouble down hu're."

"I'm already in enough trouble," I said dryly, pointing to my protruding stomach. He smiled, which was the first time someone was happy seeing me in such a state.

"Well, alright now. I knew a lil' nice thang like you was taken. Now, ya shouldn't be on your feet like dis Lil Mama. Why don't ya lead the way."

Still no sign of Bad Habit. I hesitated then forced a smile.

"Actually, my ride is running a little late. Got a comfortable bench I could back my wide load onto?"

He smiled, pushing the cart ahead. "Of course, right dis way."

***

Four hours later, the sky was dusty pink as the sun set on my first day in Atlanta. The friendly Red Cap stopped by a couple of times to check on me. The more he stopped, the more pity I could see in his eyes. It was humiliating, but I refused to remove my forced smile. My cell vibrated in my lap and I glanced down at the text message.

ON MY WAY

I grinded my teeth into dust to keep myself from throwing the phone at someone's head.

"Are ya ok ma'am? Ya sure you don't need anything?"

I looked up at the friendly Red Cap and tried to dazzle him with my practiced smile.

"I'm fine, really. He's on his way," I said, hearing a slight quiver in my voice. His gray eyebrow rose a bit. He was no longer buying my act. Just then, an older woman with a baby hooked on her right hip stopped in front of us. Her smooth skin was the color of an ice cream cone and her salt and pepper wig came to a bob at her ears. The chocolate baby was dressed in a stained white jumper, barefoot, sucking his thumb, staring at me.

"Is this seat taken?" she asked the Red Cap and smiled at me.

"No ma'am. You just sit right on down the're."

The woman smiled and with exaggerated effort sat on the bench next to me, switching the baby to her lap. The little drooling boy smiled at me, showing off his two new front teeth. He took the drool-covered thumb out his mouth and placed his wet hand on my arm.

YUCK!

"Jacob, say 'Hi' to the pretty lady," the woman said and smiled at me. "He's such a flirt."

"Oh," I cringed, taking out a tissue out to wipe off my arm, moving further away from the kid. He giggled as if it was a game and reached for me again.

"See, he likes you. You wanna hold him?"

"No! I mean, no thank you."

She laughed, bouncing the baby on her one good knee.

"It's ok baby boo. Grandmamma will hold you."

The Red Cap rushed over to help another family with their bags.

"Just like his Daddy, a handsome devil he is."

I grimaced a smiled, looking over at the door, eager for Bad Habit.

"Me and my grandbaby just came back from visiting my susta, in North Carolina. It's real nice there. Took baby boy with me. His momma works at the Coca-Cola factory. His daddy don't do nothing tho."

"Wait, they make Coke down here? Wow!"

"No, no, no. The factory. You know, where all them tourist go with the rides and stuff. They don't make no soda there."

"Oh," I said, a little disappointed.

"So, you not from around here?"

"No, just moved."

"Well welcome!"

I winced a smile. I didn't feel very welcomed. I felt like an abandoned stuffed animal.

"So how far along are you now?"

Next thing I know, I was blurting out the cliff notes version of my story. I don't know why, maybe I just needed someone to talk to. Someone to tell me I was making the right decision. I was looking for assurance, approval from a stranger. I had reached rock bottom.

"So, y'all not getting married?"

"Well, no. I mean, I don't particularly like him. I'm just doing this because I got no other choice."

She nodded in agreement.

"That's right! You don't got no choice, you gots to be togetha!"

Her sudden passion was baffling.

"I'mmm...not understanding you."

"I tell you, you young people today! Always thinking you got choices. Well you don't!"

She shifted the little boy to her other arm, pointing down to the floor to drive in every word.

"I was seventeen when my husband got me pregnant. And he married me alright. Back then, there wasn't no choice, you had to do what you had to do. Now, we weren't all in love, I barely knew the man. But we learned to love each other. Now I gots five children, fourteen grandbabies, and one great grandbaby."

She bounced the drooling little boy on her knee and continued to preach.

"It wasn't easy, but it was the right thing to do. To marry the woman that's having your child. To take care of her cause nobody else is. You see, when you get a girl pregnant, you ain't just responsible for the child, you responsible for the girl too. Your man has a RESPONSIBLITY to be with you! Ain't no longer a choice. You gotta give them babies a daddy."

Speechless, I said the first thing that came to my mind.

"But...he's an asshole."

She laughed a big belly of a laugh.

"They all are. You love him; you just don't know it yet. Us women gotta change when we become mothers. Being a woman is all about sacrificing. It's not about what you want anymore."

What! Why do I have to change? Michelle didn't have to change!

She laughed again, noticing the war on my face.

"I tell you what, you do got two choices. You either be with a fool or be alone and a fool. Cause ain't nobody else gonna wanna be with you, taking care of some other man's baby."

Alone?

It wasn't impossible (just look at the Brady Bunch), but my options for a future mate were limited. Finding a worthy single man that wants to date a woman with four kids was like trying to find a size nine at a sample shoe sale. He would have to be a man of sainthood stature, the kind you find in the thick bushes of south, not in New York, a pretentious city of egos. She was right, no one would ever want to marry me.

Alone.

I sighed, looking at the old woman at a loss for what to do with myself. She smiled.

"Now, before I let you go, let me ask you, have you accepted Jesus Christ as your Lord and Savior?"

Huh?

"'Cause he's coming and I have something here for you..."

She dug around in her bag and pulled out some *The Watchtower* pamphlets.

Jehovah's Witness! I knew it!

Before she could finish her sermon, the sound of rushing hard bottoms came to an abrupt stop behind me.

"I've been looking all over for you! You could've told me where you were," Bad Habit snapped. He was dressed in his regular business attire, Bluetooth secured in his ear with two Blackberries attached to his hip like Batman's utility belt.

Wonderful way to start our new forced life together.

The Red Cap appeared with his cart. "Oh, I moved her over hu're so she'd be more comfortable, that's all. Ya wouldn't want your pretty wife up on her feet for four hours now, huh?"

Red Cap smirked while the Grandma winked at me.

"She's not my wife."

Ouch. Well fuck you very much.

I was ready to drive a hole the size of a Blow Pop between his eyes. I rose from my seat to face him and he avoided my piercing glare, looking around, assessing the suitcases.

"Is this everything?"

"Yes sir. I can load it up on the cart and bring it out to your car if you'd like?" The Red Cap raised a curious eyebrow at me.

"Yeah, that would be great. Thanks," Bad Habit replied in relief, saving himself from manual labor. He started to lead the way until he noticed I wasn't following and stopped short.

"Uhhh...the car is this way."

I folded my arms across my chest. My pressure was so high I could spit flames.

"Are you sure you want me to follow you? I mean, I'm already at the airport. You can just leave me here, save yourself the gas money on a return trip."

The Red Cap stood nearby, torn by what to do. Bad Habit sighed and rolled his eyes.

"My truck is sitting outside door A, an Escalade. Can you meet us there?" He slid a tip into the Red Cap's hand. Red Cap nodded and pushed the cart away, taking one last glance over his shoulder at me.

Bad Habit turned back to me with a groan.

"Sooo what are you gonna do? Stay in the airport?"

"Why not? I've been waiting here long enough."

He glances at his watch as if I was wasting his time.

"My cousin was supposed to pick you up because I had a meeting. He forgot, so I came as soon as I could."

"You sent your cousin...to come get me?"

"Yeah, my cousin Paul. He knows what you look like. No big deal."

So I'm not important enough to pick up from the airport?

"That's not the point."

"Well, what is the point?"

"The point is it should've been you!" I shouted, throwing my hands up. "Damn a meeting! I'm the one who just moved her entire life down here. I'm the one who's pregnant! The least you could do is pick me up YOURSELF!"

The crowd of travelers surrounding us stared and he rolls his eyes again. My heart raced, feeling a dramatic sob building in my throat. Those ridiculous kinds of sobs accompanied by snot. Hormones were killing the part of me that held my self-respect.

Why am I about to cry? Bad Habit is always late. This is nothing new.

When you have a Bad Habit, they tend to make no apologies for their actions, as loud and blatantly disrespectful as those actions can be. Because at the end of the day, whose fault is it really? That's right, yours, for agreeing to deal with him. I glanced at Grandma who was pretending to be engrossed in her grandson, but I knew she was listening.

I closed my eyes to shut him out of my thoughts and checked myself.

I don't have a choice... Babies need a father.

"Do you need to sit down...or something?" Bad Habit mumbles.

Pulling myself together, I opened my eyes. He was halfway turned, staring down the hall in the direction the Red Cap exited. I didn't respond, instead I walked by him, ignoring his presence altogether. There was no use in waiting for an apology that was never going to come.

Be alone or be a fool...

I chose the lesser of two evils. Or so I thought.

***

The clock read nine thirty-five, but you couldn't tell by the sweltering heat. I stood in the middle of Bad Habit's driveway drenched in sweat. He struggled with my luggage while I took a moment to absorb my new suburban surroundings. I had never been to Atlanta. In fact, the furthest I had been past the Mason Dixon line was D.C.

The street was a cozy cul-de-sac with a mixture of brick front homes, landscaped yards, and basketball court driveways. It looked like a scene out of a movie, the ideal space to raise your two point five children.

Uhhh...so where's the subway?

Being a city girl all my life, I've never trusted the silence of the suburbs. You never know what's lurking behind the rose bushes. And I was almost certain the block looked exactly like the one from *Nightmare on Elm Street.*

"Shit, Alexandria. What the hell do you got in here?"

Bad Habit's two-story colonial cream and brick faced home was one of the larger ones on the block. It had a large wraparound porch with black shuttered windows and a black iron balcony on the second floor. The massive front yard had several obscure shrubs, clearly planted by the realtor who sold him the place. There was a white cobblestone path leading from the detached two-car garage to a red front door. I peeked inside the neighboring window at the happy white family sitting at the dinner table. The proverbial father and mother holding hands while the kids chatted over meatloaf and mashed potatoes, as picturesque as a Norman Rockwell painting.

Wonder if that'll be us someday.

The unrealistic thought startled me and I prayed I didn't say it aloud. I waited for his sharp reaction but was met with eerie silence. He was gone, abandoning me on the driveway. I rushed towards the open door, frightened by the solitude. Maybe it was my wary spider senses but the street was suspiciously too perfect for my liking.

Bad Habit's house had a mixture of bachelor pad and old school mama decor. The large living room walls were adorned with African American art reprints and New England Patriot memorabilia, surrounding an L-shaped chocolate micro-suede couch, facing a mounted fifty-inch flat screen. Past the couch was a disorganized office.

I stood in the foyer beneath a crystal chandelier, peering down the small hallway leading to the kitchen on the right. It had high gloss pearl cabinets, granite counter tops, and stainless steel appliances. The white marble floors stretched towards the sliding glass doors hidden by vertical blinds leading to a deck in the backyard. A kitchen nook table sat in the corner covered by old newspapers and junk mail.

"Fuck," Bad Habit grumbled from the first staircase landing, heaving my bags up. I giggled with pleasure seeing him wrestle with my wardrobe. His eyes narrowed and I straightened my face. Dragging the bag up the rest of the stairs, he glanced down at me from the balcony railing then proceeded to walk down the hall out of sight. Holding my stomach, I raced up the stairs to catch up with him, excited as a kid on Christmas morning about my new room. I even packed some of my trinkets and scarves to decorate the place with and Mom promised to send some of my framed paintings.

The only light shined through the double door entrance of a master bedroom. Bad Habit threw my bags in the corner and disappeared into a walk-in closet. His familiar king sized bed sat in the middle of the room surrounded by matching nightstands and adjacent dressers. A cream leather recliner sat alone by the windows facing the front yard. He came out of the closet shirtless. I couldn't help noticing how his well his back muscles were defined before he opened the door to the master bathroom.

Wait? What's he doing? I'm confused.

I leave his bedroom in search of my own. Guess I was expecting too much if I thought he would be polite enough to show my room first. Manners are not a part of Bad Habit's religion. I walked down the hall and began to open the remaining bedroom doors. The place was huge, twice the size of my parent's house, with high ceilings and massive windows. But when I reached the end of my self-guided tour, all three spare bedrooms were devoid of furniture.

"They're all empty," I said, rushing back into his room. He had just plopped on the bed after changing into some gray sweats.

"Yeah, I know," he replied and grabbed the remote, flipping to ESPN. My feet were glued to the entrance, like a force field was keeping me from stepping one foot into his lair.

"Sooo...where am I supposed to sleep?"

"In the basement. It's unfinished and a little damp, but I'm sure you'll be fine."

I don't know what happened next, but all I know is that my purse flew from my hands and lunged itself at his head. He ducked right before it hit him.

"Well, I see I need to hide all sharp objects."

I crossed my arms, tapping my foot, while we held a staring contest. Two minutes passed before he rolled his eyes.

"It makes no sense for me to buy you a bed. Don't you think we'll need all the room we can get with that team you're carrying?"

Damn. He has a point. I hate when that happens.

"But I thought I made myself clear, this is a strictly business type relationship. I don't think you sleep in the same bed as your business partner."

He smiled mischievously and turned back to the television.

"Sure. Right. Business. Whatever you say Alexandria."

Wary, I took my first step inside the room toward my bags, eyeing him, ready to rip his head off if he made a wrong move.

Involuntary manslaughter due to raging hormones.

He dropped the remote and slipped off the bed.

"Come here."

"Why?"

He walked towards me, a smirk growing across his lips.

"Cause I said so."

Uh oh.

I recognized that "I'm about to blow your back out" look and before I could come up with a clever response or defense, he backed me into the corner by my suitcases, hands pressed against the wall on either side of me, his smell overwhelming me.

"What's wrong Alexandria? Why so tense?"

His juicy fat lips grazed that soft spot on the side of my neck. He trickled his fingers down my stomach, slipping into my leggings then past my underwear until he was so deep inside that I thought he pressed right through me.

"No...don't," I stuttered, gasping yet pushing harder against his fingers.

"Really? Tell me you don't want me and I'll stop."

He slipped another finger in, stroking. His lips moving by my ear as he leaned closer, his other hand moved up my shirt and grabbed my breast like it did something wrong. I panted loudly, grinding harder against his fingers. He moved my shirt up, tilted his head down, and wrapped his lips around one nipple and flicked his tongue.

I came so hard, fast, and loud that it was embarrassing. He slipped his fingers out of me, straightened up, and smirked again while the weak words trapped in my throat sputtered out in between my gasps.

"Stop."

He shook his head with that cocky smile I hate yet love and strutted back to the bed like he didn't just rock my world.

"By the way, I made space in the closet for you."

***

The next day Bad Habit took me on a mini tour of Atlanta. Mini in the sense that it was all of ten minutes long and I was pretty sure there was more to see besides a strip mall and a Publix. (Not to be confused with PUBIC. Still, it grosses me out to shop for food at a place whose name closely resembles unwanted genital hair.) We didn't have much time for pleasantries. I had my first appointment with a new doctor. Thanks to some research done by Dr. Carroll, my records were transferred to an Atlanta practice that specializes in high-risk pregnancies and they were eagerly expecting me.

Bad Habit pulled up to the front of a glass medical facility and put the car in park, engine still purring.

"You're not coming in?"

He sighed and avoided my eyes while fidgeting with his phone.

"Well, you said they were going to perform a whole bunch of tests on you today and waiting areas are generally not that comfortable sooo...I figured I'd just pick you up in an hour or so."

Oh you poor thing! You have to sit and wait while my fat ass is poked and prodded. I feel so sorry for you.

I opened my mouth to protest and his phone rings. He clicks on his headset.

"Hey man...oh nah nothing...just dropping someone off at the doctor. What's up? Yeah, I'm selling those two properties tomorrow. Just drawing up the paper work...Yeah man, I don't have time. I gotta get this dough..."

His smell was overwhelming me again and I had to resist taking his clothes off in public. I stalled at the door handle, hoping he wouldn't be long so I could convince him to come with me. I was willing to brave most situations on my own but this was serious unknown territory. My nerves were making my hands shake. He glanced up from his phone and frowned, confused by my presence.

"Hold on one sec," he said then turned towards me. "Well, go on. You're going to be late."

Asshole!

With a huff, I opened the door, slamming it shut with just enough room before he took off. He sped down the street and I stood surrounded by the dust cloud he created caressing my bulging gut.

"Looks like we're on our own."

***

The nurse's icy hands spread the thick clear jelly on my stomach for yet another test. I was on hour two at the God-forsaken place and regretting my decisions on various levels. Dr. Justin Turner was medical Hollywood; he was the top perinatologist in the state of Georgia and third in the entire country. He had delivered several multiple births. Pictures of the sets adorned his office walls, next to a multitude of plaques and degrees. I would be his first quadruplet delivery and the first quad set without in vitro fertilization. And he was as excited as a drag queen in a wig shop about my case.

After formal introductions, he went over his process in great detail and explained the reasoning behind the torturous regiment of tests. A nurse proceeded to ask me an endless amount of questions about my family history. I couldn't provide a single detail on Bad Habit's history.

Dr. Turner's staff was uncomfortable with my sulky sarcasm. My lack of enthusiasm regarding the process was unusual in an office that specialized in getting women pregnant. I was not interested in seeing the pictures from the ultrasound nor fascinated by the babies' heartbeats. What I was could be summed up in one word: miserable. I was tired of throwing up every morning. Tired of being parched like I had walked through the Sahara in a wool one piece. Tired of the nonstop drilling on my temples. Tired of the violent back pains. I couldn't take a shit without agonizing strain. It literally hurt just being near light. I was certain I was turning into a vampire, but my various attempts to end my suffering by stepping into the sun proved otherwise.

"It's called hyperemesis gravidarum and I'll be honest, it's a woman's worst nightmare," Dr. Turner explained. He was in his mid-forties, tall, fit, and resembled a Ken doll with his striking smile.

"It's an extreme case of morning sickness. About one in every thousand have it."

"Oh, so I'm just keeping up with my anomaly themed pregnancy I see?"

He laughed at all my jokes, which made him a winner in my book.

"We can give you some medication so you can at least keep some of your food down. But you need to keep hydrated and stay off your feet. You'll be extremely hormonal, by the way, so you should warn your family. They may start to think you're unstable."

"Trust me, they already do."

Another nurse dressed in SpongeBob SquarePants scrubs walked in, pushing a cart with a tray hidden by thick blue paper towel.

"Ok Alex, this is the last test of the day and then you can go home."

"Great, sure, bring it on!"

I wonder if he's waiting for me downstairs. Or maybe he's come up already.

I fidgeted with my hospital gown. It was too small to completely cover my naked body. Dr. Turner turned to the nurse as she lifted the towel, giving me a clear view of the biggest needle ever made in history. I leaped off the table like I was hopping a fence.

"WHAT THE FUCK IS THAT?" I screamed, backing into a corner, my bare ass pressing against the wall.

Startled, Dr. Turner cautiously approached, the nurses flanking him.

"It's ok. There's nothing to be—"

"You're crazy if you think you're coming near me with that thing!"

"Alex, please try to remain calm—"

"Remain calm? You can draw all the blood out of my body! NO! I will not remain calm!"

The first nurse's eyes measured me and I picked up the closest weapon near me, a tongue depressor.

"No, Alex, we're not taking your blood, ok? It for a CVS—"

"What...why are you talking about drug stores NOW?"

They had me surrounded like they were trying to catch a wild animal.

"No, a CVS is a type of test. We are going to take tissue from your placentas so we can run tests on the fetuses. Check for any abnormalities—"

"Placenta! That's in my stomach. You're gonna put that thing in my stomach? Hell fucking no!"

"Alex—"

"I'm pregnant with quadruplets. That's abnormal enough! Mystery solved!"

The SpongeBob nurse glanced over at the other one, signaling with her eyes.

They're plotting against me. Bad Habit's probably in on this too.

The nurse charged forward and I fell into a defensive stance.

"I'm telling you right now bitch, if you come near me with that sword like contraption, I'll stab you in the eye with it."

The nurse stopped short, her eyes threatening. Dr. Turner chuckled, nervous about a potential throw down with him being the odd white man out.

"Alex, we can do it now or we can do it later. Either way, in your condition, it is a must," he said, inching towards me with his hands held up over his head. "Now why don't you come and sit down and I'll tell you all about it. I'm sorry you saw the syringe first. It was not our intention to scare you."

It took another twenty minutes of convincing before I finally came down from the ledge.

***

Less than twenty-four hours in Atlanta and I was ready to go home.

Bad Habit pulled up in front of Dr. Turner's building, looking refreshed and well rested. I was waiting for him outside, as far away from the building as I could get.

"How'd it go?"

I somehow stopped myself from slapping him. Instead, I gave him a spiteful look and turned to fasten my seatbelt.

"O...k. Sooo...what did they do?"

"A whole bunch of tests...with needles."

I flipped down the sun-visor to check my makeup in the mirror. I had wiped most of my runny mascara off in the bathroom but I still looked awful. It was a jaw dropping experience, watching the needle penetrate through my skin, mere inches away from a baby's head, petrified of what would happen if the doctor messed up. What if he poked one of them in the eye or something? The kid would have to walk around with an eye patch like a pirate. But I wasn't crying about the test, I was crying about doing it alone. The nurse held my hand through it rather than the man who helped put me there.

"Ohhhh," he said. If he knew one thing about me, he knew my feelings on needles. "So they took your blood?"

"Yeah, and the babies' too. Really wish I saw that coming."

"The babies'? Oh well...maybe I should stop by then."

"Stop by for what?" I yelled.

Why would you go when I'm not even there you dumb bastard! You're about an hour late for when I needed you!

"To give them some of my blood. So they can run...tests."

I stared for a moment before realizing what he was referring to.

"You mean like a paternity test?"

He sighed, smoothing down the waves in his hair.

"Relax, it's a perfectly legitimate test."

"That you don't need since you ARE the father," I snapped, slamming the sun visor shut.

"Right," he said under his breath. "Well, just to be sure, it doesn't hurt."

"Actually, you asking me for one does hurt. Plus, I'd rather wait for you to find out on the *Maury Povich Show* anyway."

He rolled his eyes and drove in silence, the striking ATL skyline in the distance. He turned a couple of more corners and we pulled up to the end of the driveway.

"You're not coming in?" I asked, wondering why the jerk stopped so far from the door.

"Nah, I have this thing I gotta go to."

"Oh, well, I'll come with you. Let me just change." I hadn't even unpacked yet, but I was already planning an outfit in my head. My turquoise maxi dress from Zara was long enough to cover my swollen feet and my gold Louis bag would be a distraction from my belly.

"No, it's at a club. I don't think it's wise."

"At a club?" I checked the time. "What club opens at five?"

"Happy hour," he said, smiling. Shaking my head, I opened the door.

"Do you have an answer for everything?"

"Pretty much, yeah."

I stepped back and slammed the door shut, hoping the glass would shatter and hit him in his cocky face. He threw the car in reverse and sped off.

Jerk. He couldn't even wait to make sure I made it inside.

With a groan, I waddled toward the house, realizing that this would be one of many nights he planned on leaving me alone.

***

Dear Me,

Atlanta is hot. Scratch that, it's not just hot, it's boiling fire blazing hot, like the sun shines a specific beam of heat here and nowhere else in the universe. Besides the glamorous buildings downtown, the rest of the surrounding neighborhoods are lined with broken down boarded up houses, chicken wing shops, and crusty strip clubs at every other stoplight. I had my first *Player's Club* moment when a woman standing behind me at a supermarket, fully aware of my condition, offered me a job. I, respectfully, declined.

The girls down here fall into three categories. First, are the hardcore southern girls who wear loud, tight, obnoxious clothing that never fits, tri-colored laced front wigs, and gold teeth. Their attitudes, just as loud. Second, are the ruthless top model video vixens with their oversized sunglasses, designer imposter handbags, and jet-black ass touching weaves. The sheen on the apples of their cheeks makes them look like they are constructed from Barbie plastic. Third are the Ladies; the Jack and Jill-Links-Delta Sigma-Alpha Kappa-Grandma's pearls wearing-church eight days a week women made of old money. Their noses so high up they can smell the moon.

In any case, they all stare at Bad Habit like he is made of Godiva chocolate, right in front of me, with no qualms

about making their feelings known. And that's just at the damn supermarket! I imagine the rest of the city is a pussy playground for him. Thus, I have concluded that if he flirts with another one of these broads in my presence I will rip off his eyelashes and smack the hair off his chin.

Make that money. Don't let it make you,
Me

***

"If you keep eating like that you won't have enough food to last the weekend," Bad Habit said while coming down the stairs, carrying an overnight bag. I looked up from my plate of barbeque chicken wings, sucking the remnants off my fingers.

"And it's only nine a.m." he added while trashing the empty cartons of orange juice I left on the counter.

"I'm eating for five. Piss off," I snapped, my mouth full of smothered meat. It had been weeks since I had a real appetite and now all I was craving was chicken. Mountains of chicken. Legs, thighs, wings, breast stacked to the ceiling.

He shook his head in disgust. "Weren't you in the kitchen earlier this morning?"

He must be referring to the six packs of his favorite instant oatmeal I ate at four-thirty.

I nodded my head in between bites.

"You were asleep. I guess another looooong night. Humph!"

Bad Habit left for work every day like clockwork and he went out almost every night. A mixture of various undefined meetings, happy hours, and random fuckery kept him out late while I stayed home alone for thirteen hours a day. He ignored my side eye and zipped up his bag.

"I'm heading to Vegas for a conference this weekend. I'll be back Sunday."

"Sure, whatever," I said with zero care while scavenging through the fridge with my sticky fingers.

I could've sworn we had some potato salad in here.

"You know," he began. "Maybe you shouldn't be eating so much."

I froze and spun around, catching him checking out my ass.

"Why not?"

"Well, maybe you should...exercise a bit."

My mouth dropped and the relief of the cold breeze from the freezer vanished.

No. He. Didn't.

"Are you calling me fat?"

He shrugged while walking toward the pantry.

"No, but you have been eating a lot more lately. And aren't you supposed to be taking some vitamins or something?"

"They're horse pills. You take them. And quit changing the subject. You think I'm fat!"

"No, but...well...it may just help with your...anxiety."

He took out the last pack of instant oatmeal and waved the empty box at me. Furious, I held my hands on my hips.

"Oh well gee thanks for the marvelous advice! Let me just unzip out of this fucking fat suit and go for a brisk run. Hmmm...can't seem to find the zipper. You think you could help me out?"

Rolling his eyes, he grabbed his bag and headed for the door. I followed.

"Alexandria, it's perfectly acceptable to engage in physical activity while you're pregnant. Plenty of women do. I've seen them at the gym."

"Yeah, well THOSE women aren't the size of a damn planet at four months!"

You never ever call a woman fat, especially when she's pregnant! Even callous bastards like him should know that much.

He stopped at the hall console to comb through an unopened pile of mail. I stood behind him.

"What, no response?"

Say something. Anything. Please give me an excuse to rip out your tongue with rusty pliers.

"Given your current condition, I've chosen to disregard your shenanigans as mere hormonal outbursts," he said using his normal cold formalness.

He finds his car keys and turns around with a smirk.

Ugh. His audacity disgusts me.

"I may be pregnant, hormonal, and maybe even fat, but this is temporary. You however are a permanent dick! How about you try not to say or do anything stupid from now on?"

He grinned, amused by my outburst, and opened the door.

He thinks this is funny. So I'm a joke now?

"Alexandria, do you need another spanking?"

I gasped, mortified by what we did the night before and took a step back. He laughed.

"That's what I thought. I wouldn't mind, but I have a flight to catch. Be back on Sunday. Hopefully the food will hold out until I return."

And with a smirk, he shut the door behind him.

***

Dear Me,

Fish, coffee, soda, sugar, alcohol, herbal teas, tap water, raw meats, and eggs. This is just the shortened version of a long list of foods I can't have. As if being pregnant wasn't bad enough. I'm dying for a rare T-bone steak and sunny side up eggs. I've just about devoured every morsel of food in the house and Bad Habit doesn't come home until tomorrow.

More good news! I finally found an appropriate name for the little life suckers growing inside me. I will now refer to them as Aliens 1, 2, 3, and 4. I have a feeling they are plotting against me to divide and conquer. Alien 1 is responsible for my gas and heartburn. Alien 2 is responsible for my swollen hands and feet. Alien 3 is the troublemaker who twists and turns my organs so I feel the need to piss every twenty minutes. And Alien 4 is in charge of my aches, pains, and all around miserableness. Together they are a destructive team. Hopefully I'll be able to harness their power to conquer their father when they're born.

Love,

Sugar-Free

***

"I'm bored," I said out loud for only the walls to hear and collapsed into the recliner by the care package my mother sent filled with books I found as interesting as calculus. *What to Expect When You're Expecting, 1000 Baby Names, Healthy Nursing*, blah, blah, blah. She even switched my *LUCKY* subscription to *Pregnancy Magazine.*

'10 Things to know about Cloth Diapers'? Lawd, take me now!

My life was pregnant everything and I was drowning in it. It was like I stopped existing. No one was interested in me. They were only interested in the bulge.

I needed something to ease my anxiety and impatience. Something to make me forget about the Aliens growing inside of me and all the things I couldn't have or do. I missed the sounds of clicking computers, hectic deadlines, conference calls, and office gossip. Managing projects, ten-hour days, and rushed lunch hours. I've had a job ever since I was thirteen, sitting idle is a foreign concept.

Boredom reaching a new high, I decided to call Ralphie and see what was happening at the office. I dumped out my purse, searching for my phone and the *Watchtower* pamphlets fall into my lap. The old lady's words had been ringing in my head since I left the airport.

"You love him you just don't know it yet."

Bad Habit and I had the ultimate love-hate relationship. It seemed my very presence in his world irritated him and vice versa. One minute we're hoping for each other's slow death, the next we were ripping off each other's clothes. We'd never fit the stereotypical fantasy.

But is it possible that I really do love him, more than I'd like to believe?

Instead of calling Ralphie, I decided to try out the theory on the one person who would listen.

"Hey! I was just about to call you," Kennedy said after the second ring. "Did you know that during labor you could actually shit on yourself? So you're pushing out a kid and taking a shit at the same time. What a way to start your life, sliding head first into shit!"

"I'm having a C-section."

"Oh. Well good! You can ask for a tummy tuck."

"Ken, do you think I'm in love with Bad Habit?"

"I'd freaking hope so. It'd be the only explanation for you putting up with his bullshit all this time."

"Jeez! How could you let me to fall in love with an asshole?"

"I tried to stop you! But his name is Bad Habit for a reason. It took Whitney Houston twenty-five years to kick that crack rock."

"Well...do you think he's in love with me?"

She laughed.

"Remember last year on your birthday, how you made him promise to take you out. You bought that pearl pink Betsey Johnson dress, even made the reservation for him and scheduled it in his phone, sent him reminders, and he still showed up dumb late without so much as a card, flowers, or explanation?"

"Yeah."

"Oh, this is a good one! Remember the time he left you stranded at the airport because he forgot to pick you up. You were waiting there for like three hours before you decided to call me. And you forgave him for, like, the millionth time?"

"Yeah. So?"

"Yeah, so no. I don't think he's in love with you. Idiot."

Kennedy can be brutal in her tactics.

"But maybe...maybe it's like the little boy who bullies a girl he likes."

"He's a grown ass man, fool!"

"Be with a fool or be alone and a fool..."

"But don't you think it's strange Ken, that after all this time and me getting preggo, that maybe it's fate? That maybe we were meant to be together?"

"Hello?"

"Huh...hello?"

"Hello? You're breaking up."

"You're on a land line."

"Hello? Call me back when you've come back to your senses."

She hung up and two seconds later, I had a thought that spawned a litany of piss poor decisions.

If he really did love me, I could wind up marrying my Babies Daddy!

A part of me questioned my sanity, but my raging hormones had already taken over the part of my brain that thought logically. It was the perfect solution to get the perfect life. With no job, I decided to put all my wasted energy into another challenge...Bad Habit.

I jumped up to start my mission, but was brought back down to Earth with a thud, my knees giving in to the extra weight.

Damn, forgot I was pregnant again.

I shook my head in defiance, not willing to let some swollen belly get in my way.

My mother should have sent another book: *He's Just Not That Into You.*

***

Dear Me,

To make one fall in love with you, you must unmercifully kill him with kindness. And today, you outdid yourself. You were the queen of the duster, empress of the mop and ruler of stain remover. You were able to scrub this four-bedroom shack until it sparkled and shined. You whipped up a three-course roast beef dinner and even called your mother to get her famous candied yam recipe. You fixed your face, did your hair, and you were able to squeeze into the one cute outfit you have left that accentuates your new boobs. The candles are lit and the table is set. You are a rock star! This being a mom/wife thing will be a piece of cake! He won't know what hit him!

Love,

Alexandria the Great

***

Smoke swirled around the bathroom and I shrieked.

The roast!

I ran down the stairs in my heels, which screamed at my feet for being too big to fit in them. The kitchen was a massive chimney. I swung open the oven door to let the smoke clear. A crispy shell capsulated my roast beef. Besides the burnt cow, the yams were soupy, and the greens were better off coming from a can. I glanced down at my ridiculous outfit. My V-neck lace top looked more like a corset and I couldn't breathe in the matching skirt that used to be knee length, but now looked more like a mini.

I opened the backdoor to let the smoke out just as I heard the front door slam.

"What's burning?" Bad Habit shouted, rushing into the kitchen.

"Hey! You're back," I said as if the house wasn't on fire. He wasn't alarmed or even excited the moment he saw me. Just his usual ambivalent self.

"What happened?"

I waddled over, forcing myself upon him for a hug. It had only been three days, but I surprisingly missed his smell and buried myself in his warm chest.

Bad Habit froze under my touch, arms extended out, leaning away like I was made of poison oak. I looked up, trying to dazzle him with a flirty smile.

"What are you doing?"

"I'm hugging you. I missed you," I said like a psychotic cheerleader.

He pushed me away, backing out of the kitchen as if he was preparing to be attacked.

"Ok, what's wrong with you?"

I chuckled and stepped closer. He took another step back.

"Nothing's wrong, I'm just happy that you're home. Can't I be happy?"

"No. You can't. You're never happy."

I laughed a bit, before turning back to the stove, remembering to keep my cool around his digs, accepting that I would have to ignore and swallow his daily bullshit in order for my plan to work. If I snapped, he'd get angry, pushing me further away from the goal.

He has to fall in love with me before the babies are born. First comes love...then a baby carriage.

"Come to the table. I made dinner. Well...sort of."

He stared and hesitated before following.

"What's the catch?" he asked while walking into the dining room to a fully prepared table I mimicked off of HGTV. Stunned to disbelief, he watched me place the shamefully burnt cow on the table. Luther Vandross was playing in the background. I was laying it on thick.

"No catch. Go on. Sit down. Your soup is probably cold. But no worries."

Bad Habit eyes tracked my every movement as he sat at the head of the table. He picked up his spoon, swirled around the creamy lobster bisque slowly. His eyes were bloodshot and drained, indicating he did more than just attend a conference in Sin City. Suddenly, he dropped his spoon and leaned back in his chair.

"You're trying to poison me."

"What? I am not. It's not poisoned and no I'm not trying to kill you!" I laughed while attempting to carve the roast, nearly breaking the knife. "Can't I just cook for my man?"

He raised an eyebrow and tore off a piece of French bread, dipping it into his soup.

"Aight, Alexandria. For real, what's the catch? What do you want?"

I sighed, feigning innocence, and I sat next to him, kicking my heels off under the table.

"Nothing. It's just...well, since you're at work all day and I'm at home, I figured I would add an amendment to our...agreement. I take care of you and you take care of me."

He frowned as I laid a napkin on his lap.

"An amendment?"

"Yep. It's only fair, right?"

He exhaled, taking another bite of his bread. He was skeptical but couldn't do anything about it. I carried on like I was drinking a Prozac shake.

This is only the beginning.

"So...how was your trip?"

***

My dreams were so vivid and lucid in some ways that I couldn't tell if the sound of shattering glass was real or not. Uneasy with the disturbing feeling, I leaned up on my elbows in the dark room, lying next to a snoring Bad Habit. He had been complaining how my sleep talking was disturbing his precious slumber so I was relieved that I hadn't bothered him.

Until I heard it again, the distinct sound of glass hitting tiles. My heart stopped, staring at the open bedroom door.

Someone's breaking into the house!

I shook Bad Habit and he groaned.

"What?"

"Did you hear that?"

"Hear what?"

"I think someone's downstairs."

"Oh my God Alexandria! Go back to sleep, you're hearing things again," he moaned groggily and turned to his side, lifting the covers over his head.

"I'm serious! You don't..."

Glass crashing silenced me. One of those scared shitless types of silences. Bad Habit slowly removed the blanket from over his head, staring in disbelief at the half open door.

"Shit," he whispered and sprung up, throwing on a pair of basketball shorts.

His ass looks pretty good in those shorts. Ahhh...damn it Alex. Focus, we're under attack!

"What are you doing?" I whispered, clutching my knees to my chest. Another sound echoed from downstairs. Low murmuring voices.

"Pass me my gun. It's on your side underneath the mattress," he ordered while slipping his bare feet into some sneakers.

"I'm sorry, did you say gun? I believe you meant to say hand me my phone so I can call the police."

"Stop fucking around Alexandria and give me my goddamn gun."

"Wait! You're not going down there! You don't know who's down there or what they got! They could kill you!" I shouted under my breath. Even in my supposed high emotional state, I knew the difference between logical and plain old craziness. If he went down stairs like Rambo, there could be dozens of men, ready to attack him.

They may have the place surrounded. Like ninjas!

Losing his patience, he jumped over to my side of the bed and lifted the bed skirt. He pulled out what I could only guess was a Magnum and shoved in the clip. We looked like a 50 Cent video.

"Go to the bathroom and call 911."

"You're gonna leave me here by myself? No way!"

He grabbed my arm, yoking me from the bed. I snatched my cell phone off the nightstand before he pulled us into the bathroom and eased the door shut.

I raced to the window and peered out of the shades. Not a moving car in sight.

Damn suburbs, I knew this was a bad idea.

"Stay here and DON'T move!" he said, inadvertently pointing his gun towards me. I remained frozen and he closed the bathroom door behind him.

This is insane! He's going to get himself killed and leave me here defenseless. Or worse, a single mother of four!

I triple checked the door and rushed back to my seat on the windowsill, at a loss for what to do with myself. The bathroom was eerily silent as water trickled from the showerhead. My teeth chattered and I threw on my terry cloth robe to ease the chill. I peered out the window again. It was at least a twenty-foot drop to the ground below, but with my fat ass, it'd be a fast fall to my death if I tried to escape.

Trapped in a bathroom. Perfect. I'm officially the dumb blond who runs up the stairs in a horror movie.

I suddenly remember the cell phone in my hand.

"9-1-1 what's your emergency?" a woman with a squeaky voice responded.

"You have to help me. Someone broke into my...I mean our...his...the house!"

I climbed into the bathtub and pulled the curtain closed.

"Ok ma'am. Just remain calm."

"No, you don't understand. He went down after them. He has a gun and he's gonna get himself killed, and I'm four months pregnant and I—"

"Ma'am, can you tell me where you are?"

My teeth chattered and my hands trembled like I had Parkinson's. I couldn't think straight.

"Ummm...Atlanta. Yes, that's it."

"Yes, ok ma'am, I know that, but can you tell me your address?"

Oh shit.

It dawned on me that I had been living with Bad Habit for a month and had no idea what his address was. I didn't even know the house number. I peered out the shade again in search of a street sign.

"I...I don't know. I don't know. Oh shit...I'm, I'm in a house, it's brick and white and I just..."

The walls of the enormous bathroom started closing in on me. I braced the sides and tried to breathe, desperate for safety. I needed Bad Habit. No idea why, as he made me as comfortable as a Motel 6, but I needed him.

"Ma'am? Ma'am, are you there?" the voice pleaded.

After a quick calculation of my impending doom, I sighed before answering.

"Can you track me by my phone?"

"Yes ma'am, we are working on it right now."

"Good," I said and set the phone on the counter.

"Hello... Ma'am... Hello?"

What kind of woman would I be to let my man die alone? Ugh, how dramatic!

I unlocked the bathroom door and let it creak open. It couldn't have been more than five minutes but the house was silent. No voices, no gunshots, no glass. The room was empty. The bedroom door was a wide-open invitation, the hallway a black hole. I tiptoed out and peered over the banister. Light glowed from the kitchen.

Burglars turn on lights?

I rushed back into the room, silently closing the door behind me, struggling to make sense of things.

What if they captured him? What if they're gagging his mouth and torturing him, cutting off his fingers and toes one by one?

A part of me suspected there was something much more logical, but my overemotional state had already taken full control.

Bad Habit wasn't the type to buy just one of anything. Quietly, I began to search the drawers for another gun when there was another shattering of glass, sharp and violent, like a bottle broken over someone's head. I ducked as if the glass was being hurled at my neck and curled up to the nightstand.

Hide you idiot!

I tried to crawl under the bed, but it was like fitting a fat round peg in a small square hole. Doubling back, my hand slid and rammed into a mental box under the bed, breaking several nails. It took a moment to realize what I found. I seized box and pried it open. The glistening gun stared back at me, cold, ruthless, smelling like spray paint.

This is it. I'm going to die. In Atlanta, go figure.

I held my breath and grabbed it like it was a pair sweaty socks. Using the bed to help me stand, I left the room and tiptoed down the stairs.

There was mumbling coming from the kitchen, voices I didn't recognize. Pressing my back to the wall, I crept towards the entrance like the cat burglar. I raised the gun, readying myself when something small yet sharp hit my stomach. It was quick, but distinct. I curled back like turtle.

Oh God...I've been stabbed!

A horrified whimper escaped my lip. Frantically, I searched for the dagger one of the ninjas launched at me in the darkness. But there was no blood. I patted down my rounded belly when it happened again. The stab wasn't coming from the outside pushing in. It was from the inside trying to push out.

Was...that a kick?

It was just plain creepy. Proof that something really was growing inside of me, alive and aware. The kick was also a frightening reminder. I wasn't just putting myself in danger.

The Aliens will never see the light of day if this goes bad.

But there was no turning back. I accepted my fate, only upset that my mother would read about me in the papers. With a deep breath, I closed my eyes and charged in the kitchen, preparing to open fire.

"What the fuck are you doing!" Bad Habit roared, bringing me back to reality.

Bad Habit stood next to a man I could only guess was a relative since they looked so much alike. His eyes were droopy but filled with panic at the sight of a crazed pregnant chick holding a gun aimed at his head. Standing next to them were three other men, dressed in standard issue hood gear of baggy jeans, oversized t-shirts, and boots. Their hands raised to surrender.

"Alexandria put the gun down. It's just my cousin and his boys."

Cousin? Boys? No ninjas?

Bad Habit was fine. No cut off fingers or multiple stab wounds.

"I...I heard glass breaking?"

He rolled his eyes, looking back at his cousin who was swaying like a balloon.

"Dumb ass is drunk. He broke a window, a vase, and some glasses. His friends were just dropping him off."

I eyed his friends, giggling like schoolgirls. They covered their mouths, muffling their chuckles. I lowered the gun. There was nothing funny about this.

"Well why would he come here? This late?"

"He lives with his moms. He can't walk in like..."

"Ohhhh snap," his cousin interjected, slurring his words with a thick Boston accent. "This must be the bitch you knocked up."

"Excuse me?"

"Oh my bad babe, my bad. I mean no disrespect." The Patron was sweating out of his pores. He turned to Bad Habit. "Yo, she's cute. You gonna have some pretty ass babies man, congrats, man! What was you all worried about? Shit, I'd hit that too."

Bad Habit punched him in the arm.

"Hey Cuz, I mean no disrespect man, you know me. But damn, look at those thighs. Wooo...and I can see that ass from the front."

That did it. The boys busted out laughing over each other. All except Bad Habit. He closed his eyes, pinching the bridge of his nose.

"Alexandria...can you close your robe, please?"

"Huh?"

I looked down at my and gasped. I never tied my robe before leaving the room, exposing my bright pink underwear and see through white tank top that only partially covered my rounded tummy. Mortified, I snapped the robe closed and shot Bad Habit a disgruntled look.

"Now, don't get all upset," his cousin slurred while laughing. "I've seen enough titties and ass in my lifetime, relax. So cute, look at you, standing there with the burner, just ready!" He turned to Bad Habit. "Let me find out you got yourself a ride or die chick! Lady in the streets, freak in the sheets, especially to keep your ass around."

Bad Habit suddenly smirked. I still failed to see the humor. He shrugged, shaking his head at me.

"So you came down here to save me, huh?" he asked with a mischievous smile that melted the ice around me. I shrugged, amazed how he could make me gush with just a smile.

"Nah, I was saving myself. You didn't even cross my mind. I couldn't leave it all up to you to fuck up."

His cousin shook with laughter and playfully punched him.

"Hey Cuz, I like her. She's a good look for you."

Bad Habit smirked and walked over, reaching for the gun.

"She's alright," he said and stared down at me proudly. I almost exploded with joy. It was the first time that I could recall him outright approving of me. I wanted to live in the moment, throw my arms around his neck and tongue him down, but he was not into public displays of affection. I'd be pushing my luck.

Then, all of that relieving joy came to an abrupt end.

"Man, what the fuck?" His inebriated cousin shouted.

I followed his gaze over us towards the living room. Flashing blue and red lights danced hectically in the windows. Bad Habit turned to me, enraged.

Uh oh.

"You called the cops!"

"You told me to!"

His cousin and entourage scrambled to empty out the contents of their pockets into various drawers in the kitchen. A knock came from the front door.

"Oh shit, they got us surrounded!" His cousin shouted. His hysteria fueled by his drunken stupor as he paced in a circle. Bad Habit grabbed the gun out of my hand. Another knock, this one closer. We froze, then turned to the sliding glass door where an officer was standing in full view of our after party, flash light in one hand, gun in the other.

"Good job with the blinds, Derrick," Bad Habit hissed as he slowly set the guns on the floor and raised his hands. Derrick and friends followed his lead. I sucked in quick breath and walked over, sliding the door open.

"I'm sorry Officer, there's been a misunderstanding—"

The young officer brushed by me and began screaming.

"Everyone, down on the ground. NOW!"

Derrick sucked his teeth and bent to his knees. Bad Habit did the same. The front door cracked and heavy footsteps rushed to the kitchen. Three other officers surrounded us. It was like a mini army.

Wow! You'd never get this type of service in New York with one call.

"Wait, Officer. I can explain everything—"

The officer kicked the guns out of reach while the others held their positions.

"Search them!" he barked.

Bad Habit flinched, his bare chest on the cold marble. I jumped in front of him.

"LISTEN TO ME! This is my...boyfriend, alright! This is our house! These are our guests! You're not going to search anyone! It was just a misunderstanding. It was just his cousin coming in late. Everything is fine!"

The officer blinked a couple of times, breaking out of his search and destroy trance and stared in disbelief.

"Ma'am, are you sure?"

"Yes, I'm positive. I forgot to call you back—"

"Yo, man, get your foot off me!" Derrick shouted at the officer with his boot on his back.

"Alexandria, just don't—"

"Stop that! Please!" I turned to the officer. "Can they get up now?"

The officer glared at me then peered down as my robe started to unravel.

Of course the sight of my new boobs would be a distraction. They are like sagging watermelons with nipples.

"Lower your weapons," the officer ordered the others and they too snapped out of their trance. "Alright, on your feet."

Slowly, the boys rose, watching me from the corner of their eyes.

"Where'd you get the guns?" The officer asked Bad Habit.

"I bought them. I have the proper paperwork," he responded frigidly.

The officer looked displeased with the news.

"I'll need to see them."

"Duly noted. I'll need to see your badges as well."

The officer, irritated, turned back to me.

"Ma'am, are you SURE you're alright?"

I mustered out a nervous laugh in the tense air.

"I'm fine, really. You know us crazy pregnant ladies. Ha ha ha!"

Other than the static calls from the walkie-talkies, the room went silent. The officers and the boys facing each other like a Mexican standoff.

I coughed up another nervous laugh. "Uhhh...would anyone care for a late night sandwich?"

Five Months

After breathing, sex and food were my main priorities in life. Bad Habit, on the other hand, wasn't the type who needed sex on a daily basis, which was just plain irrational. So when I woke up, startled by him grasping at my nightshirt and kissing on my collarbone, I more than happily obliged.

He pressed hard against my inner thigh and I lifted my leg to let him inside. He eased in and I uttered an uncontrollable moan, my deprived hormones praised his godly dick.

Of course he wants to sleep with me, who wouldn't want a piece of this granny panty action?

He slid all the way in, letting me adjust to his length before he started to thrust. I pulled at his shirt, touching the muscles. I wanted more of him, all of him. I needed him to scratch an itch I couldn't reach. Like an unknown craving my mouth watered for, driving me insane with thirst. I stared, anxious for him to kiss me, ready to melt into him. But just as his lips tickled mine, his eyes went wide and he came to an abrupt halt.

"What the fuck!" he shouted, startled yet still snuggled inside me.

Huh...did I miss something?

I sat up on my elbows, winded and confused.

"What...what is it?"

It took him a moment as he caught his breath.

"Did...did you just do that?"

"What? What are you doing? Don't stop—" But as soon as I tried to grab for his neck again, a soft yet striking nudge pressed my stomach. His dick went limp inside me within seconds.

"THAT. Was that the...baby?"

Defeated, I fell back on my pillow with a thud. He pulled out and covered himself.

I didn't want to admit that it wasn't anything new. Kicks were normal. There were four of them in there after all. But I was sure it was Alien 3, the troublemaker. I held my stomach with a sigh.

"He must be kicking."

Bad Habit stared at my stomach like it was the Creature from the Black Lagoon oozing blood, mud, and alligator carcasses. He hovered above me, spooked.

"Did I hurt it...him?"

His stuttering was somewhat amusing.

Ha! Mr. Know-it-all is in uncharted waters.

"No, you can't hurt them." I tried to sound upbeat, like it was no big deal the tiny humans inside me were feeling his every stroke.

"Well, why did he kick?"

"Cause he felt like kicking...I don't know," I said, frustrated, trying to pull him closer. "Now come on, you won't hurt any of them, I swear."

Bad Habit went cold to my touch.

Jeez, this really freaked him out.

"Nah...I'm tired. Let's just...call it a night." He jumped up before I could protest and rushed to the bathroom, taking the dick I desperately needed with him.

***

Dear Me,

I'm pretty positive that the woman who wrote *What to Expect When You're Expecting* couldn't have possibly been pregnant at the time. Or at least not pregnant with multiplies with her happy-go-lucky Care Bear sounding self. Oh and her advice sucks.

Bad Habit won't touch me. Just because he felt a little Alien kick. I pretty much tried to rape him last night. But it was more the equivalent of a sumo wrestler pouncing on an unsuspecting emaciated victim. Not exactly the sexy effect I was going for and he swears I broke a rib.

I'm about to hit the street corners. Someone out there must be willing to fuck a pregnant girl. I won't even charge.

Love,

Call Girl #9

***

"Mrs. Konick from next door is coming over this afternoon," Bad Habit announced from the breakfast nook. I stood over the stove, flipping his last pancake. I'd been getting pretty decent at the whole cooking thing, attributing it to all of the Food Network I digested daily.

"Who's Mrs. Konick?" He had a habit of speaking people's names as if I knew whom he was talking about since I was expected to be a mind reader on top of everything else.

"Mr. Konick's wife, Jill. She lives next door, the one with the two kids. She wants to welcome you to the neighborhood." I turned just in time to see the smirk on his face before he hid it behind his newspaper.

"Isn't it a little late? I've been here for almost two months."

But we both knew where her curiosity stirred from. Ever since our episode with the po-po, a certain drunk cousin, and his minions, the neighbors were extra interested in us. I noticed Mrs. Konick watching us from her window. It was entertaining, the only real entertainment I got.

"Well, guess I can't sit around in my robe all day. Oh goodie, company. Let me break out the fine china!"

"Knock it off. She's just trying to be nice." His voice was laced with a 'don't embarrass me' warning tone.

"Relax," I said, dropping a plate in front of him. "I'll be on my best behavior. Plus, I really wouldn't mind the company."

The weeks were flying by and being cooped up in the house was giving me a serious case of cabin fever. At even the mere suggestion of going to the store, Bad Habit would beat me to the punch and bring home more groceries than the two of us could really eat in a week. The only time I was allowed out of prison was for my bi-weekly doctor's appointments, a.k.a "visiting hours."

"I'll be home late tonight." That was his way of telling me not to expect him home for dinner and another lonely night with the television, which I nicknamed Eddie.

"Big project?" I craved interaction with the outside world, particularly his world.

"Something like that," he said without looking up from his plate. Bad Habit was always careful not to lie but he danced around questions like a ballerina. "Meeting with my broker."

"That's the fourth meeting this month. Business must be going well, huh?"

He stuffed his mouth with bacon.

"Uh huh."

Well, so much for small talk.

There weren't many times where I'd seen Bad Habit relaxed. He was always as stiff and serious as concrete, taking a business approach to every aspect of his life. It was what I liked about him, at first. His drive matched my own.

I pushed myself up to grab his lunch knowing he was leaving soon and it would be my last opportunity to leave an imprint before work. I pulled out the lunch bag packed with last night's meat loaf, mashed potatoes, and string bean leftovers along with a cupcake.

Not bothering with the empty plate, he slid his chair back from the table and walked across the living room to his office to grab his briefcase, never appreciating that I always packed it for him while he showered. I grabbed his keys and took my place by the door like a faithful puppy.

Bad Habit emerged from his office, sighing at our inevitable morning routine. It took him a couple of days but he finally humored me. He dramatically stopped in front of me and I grinned.

"Your jacket." I handed him his chocolate blazer and he slowly put it on, one eyebrow remaining arched.

"Your lunch." I gave him the bag. I had been leaving small love notes laced with my perfume tucked inside. Though he hadn't responded to the previous ones, I was sure he enjoyed them.

"The door." I opened the front door, letting the humidity hit me like a brick.

"My kiss." I grinned and pulled him closer, raising my chin. On most days, he kissed me with apparent unwillingness. Like I was forcing him to kiss a toad. Which was why I always saved the keys for last. Yes, it was entrapment, but I was playing with the only cards dealt.

After a long sigh, a mischievous smile crept over his lips and he cupped my face. His lips started slow, gently taking my breath away. I curl and suction around him, his tongue gliding around mine before nipping my bottom lip. The room grows hotter. Eyes closed, head spinning, I almost fall forward when he let go.

"Better?" he asked smugly once done. My eyes flew open and I tried not to gasp at his close proximity.

He smells way to enticing for his own good.

"Much better," I breathed then smiled.

"Keys," he said and he held out his hand. My bliss turned into a sulk and I dropped the keys into his hands.

"Keys."

He didn't give me another glance before running out the door, never knowing that this was the best part of my day.

***

The knock was faint, but the repeating doorbell was loud and clear from the second floor.

Damn, doesn't she know I'm pregnant and my motor skills have slowed dramatically?

"I'm coming!" I snapped, descending the stairs breathless and exhausted. After Bad Habit left for work, the rest of my morning was spent cleaning and preparing for my impending company. First impressions are everything, but it was hard to do anything in my condition.

How women are able to function pregnant with one baby let alone four is madness.

I peeped out of the window before opening the door. The smell of fresh baked apple pie hit me and I wiped the drool off my chin, not even noticing the bleached blonde holding it. Mrs. Konick was tall and slender with over baked skin that cracked around her blue eyes like old paint. She was cut and lean, but seemed much older than her body gave her credit for.

"Hi, you must be Alexandria. I'm Jill, I spoke to your...boyfriend and told him I wanted to come by and welcome you to the neighborhood."

Boyfriend was the wrong title, more like fellow scam artist as we had somehow perpetrated being a happy couple. But it was too early in the day to snap at my only company in weeks.

"Hi Jill, it's Alex, pleasure to meet you. Come in, please."

Her eyes fixed on my stomach, while I fixated on the pie. I was wearing an extra-large plus sized peach housedress that once belonged to my overweight cousin. After many hours of research, I found there are no designers that catered to obese pregnant fashionistas, so I had to take what I could get.

"I am so sorry I haven't been by here sooner," she lied in her thick Georgia peach accent as I closed the door behind her. "It's just with the kids' schedules, running the PTA, being the president of our women's group, book club, and trying to keep the house in some type of order, time just gone and flew by so fast. But I baked a pie, so surely that'll make up for it." She laughed with a small snort.

Humph, damn do-it-all woman. She'll put me to shame!

Alien 2 kicked. The moment I'm about to lose my temper, the Aliens would communicate by using my organs as punching bags.

"Oh it's fine, I've been trying to adjust myself."

"How you liking Atlanta?"

"It's...interesting. Hot."

"Hot it is! New Yorkers always have a hard time adjusting at first but learn to love it. And in your condition you shouldn't be out in no sun no way and...oh my!"

She stared at my stomach, her eyes filled more with green envy than shock.

"Wow! I never realize how far along you were sweetie! When yah due?"

"Well, not sure yet, it'll probably be early, since there isn't much room for them to grow properly and all," I said, quoting Dr. Turner's words. I motioned towards the kitchen and she happily led the way.

"Oh you're having twins? That's wonderful. Heather Richardson, 'bout two houses down, had twins last April. You ought to talk to her for some tips. Those boys of hers are sure a handful."

He didn't tell her. Why?

"Well...actually, I'm having quadruplets," I said painfully, like I hit a funny bone in both arms. Her mouth dropped.

"Well, as my daughter would say, O M G!" She squealed like a little girl, almost breaking my eardrum. "That is amazing! How in the world..."

"Fate, I suppose," I said with a shrug.

Wait. Did I just say that?

"That's just unbelievable!"

Oblivious to the displeasure in my voice, she placed the pie on the counter and proceeded opening all the cabinets. I slid onto a barstool at the kitchen island.

Damn, she's really making herself feel right at home isn't she?

Alien 4 kicked my side.

"To think about just how amazing all this is. You couldn't be no more than, what, twenty-four?"

"Twenty-five."

"Twenty-five, oh right, sorry. As I was saying, you're twenty-five and y'all already have a full house of kids. When your man bought this house 'bout six months ago, he was a bachelor, clearly living the single life, if you know what I mean. And look at him now, with a beautiful gal, hopefully wife to be, and four little ones on the way."

She set two plates down in front of me with a wink.

"Clearly living the single life?"

"Oh yeah sweetie, your beau was definitely a ladies' man. He's always been a pretty private person, but we've seen some casual lady friends come out of here once or twice. In fact, you're the first consistent girl we've seen around here. But I'm sure you knew all that." She stood, reveling in her gossip. I grabbed the edge of my seat to keep from lunging at her neck.

"Oh," I said, trying to compose my face.

No wonder she hasn't been by yet, she thought I was one of the many smuts he's had in here. Here I am trying to be on my best behavior so that I wouldn't embarrass him and he beat himself to the punch by being the whore of the neighborhood.

I glanced around the kitchen and nothing seemed the same. It disgusted me to think of some other chicks roaming the very halls that have entrapped me for the past two months. That they've had his body the same way I have. The heat rising to my throat was nothing more than pure jealousy.

"All seems...really fast. If you don't mind me asking, how long were you trying for?"

"Trying?"

She grinned liked a teenager digging for secrets.

"You know...to have a baby?"

I stared in silence and gripped the seat tighter, nearly breaking the wood. She continued, numb to the tense air.

"Oh don't be ashamed sweetie, many gals do it. Why, just the other day I was talking to—"

"No in vitro."

If it wasn't for the pie, I'd kick her out, but I feared she'd be smart enough to take it with her.

"No in vitro?"

"That's right, none. No hormone medications, no special voodoo, nothing. Just plain old sex did it for us."

She stood motionless and amazed, her smile quickly fading.

"Oh, I just thought, well, never mind...I guess."

Her eyes dropped down to her hands while she played with the empty plate.

"You know, it always shocks me, how some people just have such an easy time getting pregnant and others...well...it could take a life time. I mean look at you, twenty-six. My God, you know...some women can't even have kids until they're in their forties..."

Her voice cracked and she turned away, searching through the drawers for forks. My heart sank to my stomach. Of course, she was taking about herself, trying to own up to a perfect life and unable to bare children. And there I was, an unwilling oven with four aliens baking inside. She was worried about PTA meetings and I was worried about Bad Habit and his smuts.

"Well, if you know anyone who needs a baby, let me know. I have plenty to spare."

She turned with a smile, her eyes glazed with tears.

"I'm sorry. Me and my big mouth, always getting the best of me." She pulled out two forks and placed them on the table. "I didn't even come over for all that. I came because your man said I should talk to you 'bout making one of those Facebook sites for our book club."

I paused before responding, wondering what man she could be referring to.

"He DID?"

"Yeah, he said you were real, real good at that social media stuff and I don't know nothing 'bout it. How much you charge?"

I'd mentioned to Bad Habit that I wanted to freelance from home but I didn't think he was listening since he didn't respond. It's like talking to a Chucky doll sometimes.

"Uhhh...can I get back to you on that? But until then, why don't you tell me more about it."

"Well of course! Why you may go ahead and join!"

I smiled, glancing at the golden crust pie, picturing the warm granny smith apples and cinnamon sugar inside.

"This pie looks delicious, Jill," I said, drooling again.

"Why thank you! It's a family recipe, passed by my Mama. Now, where do you keep your cake knife?"

"If we have one, it may be in that first drawer, next to the fridge, behind you."

She turned, continuing her chatter. "Anyway, this is the perfect place for you to raise your little ones. There's plenty of kids in the neighborhood and the school..."

Her voice trailed off and though her back was facing me, I knew something wasn't right. She stared into the drawer like it was an open grave.

"Something wrong?"

She jumped and slammed it shut, spinning around. Her eyes loaded with a strange look of bewilderment and her mouth hung open, large enough for a bird to fly in and build a nest.

"Jill? Is there something wrong?" I repeated, not knowing what else to say.

She gripped the counter behind her, pinning herself, attempting to be as far away from me as possible.

"Umm...nothing! I...I...I actually have to go."

"Go? But you just got here. We haven't even had pie yet."

I didn't want to admit it, but I enjoyed the company. I hadn't interacted with another human being other than Bad Habit in weeks. I wanted to keep her locked in the basement *Silence of the Lambs* style.

"At least stay for a—"

"NO!" she shouted, startling even herself. I remained silent.

The bitch is crazy.

"I'm sorry…I just have to go. I…forgot I have to pick up my son from school today," she begged, backing out of the kitchen. I glanced at the clock, which had just struck noon.

What school lets out this early?

"Jill, it's only—"

"I'm sorry, I just really have to go," she insisted, continuing to inch away, bruising my ego with every step.

Fine. If you want to go, then go. But I'll be damned if you try to take this pie with you!

I slid off the stool and she froze, holding her hands out towards me as if to protect herself.

"NO! Just stay where you are! It's ok, I can see myself out."

My eyes dart between her and the pie between us.

"Take care, enjoy the pie," she sputtered out and spun on her heels. I waited till the front door slammed before peering out the window in time to see Mrs. Konick race across the lawn in full track star sprint like I was chasing her with a meat cleaver.

"What the hell was all that about?"

Alien 4 kicked me.

"Oh, right! The pie!"

The pie was a gleaming prize on the counter. Mrs. Konick's early departure was the perfect excuse to eat both of our portions without subjecting myself to ridicule from Bad Habit when he arrived home to find that I had overindulged yet again.

It was only when I opened the drawer behind me to retrieve the cake knife did I realize why Mrs. Konick ran. Inside, on top of the cake knife, was a large zip lock bag filled to the brim with what I could only guess was weed. It smelled sweet and tangy, so I knew for sure it wasn't parsley. Laying on top of the weed bag was an equally large gun. My mind flashed back to Bad Habit's cousin, Derrick, and the police raid...I remembered a drawer slamming shut.

Aw hell.

In Jill's defense, I probably would have ran out of the house screaming too. With a sigh, I brushed past the hash and pulled out the knife.

***

Dear Me,

I ate all of Mrs. Konick's pie. Not because it was good (it was missing allspice and needed more sugar) but just because it was there and it was hard not to. As punishment, the Aliens hit me with heartburn so severe I almost called the paramedics believing I was in the middle of a heart attack.

Mrs. Konick's visit was a wild success as she has now confirmed we are nothing more than stereotypical hood negroes. I'm sure I'll be getting a call from social services to confirm that I am, indeed, carrying crack babies. So I'm just sitting here and waiting for the cops to show up... again. Jail won't be so bad. At least I'll have company.

It's 1 a.m. do you know where your Bad Habit is? Because I sure don't.

Love,
Mom Behind Bars

***

An unfamiliar car purred outside. I tossed my journal aside, waddled over and peered out the window at a cherry red 3 series BMW parked in the driveway, its lights bouncing off the garage door, the dark tint blocking my view of the inside.

"Who the hell is—"

The passenger door flew open and Bad Habit stepped out, smiling. He bent down to look back in the car again, spoke a few words, and then closed the door.

As he strutted around the car towards the walkway, the driver's side window rolled down, revealing the driver. A gorgeous cinnamon toasted woman with a striking face perfected with makeup and a long, loosely curled blond weave, smiled wryly.

"Hey," she called out to him and he spun around. She reached her delicate, manicured hand adorned with a sparkling tennis bracelet out the window, holding the tie he was wearing earlier that morning.

The tie I tied for him.

"You forgot something."

She swung it around, like she was dancing a carrot in front of a donkey and the ass took two large strides to retrieve it. He held one end of the tie while she held onto the other.

"Thank you," he cooed with a seductive smirk.

"You're very welcome," she replied in the same tone, releasing her hold. Rolling the window back up with a wink, she threw the car in reverse and backed out of the driveway while Bad Habit watched.

I stepped away from the window to keep myself from breaking the blinds.

He is coming home...from a date?

The walk back to the bed seemed to happen in slow motion, eyes never blinking. I hear the front door close.

While I sit at home like an overstuffed penguin, he goes out on DATES?!

Alien 3 kicked my back.

"I'll try not to kill him."

I snapped on the bedside lamp. My eyes wore a red filter. Thoughts of the gun under the bed crossed my mind. Alien 3 kicked me again.

"I said I'll TRY...that's all I can give you."

Bad Habit moved about the kitchen and I could smell roasted lamb chops heating up in the microwave.

The dinner I made for HIM while he was out on a DATE with another woman!

I touched my brittle, unmanicured nails and my dry, frizzy hair that I kept almost permanently in a low ponytail. I needed a perm but that's on the 'No' list when you're pregnant. Old Navy sweat pants and tees had become my daily uniform. The only jewelry I wore was a seasick band to keep from barfing while walking and I couldn't remember the last time I glossed my lips. I was a hot mess compared to that Beyoncé wannabe.

Yet, she is everything I wanted to be.

His heavy footsteps climbed the stairs. I tried to act natural, but my body was a hot rigid stone and the room became a sauna when he entered.

"Why are you still up?" he asked casually, walking into the closet without so much as a glance.

Don't hurt him. Don't hurt him. Don't hurt him.

"Why are you home so late?"

He hesitated, but continued to change out of his clothes.

"Long day."

Oh really? I bet it was long.

"Really. So where's your car?"

He hesitated again and walked into the bathroom like a mute.

"Hello, did you hear me?"

"It's in the shop."

"So how'd you get home?"

Silence, then the shower turned on. I jumped out of bed and slammed the door open. The steam from the hot water swirled around him. He wasn't surprised to see me.

"I'm talking to you," I shouted, holding the doorframe to brace myself, coordination askew.

Bad Habit eyes pierced me before turned his back to check the water temperature.

"I got a ride."

I bet you did get a ride.

Alien 3 kicked me harder.

"Oh really, from who?"

"A friend."

"A friend? You expect me to buy that?"

Bad Habit sucked his teeth, gliding his hands down his face slow like he was trying to rip his eyes out.

"I'm tired and I need to take a shower," he moaned.

Word vomit spewed out before I could stop myself.

"You asshole! Who was that? Are you sleeping with her?"

His eyes narrowed. He yanked off his shirt and boxers, tossing them in the corner and stepped inside the shower, jerking the curtain closed in front of me. He had no intention of dignifying my questions with a response. I groaned.

Unbelievable!

Before storming away, I shouted over my shoulder.

"By the way, you can relax, the neighbors just think you're the next Escobar."

***

Dear Me,

Atlanta has something down here called Sweet Tea. Bad Habit brought some home the other day. Kinda reminds me of the stuff the Chinaman sells at the carry out in those big plastic soup containers back home. It tastes like awesome mixed with heaven. I was drinking tea and listening to the radio while cleaning the carpet this morning (on my hands and knees, mind you). After they announced the weather (101 degrees in the shade. Lord, take me now!) they played an hour worth of OutKast. And I love André 3000.

Bad Habit has been out every night and I've simply combated his behavior with utter subservient willingness. Pretending to be dumb as rocks, ignorant to everything. I'm like the black Martha Stewart, queen of three course meals, crafts, and home decor. Bad Habit, however, is the king of showing his lack of appreciation. I don't think I'm doing anything outrageous. Women have been playing this role for centuries with a 75% success rate.

I know this isn't what Michelle would do. But sometimes you gotta play your role and the way I've been acting, you'd think nothing bothered me. Not even the perfume he smelled like when he came in drunk the other night. I'm pretty proud of myself for controlling my temper.

Love,

The Biggest Loser

P.S. Ok, so I broke a couple of lamps when he wasn't around. No biggie.

***

"We need to go shopping. I need some new tops. Maybe Pea in a Pod or Izzy. I could probably fit some dresses in the plus size section of Nordstrom, but Saks has a maternity section. Hmmm, I don't know, what do you think?"

"What am I, your gay best friend?"

Bad Habit, seated in his office on a rare Saturday home, looked up from his desktop. It was a beautiful day, crisp and refreshing. There was even a breeze, laced with what I imagined honeysuckle to smell like. I was looking for any excuse to get out of the house.

"I'm serious! I have no clothes," I said, pointing to my stained, tattered t-shirt that came free with my *Entertainment Weekly* subscription. But after another growth spurt, it looked more like one of those midriff tops you buy at Rave. I hadn't been shopping in months. I was setting some sort of world record.

"We're on a budget. And you have plenty of clothes hanging in the closet."

"Those clothes are a size four, I'm a size fifty!"

"I don't think Wal-Mart carries that size."

"There's a Wal-Mart around here? Oh where! Oh please show me, I'll do anything!"

"Since when do you shop at Wal-Mart?" He raised an eyebrow, knowing my aversion to polyester.

Since you got me trapped up in here like Kunta Kinte! I'm willing to slum it.

"I...like Wal-Mart. I'm not picky."

"Yeah right," he scoffed with a short laugh and refocused on his computer.

"Pleasssse! I really want to go."

I would've fallen on my knees if I knew I could get up without assistance.

"I am quite aware of your esoteric taste, but there is no need to be sycophant. New clothes are not essential."

I have no idea what he just said, but I'm sure I should be insulted by it.

I breathed in deep, playing it cool. That's what Michelle would do.

"Sure, whatever you say."

His eyebrow arched.

"You feeling alright?"

"Yes. I. Feel. Fine. Thank. You. For. Asking," I gritted through my teeth.

He shrugged, continuing to type some biblically long email and I found myself envious of his homework.

"I finished that Facebook page for Ms. Robinson, down the street," I blurted out, it sounded just as childish as it did in my own head. But I didn't care, I was proud of it. Ms. Robinson made baked goods and was known in the streets for her sugar cookies. Within a week, she had over 1000 likes on her page and a fifteen percent increase in sales. Business was booming. She was an easy brand to market and I already created a site map for her website.

Bad Habit didn't look up or stop typing.

"I'm actually thinking of starting my own consulting firm so I can take on more clients. I flushed out a business plan and a proposal. Maybe you can take a look and—"

His Blackberry buzzed and I was nothing more than a fly in his room.

"Yo man, what's up—Nah, we splitting this party sixty-forty. My assistant just confirmed twelve VIP tables...Some Falcon players I represent...Oh come on man, really?"

"Be with a fool or be alone and a fool."

I groaned, walking away like I was cut from cardboard, chewing on my tongue to keep from screaming.

"Oh hold on one sec... Hey! By the way, what's for dinner?"

***

Dear Me,

Bad Habit put the credit card he gave me on a timeout. I spent over eight hundred dollars at Barnes and Noble in the last month. It's really his fault since I'm bored out of my mind! I've been reading all the classics, like Hughes, Morrison, Baldwin, and Hurston. I even read a biography on Gandhi, hoping it would inspire me to be more peaceful. But I think he's more concerned about the amount of fluff I'm reading as well. *Good Girls Gone Bad*,

Project Chick, and *Hot Girlz* aren't exactly Pulitzer Prize winning novels.

Now I must resort to reading Bad Habit's old law school textbooks. I figure, I might as well earn an honorary law degree, since my mind is melting into oatmeal. So far I'm up to Family Law. Did you know if you're with someone for seven years, it's recognized as a valid marriage? I wonder if I can hold out that long.

Love,

Alex Stone, Esquire

***

Relax Alex. They'll love you. Who wouldn't?

"What time is it?" Bad Habit shouted from the living room. I checked the clock on the stove as I shoved in the last tray of macaroni and cheese.

"It's six-thirty. What time are they supposed to get here?"

No response. Apparently, he only answered questions he felt like answering. Just another one of his flaws I had to ignore for the sake of our impossible union. That evening, his friends were coming over to watch some highly important game that I knew nothing about. Knowing it would be the first time I was meeting some of them, I wanted it to be special and went into full Michelle mode, pretending it's a White House dinner for our foreign allies.

Wiping my sweaty forehead, I surveyed the scene in the kitchen. The barbeque chicken was sizzling, the baked beans stewing, and the corn bread was rising. Every table and countertop had a bowl of mix, chips, or seasoned popcorn. But perhaps I over did it with the coconut cake, fruit salad, and spinach dip. (Ok, so I was nervous.)

Having your significant other's friends like you is crucial, especially when you're about to pop out four of his children. Back in D.C., his friends didn't acknowledge my existence. Bad Habit didn't help the situation, always laughing along with his friends at some inside joke at my expense. I was determined not to be a joke in Atlanta. I shuddered at those memories. The embarrassing ways he treated me, how pathetic I looked, pretending it didn't affect me. In some warped way, not much had changed.

Bad Habit walked into the kitchen like a food inspector, his eyes gazing over the spread, unimpressed. I smiled, searching for some type of approval while cutting limes for Coronas but silence was his only compliment.

It's fine. He doesn't have to pat me on the back every time I do something good. I'm not that needy. Am I?

He opened the freezer.

"Is this all the beer we got?"

"Oh, well...yes, but we can always get more...if you want!"

Lawd, what is happening to me?

He grunts as the doorbell rung, slamming the fridge shut, bolting for the door. From the kitchen, I listen their loud, joyful, clashing reunion and found myself missing home. Ever since I moved to Atlanta, a huge dividing rift grew between me and my friends. But it wasn't the distance, it was my bizarre pregnancy. Things we use to talk about seemed irrelevant now. We no longer had anything in common. My girls were too busy attending celebrity filled parties, fashion shows, shopping in Soho, and vacationing in the Hamptons to relate to my daily angst.

How do you compare your sudden fetish for broccoli and mustard with a girl who just bought three pairs of Manolos?

It had gotten to the point where I avoided speaking to them all together, since they were painful reminders of the girl I use to be. But I didn't have time to dwell on the past. I was on a mission.

Focus Alex. Focus.

I reapplied my lip-gloss in the microwave's reflection, straightened my hair, and smoothed my trembling hands down my shirt.

Calm down Alex. They'll love you. Just be yourself.

That was a hard sell, since I had no idea who I was anymore. I took off my apron and waddled into the hallway where the happy faces on the men and women in the group darkened at the sight of me. Their previous banter was nowhere to be found. Puzzled by their expressions, I took a quick survey of my clothes, trying to find the unsightly stains that would make them stare at me with such disgust. Bad Habit avoided eye contact and continued like I never stepped foot in the room.

"So. Y'all ready to watch the game?"

They all agreed, heading into the living room without so much a glance, while I stood like an out of place piece of furniture.

Ok. Don't mind me. I'm just the pregnant bitch who lives here.

I retreated back to the kitchen like I was the help. My back ached; I hadn't sat down in hours. I reached the breakfast nook, ready to collapse, when a car crashed into the living room. Or, that's what it sounded like. The crashing was soon followed by screams and Bad Habit's unmistakable groan. I stood frozen in the perpetual

154 | Blu Daniels

fear that I'd done something wrong before he emerged, his friends following. Their eyes pop, drooling over the spread on the counter.

"What happened?"

Bad Habit opened the fridge and passed around some beers.

"The TV fell," he muttered.

His friends picked over the wings and dip like park pigeons.

"Oh no!" I tried to sound extra concerned and rubbed his back (because that's what girlfriends are supposed to do).

"What do you want to do? We can bring the TV down from upstairs."

"Nah, no need. We're just going to head to a bar. I'll call Best Buy tomorrow to come replace it."

A bar? Yes!

"Great! Let me just change my shoes and I'll be ready."

His friends throw each other cautious glances. Bad Habit, noticing, grimaced.

"Ummm...I don't think that's such a good idea."

"Why not?" I whined before I could stop myself. His friends chuckled and headed towards the door, taking a few wings with them.

"Alexandria, the place is going to be packed. You can't come. Not in your condition."

Pregnancy amnesia strikes again. I glanced over the party spread.

"But I made all this food and I—"

"They got plenty of food at the bar."

He headed towards the door, glancing over his shoulder. "I'll probably be home late."

My mouth ajar, prepared to beg before my heart crashing into my stomach stopped me. The front door slammed shut as tears brimmed, feeling nothing but painful, unequivocal loneliness.

***

I ugly cried myself to sleep, curled around my body pillow. When I woke up in darkness, my back was cripplingly stiff, and my lips salty and dry from tears. A faint glow from the porch light peaked through the blinds. I rolled on to my back and almost shrieked. Bad Habit was laying beside me, wide-awake, eyes intensely focused on my stomach.

"Oh! You're back. Early?"

He doesn't respond. I don't know why but his emotionless expression as he glared at my stomach was unnerving.

"What's wrong?"

He looked up at me and frowned.

"I like having sex with you."

The words came out in a slur laced with liquor.

"Ok."

"So when we don't...it's confusing how I still sort of like you. Even though you can be a fucking nag."

"Well, whisper more sweet nothings in my ear why don't you."

He blinked then rolled over to his knees, sitting between my legs.

"Take off your clothes."

He can't be serious. After the way he just treated me...

"No."

"No? Well, if you say so."

He lifts up my t-shirt and rolls down my panties.

"Hey! What are you–"

He yanked my legs, pulling me down to him. I landed right on his ready fingers.

"Wait, I...ohhhh. Oh, ohhhh..."

And just like that, I forgot all about the tears and the food I cooked. My pregnancy induced need for sex twenty-four seven left no room self-respect.

I'm sure Michelle had this same problem.

"You're so fucking wet...all the time."

He slipped his dick in and air whistled through his teeth. He was so warm and filling, my moan was more like a scream. I straddled my legs around his neck while he held my waist and pulled me down harder and faster against him.

"Ah! Ah! Ah!"

I wiggled and kick at his chest, the pressure almost too much. He grabbed my ankle, pushing into me harder, knees digging into my ass.

"Ah!"

"Mine," he groaned, his free hand jumping over my stomach to my chest, squeezing. "Say it."

***

"I cut the crust off his sandwich this morning."

Kennedy gasped, choking on her garden salad over the phone. The TV on the fridge was set to Rachael Ray. I was learning how to make pesto. Bad Habit loves Italian.

I think.

"You did what?" she asked, catching her breath.

"I cut the crust off his turkey and cheese sandwich this morning. I also ironed all of his dress shirts for the week and made his favorite peach cobbler. I'm making Cornish hens and cran-apple stuffing for dinner tonight."

Silence came over the phone followed by a long sigh.

"Ok, Alex, you're scaring me."

"I know. I'm scaring myself."

"Should you really be doing all this WHILE you're pregnant? Aren't you supposed to stay off your feet?"

The last time she questioned my motives I broke into a hysterical screaming rant about needing him to fall in love with me. Since then, she danced around the touchy subject to spare my feelings about the idea she called a suicide mission.

"It's not that bad, really."

"Oh really?"

"Yeah."

That was a lie. Just walking from one side of the room to the other was self-inflicted torture.

"So is he your boyfriend yet?"

"Well...something like that."

"Alexandria!" Bad Habit bellowed from the foyer and I jump out my skin.

"Hey! He's home early!"

"Oh goodie Martha Stewart, perhaps he'll help you jar preserves."

"Shut up. I'll call you back."

Wiping my hands clean on my June Cleaver apron, I waddle out of the kitchen and stopped short in horror at what waited for me.

Bad Habit clutched the end of a black leash attached to a snow-white slobbering puppy.

"Alexandria, meet Sasha," he said like proud daddy.

Sasha frantically tried to charge towards me in the goofy way only adorable puppies could. But that was acceptable in TV shows, movies, and pet store windows. Not in my house. He stroked her head, coddling her with baby talk.

"It's a dog."

"You're perceptive."

"You...got a dog?"

"It's a pit-bull."

"So you plan on raising Cujo?"

"Cujo was a St. Bernard."

"I don't care if Cujo was poodle! Why would you get that beast?"

Sasha's ears poked up. She cocked her head to the side and stared back at me.

"I take it you don't care for dogs."

"Dogs are cool, from afar. But that's a beast. They have news specials and laws banning those things. She's gonna grow up and bite my face off."

"Not unless I train her."

"Train her?" I yelled. "You work twelve hours a day and travel the other half of the time. How will you have time for a dog?"

"I'll make the time."

"Right. 'Cause you make sooo much time for me."

He ignored my snide remark and struggled to hold her still while taking off the leash.

"Just remember," I warned. "We're having a baby. Actually, several of them. I hope you make the time for them too."

"I know Alexandria. You don't have to remind me. Seeing you is enough," he sneered, rolling his eyes. "It's better to get her now, while she's young."

Sasha trotted over, drooling on the carpet, and sniffed my bare feet. I sighed and glanced down at her. For a beast, she was rather cute, in a moronic kind of way. Bad Habit had a joy in his eye that I had never seen before. For once, his formal demeanor was replaced by childlike happiness.

Well, I guess she's not so bad if she makes him this happy.

But then, a warm steady stream of liquid sprayed on my foot. The stench fouled the air. We locked eyes.

"The bitch just peed on me."

He coughed to stifle a laugh and grabbed her collar.

"Maybe she's marking her territory," he said with a shrug, pulling her away.

Great, that's just what we need, another bitch in this house.

***

Dear Me,

I'm absolutely positive Sasha has Tourette's and the Dog Whisperer over here can't tame her in the few hours that he's home during the day. So far she's just about destroyed a piece of furniture in the house. My chunky leg has become her new tree trunk.

During the day she follows me around to the point where I don't even remember what my own shadow looks like anymore. She devours every toy and drop of food you

give her yet still wants more. Well, got to run, she's climbing on my lap. Time for our nap since, apparently, her bed isn't good enough.

Love,

Sasha and Me

***

Insomnia being yet another fun addition to my hellish pregnancy, I was used to being awake at three in the morning, but this time was different. This time I was wide-awake and starving like I hadn't just woofed down two steaks at dinner. Starving like children in those late night infomercials that I always sent money to. I've suffered with late night cravings before, but never so severe that death by starvation felt only mere moments away. I was hell bent on one thing, ice cream. Strawberry ice cream to be exact. The chunky kind, like Ben and Jerry's, Häagen-Dazs, or Breyers; the kind that could cure cancer. The problem was we didn't have any ice cream in the fridge since I killed it earlier in the week.

Bad Habit was knocked out next to me and Sasha was snoring on the floor when my mental sixty-watt bulb clicked.

It wouldn't be outrageous for him to get me ice cream. That's what a man is supposed to do for his pregnant wife. It's in all the movies.

Maybe that's why I decided to test the waters of his affection by waking him up with annoying arm tapping.

"Ughhhh...what?!"

Hmmm...should've thought this through before waking him.

"I...um...need you to do me a favor?"

"Alexandria, it's three in the damn morning!"

"I know, I know. But I REALLY need some ice cream."

He raised his head up to glare at me.

"Some what?"

"Ice cream."

"You can't be serious?"

With the voice as innocent as a twelve-year-old girl, I pleaded.

"Pleasssse."

"No," he snapped, covering his head with a pillow. I pouted for a moment before attempting to force myself back to sleep. But the thought of cold strawberries and cream hitting my hot tongue haunted me. With a huff, I pulled back the sheets and waddled to my flip-flops. Bad Habit stirred.

"Where are you going?"

"To get some ice cream," I said, hoping the sight of me on my feet would change his mind.

"Fine, whatever," he growled, sucking his teeth as he buried himself again.

Bruised with rejection, I waddled out of the room and down the stairs, my robe dragging. I scooped the car keys off the side table and headed out the door.

There has to be a 7-11 around here somewhere.

With no streetlights, the driveway seemed invisible. That should've been the first indication that I was about to make a mistake. But all my one-track mind could think of was ice cream and I had no intention on turning back. I thought I grabbed the keys to the spare car but instead his precious truck alarm beeped once and I stuffed myself inside. Being a city girl, I'm not the most stellar driver, and it had been a while since I'd been behind the wheel. I hadn't driven a mile in Atlanta since Bad Habit wouldn't allow it.

So really, what transpired was actually his fault.

The engine purred while I adjusted the mirrors, checking blind spots that were still blind. Alien 4 kicked me.

I know. I'm excited too. Freedom!

Overcome with my liberation, I threw the car in reverse and tried to pivot my body to see out of the back windshield. I guess I didn't realize the weight of my bloated foot and before I knew it the car jerked wildly and sped backwards. A loud roar of twisting of metal followed by ear piercing scratching, like steel on a chalkboard, filled the air. I slammed on the breaks and my stomach brutally rammed into the steering wheel.

"Owww! Shit!"

Three seconds later, Bad Habit comes running out of the house in his boxers, fuming.

Uh oh.

I turned off the engine and locked the doors like he was a carjacker.

"What the fuck are you doing!" he screamed, examining the car. I cringed away from the window and peered out at the side mirror, noticing the contorted mailbox laying on the ground.

Double uh oh.

"I'm...I'm sorry."

He circled the car twice like a lion around its dinner then stood by the driver's side door. Fist balled up, jaw clenched, eyes closed.

"Alexandria, get out of the car," he said with a forced calm, the bass in his voice reaching a new low.

Oh my God, he's gonna kill me!

I shook my head violently. "No."

"Alexandria, if you don't get out this motherfucking car right now or—"

"No, I'm scared!" I said, rambling. "I'm sorry, I couldn't see. It was an accident, I swear!"

He jerked at the door handle.

"Alexandria, just get out the car and go back to bed! I'll deal with it."

I shook my head again in response. The neighbor's lights turned on.

"Are you gonna hurt me?"

"No, I'm not. Just go back to bed."

I reached for the door then pulled back.

"But...my ice cream," I said, biting my lower lip.

He let out a painful moan.

"I'll get the damn ice cream, just go!"

Well, that was easy.

Smiling, I unlocked the door and climbed out the truck.

"Okay. So I want strawberry. Oh and fried chicken too. Oh and if they have some waffles I'd love—"

He moaned again before letting out a pent up scream. Like Sasha, I cowered away from him as if I just pissed on the carpet.

"Just get in the car," he mumbled.

"Where are we going?" I asked, picturing him throwing my dead body off a bridge somewhere after he finished strangling me. He sighed and climbed in the driver's seat before mumbling a brief response.

"Waffle House."

***

"Are you going to eat the plate too?"

Bad Habit glared with his sultry brown eyes across our booth at the grungy diner just off I-80, near City Center.

Normally, I wouldn't eat at a place where you would most likely find handfuls of gray hair in your scrambled eggs, but I made an exception since it had everything I wanted. A one-stop greasy food spot, otherwise known as heaven for the craving afflicted. Next door was a strip club offering a daily special, lunch and a lap dance, for ten bucks. Sounded like a pretty good deal.

We sat in a discreet corner, due to his insistence, in our jammies. He glanced around in his Georgetown Law t-shirt, fidgeting, afraid to be seen with me. After I ravenously devoured a plate of six crispy wings, I stuffed the last piece of my strawberry waffle in my already full mouth.

"Shut up," I said with a smile while the toothless, big-breasted waitress placed the large bowl of strawberry ice cream on the table with two spoons, grinning at Bad Habit.

Did I say anything about sharing?

Bad Habit pushed aside his cup of black coffee and grabbed one of the spoons. There was a commotion at the door as a group of drunken college kids who had been at the strip club next door piled into the restaurant. He glanced at them, envy in his eyes, before digging into the ice cream.

"You nervous?"

"About what?" I said, picking up my spoon.

He licked the remaining ice cream off his lips. Only he could make ice cream look so pornographic.

"What'd you think?"

I stared and blinked before feeling a kick from Alien 2, reminding me we weren't alone.

"Oh, right. I guess, I don't know, really. Honestly, I haven't really thought about it. Why, are you?"

His eyes glanced around in no particular direction.

"I'm indifferent."

We ate in silence for a moment before I opened my fat mouth.

"Before...all this...did you even want kids?"

He chuckled. "It's a little late to be asking that don't you think?"

"I guess."

I shrugged and we fell silent again, downing the ice cream, our spoons clinking the metal bowl. Thousands of thoughts shared but not expressed.

"I did want children, but I particularly didn't want them this soon."

"Oh, and you didn't even want them...when you were with her?"

He froze and locked eyes, pissed at the subtle mention of "she who shall not be named," his ex-girlfriend of five years.

"Wanting children is not contingent upon who I am or am not with. It's a personal decision." From the growl in his low voice it was a touchy subject that I should've never touched.

"Right. Sorry," I whispered and stared down at the table.

He continued eating while I had lost my appetite, sensing I was losing a battle in our nine-month war.

Bad Habit could've had sex with anyone, but he had sex with me. He could've got pregnant with anyone, but he got pregnant with me. That had to have meant something. And I was determined to prove everyone wrong. We're supposed to be together after all. Yet, a wave of doubt was washing over me. I was beginning to believe that even though I was going above and beyond to be perfect, he was more miserable than ever. Maybe I was the problem, not the babies, like I assumed.

Wonder if he would be happier if this had happened with her?

"I just...wanted more time to prepare and you...I mean, this just sprung up on me."

"Well, I'm sure your parents weren't totally prepared when they had you and you came out alright."

"I have no intentions on repeating my parent's mistakes," he snapped.

I gulped. "Well...life has a way of springing things on us that we're not ready for but actually could be good for us," I said, hinting more towards our potential love, our happily ever after.

Bad Habit sighed. He wasn't reassured.

"Alexandria, the mere fact that you 'haven't really thought about it' means that neither one of us is ready to be someone's parent."

Six Months

Dear Me,

    There's another *Law and Order* marathon on today. I'll probably watch that, after I watch *Real Housewives of Atlanta*. When I get these puppies out of me, I'm totally going to roll with NeNe. She makes ATL seem so fabulous! But I wouldn't know since I haven't been any farther than the end of the driveway in over TWO WEEKS and I don't think Bad Habit's noticed. I'm just some ghost who cleans his house and cooks him dinner.

    Speaking of cooking, my feet look like plump kielbasa sausages. They make me hungry every time I look at them. I'm drooling like a juicy mouthed toddler that I now have my own personalized spit cup. It's as disgusting as it sounds. You think if I asked for the spinal block now it'll last me the next three months? Perhaps that's too extreme but I'd settle for an epidural.

    Love,

    Casper

    P.S. Our freezer now looks like the ice cream section at Costco.

***

"He's cheating on me. I know he is. That cone headed, cocky, arrogant, no good son of a bitch!"

I vented to the only friend that would listen, Sasha. She sat on the floor by my feet, chewing on my suede Edelman pumps like they were made out of honey-smoked bacon. Didn't matter since I couldn't fit my bloated feet into them. I wanted to pace, but I could not support my body in an upright position for more than five minutes. I caressed my swollen deformed belly that now extended outwards to a point like a torpedo. Dr. Turner said I was doing remarkable for someone in my condition. I begged to differ.

My diabolical plan hadn't been panning out. Bad Habit seemed oblivious to my advances. It was frustrating enough to pull your weave out. Meanwhile, the idleness and waiting was killing me slowly. It left a considerable amount of time to think about my past transgressions. I tried to find something that would justify the karmic torment. Was it all the men I dated and disregarded? The babies I didn't find adorable? The women's outfits I mocked?

Or was it sleeping with a man who wasn't mine?

Pregnancy was supposed to be this profound experience. In all the books, it talked about the life changing awesomeness. But I was so wrapped up in Bad Habit that I didn't feel an ounce of maternal instinct. I was irrevocably unattached. I focused on that fact that in a couple of weeks I'd finally be able to see the faces of my torturers, the ones that have caused five months of death-like gas, back pains, and morning sickness when everyone else on the planet had two.

Three in the morning and Bad Habit still wasn't home.

So while I sit here, exhausted and unable to sleep because these kids keep break dancing on my kidney, this fool is out partying it up. Probably with some trifling ho'.

I tried his phone again before my battery died. Straight to voicemail. Just like the last fourteen times that I called. The temper and hysteria that I'd been trying to keep at bay for months was inching back in full force. I started to doze off but heard noise downstairs, like slow scratching of glass then silence. I called Bad Habit's name but there was no answer.

Guess I'm hearing things again.

Another noise echoed, like an empty soup-can hitting the marble floor. This time Sasha heard it too. I pushed my heavy body out of the recliner and peered out the window. No cars in the driveway or on the street, so it wasn't Derrick.

Oh shit robbers! This time for real!

I stumbled around the dark, frantically looking for the cordless only to realize I had left it on the counter, in the kitchen, downstairs.

Shit! They're here to jack me for my flat screen. Or worse, maybe they're baby stealers!

I tiptoed by the door, peering down the balcony. The lights were off, complete blackness.

That's right, baby stealers. I saw a special on the Discovery Channel about this. They'll smother me with chloroform, throw me in a trunk, and next thing you know I'll wake up in a tub of ice in some crack house with crooked, dirty stitches across my belly.

Bad Habit found a new hiding spot for the guns last week given my ever-changing temperament so I grabbed the closest weapon I could find, a wooden yardstick next to the window he was measuring over the weekend. The storm door snapped open, soft footsteps hit the tiles. Sasha whimpered and ran out the room.

So much for being a faithful bitch.

I waddled to the bedroom door, closing it to help give the element of surprise. Arching the stick back like a batter, I closed my eyes and took a deep breath. The footsteps tiptoed up the stairs. Palms sweating, I leaned against the wall, bracing myself. The handle jiggled and I stifled a scream. The door opened with a snap and an eerie creak.

Now or never...

With one giant swing I smacked my target in the face and the dark shadow stumbled, falling onto its back with a grunt. I pushed myself off the wall preparing to run when a familiar voice shrieked out.

"What the fuck!"

Shit!

I stood frozen in the darkness, still in take flight mode, before flicking the light switch. And there was Bad Habit, rubbing his throbbing red forehead.

"Jesus Christ, Alexandria! What are you doing?"

Sasha galloped over, jumping on him as if he was meant to be on floor for her to play with. I hid the yardstick behind my back.

"Nothing."

"What were you gonna do, measure me to death?"

I stood there, prepared to be chastised for my ridiculousness when my supersonic nose caught wind of something peculiar. It wasn't his intoxicating scent. It was more floral, like fresh roses, a vaguely recognizable fragrance.

Chanel! What basic bitch still wears Chanel?!

The familiar purring of a cherry red BMW roared in the distance. I whipped out the yardstick and jabbed him in the stomach.

"Wait a goddamn second! Where were you?"

"What?" he grunted, trying to simultaneously protect himself from my jabs and Sasha's slobber.

"Where were you? I've been up all night. Why were you so late? Why didn't you call? Who is she, huh? Tell me her name!"

Bad Habit shook his head in disbelief and stood, Sasha still attacking him for attention. He stared at me for a moment, like he was in deep analytical thought. Then, after a heavy sigh, he concluded with a confident nod.

"Yep. You're delusional."

"I'm dead serious. I'm stuck here, carrying your devil children and you're out playing doctor with some bitch. I want you out!"

"Sure," he said and he breezed by me with a mischievous smile. "I'll just pack my bags. Perhaps you should think about calming down."

I. Really. Hate. Him.

"No, you need to tell me where you were!"

"I was at work, and on contrary, I don't have to tell you anything. This obsequiousness you are in search of is absurd. If I want to have relations with a woman, it would be none of your concern and there will be no signs of contrition for it," he said smugly, unbuttoning his shirt.

Fuck him and his polysyllabic SAT words!

"We had a deal," I scoffed. "You should've called!"

"Alexandria, it's late and I don't feel like arguing with you. I've been working all day and I—"

"Yeah right, working on some bitch!"

"Why are you—"

"You can't keep on treating me like this! Would you want some guy doing this to your daughter? Would your father—"

"I wouldn't know what the fuck my father would do! When you find him, you can ask him!"

I bit my lower lip, not knowing how to respond.

"Oh. I'm—"

My Crackberry buzzed on the charger as he walked past me.

"Whatever, I'm done talking with you."

"But I'm NOT done talking to you. This isn't—"

I scrolled to the text message from Kennedy and with one look, I burst into an uncontrollable sob.

"AHHHHHHHHHHHHHHHHHHHH!"

"What? What is it!"

"Look! Just look!"

I shoved the phone in his face. He stared at the picture for a moment then looked back at me.

"It's a shoe."

"'It's a shoe? It's not just a shoe!"

"Ok, it's a red bottom. So."

"It's a Louboutin! Not just any Louboutin, it's an AUTOGRAPHED LOUBOUTIN! Signed by Christian Louboutin himself!"

I dropped my phone and cried into my hands.

"Are you seriously crying over an overpriced shoe that has been graffitied with a Sharpie?"

"You don't understand—"

"Whatever, I'm going to bed. I highly suggest you do the same."

He passed me without uttering another word and turned off the light, leaving me standing in the dark. It was the straw that broke the pregnant camel's back.

***

My phone held the last photo taken of me before I died.

It was the last photo of my former self. In fact, scanning the entire album was like flipping through my own funeral program. With my nose widening as far as my hips and my hair transitioning into a fro, I looked nothing like the perfect girl in the picture. She no longer existed.

The picture was taken during Fall Fashion Week, about a week after I started my new job. I remember the day well. I was wearing a bright kelly green shift dress with a pair of gold patent leather Tory Burch platforms and a matching bag. The fresh perm made my hair bone straight and shiny under the spotlights. I looked hot, in that not trying-to-be-but-elegant-and-classy way. I was sitting second row at the Gucci show, the tickets and seats, priceless. Kennedy, visiting that weekend, took the picture of me while I held a pose. I was smiling, glowing, beautifully happy, and ignorant to my pregnancy. I examined the photo like a detective, trying to see if there was any noticeable difference, some hint I should have realized sooner of my impending demise. But there was none. I looked normal.

Not the fat shell of a woman I am today.

Jill knocked on the back door and let herself in.

"Hi there! Whew! It's real real hot out today boy."

Sometimes her heavy accent makes it sound like she was raised in some white trash trailer park but I never ask.

"Your beau asked me to come and check in on you. I brought you some sweet tea."

Just the word tea made me parched. I grabbed it from her and gulped it down in an unladylike fashion. She sat and stared at me with a smirk.

"What?"

"I, well...I just don't know how you gonna do it."

"Do what?"

"Well, when me and my man first had our little Mira, it's was rough," she said, drifting off to a lost memory. "All the fussiness, the crying, the diaper rash, the leaking nipples."

Leaking nipples? I've heard enough!

"Oh and our house was just a mess," she continued. "We've had sex once in six months, and let me tell you, we were making love 'bout three, four times a day till my water broke. Henry always said he was the one who pop my water balloon, if you know what I mean."

I let out an uncomfortable chuckle.

Talk about T.M.I.

"Anyway, I love my Mira, but boy she was a miserable baby. Like everything I was doing was wrong. And you, well, y'all having four of them. At once. Boy, I tell you I'd just about shoot myself in the head with a shotgun if I was you. Henry took two weeks off when Mira was first born. That measly two weeks was nothing. Not like he could breastfeed her or change a damn diaper right. Can't even cook. I had to do everything! What you gonna do with your man?"

I sat in stunned silence. She broke out of a trance from her long tangent and chuckled.

"Boy, I just don't see how you gonna manage."

Well who asked you?

She stood up and adjusted her shirt with a sigh that reminded me of Scarlet from *Gone with the Wind*.

"Well, gotta go. I'll come by here a little later to check on you. 'Kay?"

She turned in her clunky sandals and walked out. I had been constipated in the morning, but now I was scared shitless. How WAS I going to manage four babies? Alone, while Bad Habit worked all day, playing around with Beyoncé Wannabe, or some other foolishness. I pictured myself in a disheveled kitchen with four babies in their high chairs, crying in unison. Me, standing there, wailing with them, covered in sweat and baby puke. The house would be in complete disarray and I may never leave it since Bad Habit would never be there.

I was nowhere near prepared for motherhood. It never occurred to me the weight of the responsibility that I was taking on. That the creatures growing inside me would be solely dependent on me for survival. Suddenly, four babies seemed excessive.

We really don't need four, maybe two. Maybe we can re-gift one for Christmas?

And what happens when they start getting older? What happens if my plan fails and Bad Habit doesn't want me? How will I ever date again?

Who would be crazy enough to date a woman with four kids still living at her baby daddy's house?

Frantic, I flipped through my contacts. If this was prison, I needed to make my one phone call to the only person that could post bail.

"Alex! This is a surprise. How are you?" Ellen sounded confused and a tad bit annoyed.

"I'm...ok. How are you?"

"I've been well. You caught me on one of the rare occasions that I'm in my office but I have a meeting with a potential client in a few."

I clutched the phone tighter, nervously trying to build up the courage.

"Great. Well, listen, I need your help with something."

"How can I help you? Last I heard you made the move to Atlanta. Not sure what I can do from here."

"Yeah, well...about that...after some consideration...I think we should move ahead with the original plan we discussed."

"Oh...things are not working out?"

"Not exactly. And I just wanted to know if..."

"If I would still take you on as a high risk?"

There she goes again, using the 'r' word.

I was sitting at the breakfast nook, staring at the lunch I packed for Bad Habit that he left on the counter after I reminded him twice. He left it out of spite, I was sure of it. Nothing could be more disrespectful than disregarding prepared food.

"Well, like I've told you, neither one of us are interested nor prepared for children. But I'm sure you know someone who is."

"Hmmm..."

"And I'm six months, so I'm sure time is of the essence."

"I suppose."

Patience not being one of my strongest assets, I snarled. I was tired of beating around the bush.

"Okay, no offense Ellen, but I don't get you! I have four good as new babies I could put on eBay and make a killing off of but instead I'm offering them to you and you keep turning down a perfectly good commission. What's your problem? Do you do this with every girl or just me? Am I being hazed or something?"

Ellen waited five seconds to make sure I was through with my rant. Then she responded so calmly you'd think she was asking for tea.

"Alex, do you know what 'guilt' means?"

And there she goes again, another damn lesson.

"Guilt is a permanent self-appraisal emotion," she continued. "Permanent meaning it remains with you always, no matter how old you get or how much money you have. You'll never be rid of it. Self-appraisal meaning it will define how you see yourself. When you see you, you will always see that guilt."

"Sooo you're saying I will never be able to forgive myself for that candy bar I stole from Ray's back in the fourth grade?"

She snickered.

"I see a lot of myself in you Alex. I, too, was the queen of sarcasm. I didn't learn till later that it was all to deflect from what I was really thinking."

"That's not what I'm—"

"So let me be clear. Giving up children that you KNOW you want outweighs a stolen candy bar, a million to one."

How does she know I want them? And why do I want them?

A part of me wanted to reach through the phone and snuff her. The other part, wanted to hug her. Maybe I just needed a hug all together. I sniffed the air and tears that I didn't realize had formed fell.

"Well..." I croaked. "If you're a lot like me, then I'm assuming you have something pretty big to be guilty about."

"You're right," she admitted. "But I've never been a mother. Close...but I didn't have someone to tell me otherwise. It may sound a little inappropriate, somewhat unorthodox too, but another part of my job is identifying who would make a great parent and who would not. There are certain key qualities to look for. And if I believed you'd be a failure, I wouldn't invest the time in telling you otherwise."

The pent up emotion boiled over. I started to sob.

"This is just so...frustrating. I don't know what I'm doing anymore. I'm just so lonely and...exhausted! I'm tired Ellen. I can't do this..."

"Have you had a real conversation with the father since you've been down there? A conversation about expectations and needs not just demands and illusive wants?"

I nodded my head as if she could see me.

"My advice, talk to him. Get out of the house to change the environment and have a rational discussion."

Get out of the house? Impossible!

"He won't take me anywhere!"

"Then go where he is."

"I can't! The only places I know he goes to is home and the office."

"Well, it's not ideal, but if you feel he's left you no other alternatives, the office will have to do."

***

Dear Me,

Sooo Bad Habit left his lunch on the table today and I REALLY don't want it to go to waste 'cause I'm sure he'll starve without it. Maybe I should take it to him! Why, that's a splendid idea! Why didn't I think of that before? I'm sure he won't mind. He'll be happy to see me, like a fun surprise!

Love,

A Genius

***

It was approximately twenty thousand degrees out. Beads of sweat littered my face as I waddled out to the car. Gasping at the oppressive humidity, I stuffed myself in and programmed the navigation system. I was supposed to be finishing Ms. Robinson's website, but Bad Habit's starvation was a priority matter I just had to deal with! Okay, that's a lie. Ellen was right. We needed to talk. I needed to renegotiate the terms of my imprisonment.

They say everything in Atlanta is only twenty minutes away from each other. Two hours later, (I was never good at following instructions) I arrived downtown. Bad Habit's firm was located in a gratuitous glass building on Peachtree Street, a block from the Fox Theatre that looked like the Apollo Theatre back home.

The revolving doors spit me out with my beige elastic waist capri pants under a lime-green t-shirt stretched over my torpedo. I was a massive stain the spotless lobby. Which is exactly why the overweight bow-legged security guard stopped me by the elevators.

"Morning ma'am. How can I help you today?"

"I'm looking for the Etose Firm. I think they're on the fifth floor."

"Do you have an appointment?" he asked, peering down at my protruding belly with skepticism. I fidgeted with the lunch bag.

"No, I'm just dropping off my...uh..."

Boyfriend, friend with benefits, husband to be, baby daddy, sponsor?

"My...friend's lunch."

The pudgy security guard stared then asked for ID. I searched through my caramel Coach hobo. I found my wallet then I dropped it just as fast. The security guard noticed the look of utter despair cross my crushed face, watching it tumble to the floor in slow motion. Picking things up off the ground was so much more of a hassle given that I couldn't see my own feet. I wasn't even sure if I had on matching flip-flops. He jumped from his seat and slowly picked it up. He, too, looked like he was having a hard time bending past his own stomach.

Hmmm...must be carrying twins.

"It's ok ma'am. I got it," he said, pity laced in his voice.

He handed over the lost wallet, glancing at my shoes with a raised eyebrow, confirming they were definitely mismatched.

"Why don't you just go on up. Don't want you standing 'round he're waitin.' Just sign your name in the book. I'm sure he's expecting you."

"Thanks," I grinned and made my way to the elevators.

The Etose Firm's intricate designer rugs and large floor to ceiling windows made me dizzy as soon as the elevator doors opened on the thirty-fourth floor. The walls were covered with posters of artists, plaques, and other memorabilia. The size, décor, and clientele said one thing, money. Bad Habit's first and maybe only love.

I reached an empty reception desk that sat in the middle of the hall underneath the Etose logo, blocking my view of the rest of offices behind it. Unsure if I could walk past, and wanting to avoid another run in with the law, I sat in the designated uncomfortable waiting area by the windows.

The place was impressive. As big of an asshole as he was, no one could tell him he isn't driven.

If Bad Habit's working here, he's doing rather well for himself.

To him, work, business, and money came first, before everything else. That was pretty hard to compete with. I wasn't exactly the better investment and the only return he'd see from me was a couple of screaming money-draining infants. As Ellen puts it, I'm high risk.

After the babies are born, I figured wouldn't be able to re-join the work force for at least another eight to thirteen years, depending on the age Bad Habit feels it's appropriate to leave them alone. If it were up to me, it would be two.

Thirteen years...

That's a lifetime in my field. My career would be on a permanent pause. Even if I could get the consulting business off the ground, I'd be starting from scratch. And here was Bad Habit, following his dreams without a hiccup. I mean, Michelle gave up her career to be the First Lady, but this was different. Envy brewed like bad coffee. I fumbled with his lunch as I heard the footsteps of my worst nightmare.

"How can I help you," The Beyoncé wannabe's voice purred out from behind the desk. My mouth dropped.

She works here? Oh no.

I sat his lunch beside me while using my remaining upper body strength to push myself up as gracefully as I could in front of the size two she-devil. Even up close, she was flawless. Blemish free, lips perfectly lined, that expensive hair twinkling with shine. She sat down, crossing her stunning stems beneath her tight fitting crème pencil skirt and plum satin sheen button down top.

What the fuck? That was the only phrase that crossed through my mind, but instead I confidently asked to see Bad Habit. She hesitated and gave me the ghetto girl once over.

"Ummm...do you have an appointment?"

Hello! I'm carrying his damn rugrats!

"No...but I shouldn't need one."

She raised an eyebrow at my tone and turned to her computer screen.

"Ummm...he's in a meeting at the moment. You can come back later or I can take a message."

Come back later? Does it look like I can come back later?

"No thanks, I would much rather wait in his office if you don't mind."

"Ummm...I'm afraid I can't let you do that ma'am."

She rose from her seat like she was preparing to attack. Even with four buns in the oven I knew I could still take her scrawny ass down if need be.

"Well, I'm not going to wait in this hallway. So you might want to let him know that I'm here."

"He's in a meeting and it doesn't look like he was expecting you."

Her eyebrow arched, daring me. There was a sharp kick. Alien 1 was trying to check my attitude.

"Listen, no he wasn't expecting me, but he left his lunch at HOME and I wanted to bring it to him." I made sure to emphasis the word 'home' just so she knew where I was coming from.

That's right! OUR home.

It worked. The look on her face was a mixture of disbelief and confusion.

Take that Beyoncé Wannabe.

"Well...you could leave it here and I'll be sure to deliver it to him."

"No. I rather deliver it myself, thank you."

"May I ask your name and in what relation are you to Mr—"

"Alexandria Stone and that's none of your business," I shot back quicker than I intended to. She glanced at my left hand, sucked her teeth, and rolled her eyes.

Real classy.

"Look, MISS Stone, he's in a very important meeting and I'm afraid I cannot disturb unless it's an 'urgent matter of great importance'. His words, not mine."

"Well, MISS, I guarantee you that I am important enough."

She cut her eyes and sucked her teeth, writing my name down on a post-it.

"I'll let him know you're here," she mumbled and sashayed back the way she came. I exhaled and stared down at my white knuckles clutching his lunch.

I'm sure he'll be right out. He'll probably be upset about me driving but it'll be ok. Though he'll have some explaining to do about this heffa.

She returned without an ounce of urgency.

"He'll be right out. You can have a seat."

I didn't want to sit, but my knees started to give in to my weight and Alien 2 was kicking my back. I waddled back to my seat, plopping down much harder than I anticipated. She smirked and she stared at her computer screen, pretending to work.

The art deco clock on the wall said twelve-thirty. Thirty minutes before my scheduled naptime. But with the combination of heat and stress, sleep was inevitable.

***

It was the ring of the elevator bell that woke up and startled me. A Fed Ex driver stepped out, pushing his cart.

"Goooooooood afternoon Ms. Victoria. Whew, it's hot out there boy," he said, beaming at the she-devil.

Victoria? Is that her name? Figures. She looks like a Victoria. And a stripper.

"Hey Bill, how ya doing? What you got for me today?"

"Oh you know, same as usual. Your boss sure be orderin' a lot of stuff."

"Tell me about it," she said with a smile, signing his clipboard. "Hey, can I get you anything before you head back out on the road. Water, juice maybe?"

Humph, bitch didn't offer me any water.

Just the word water made tongue burn. My mouth was filled with hot sand, covered by ashy chapped lips and my back ached, as if I had been sitting in the same hunched over position for hours.

Wait a second, how long have I been waiting?

I turned to focus on the clock, but was sure I was seeing things since. Because I was sure that clock didn't say two.

Because I know he hasn't had me out in this hallway with Beyoncé Wannabe and no water for an hour and a half waiting!

Bill the Fed Ex guy smiled as he passed, walking towards the elevator. I looked back at Victoria, who didn't acknowledge my presence or thirst. In fact, she probably got a kick out of seeing me slumped in my seat, mouth hung open, and snoring, sounding like an airport runway. Humiliation in front of her was one thing, but to be so disregarded by Bad Habit was another. Apparently, whatever meeting he was attending was ten times more important than me.

Just like everything else, I suppose.

Victoria collected and balanced the packages then walked towards the back.

Now's my chance!

Fumbling with his lunch, I quickly rose from my seat, stepping a few paces behind her, surprised she didn't hear the shuffling of my

Dumbo feet. I waited till she was out of sight before creeping down the hall.

The offices had glass walls, making it easy to see how gorgeous every person who sat behind their desks were. I walked like I knew where I was heading, though it was clear I didn't belong in the sea of sexy office apparel. I missed my office, my power suits, and my Marc Jacob's tote.

There were a few curious glances but most seemed too busy to care. Just ahead, was what appeared to be the epicenter of the floor, a large fishbowl conference room, with a long mahogany table and black leather swivel chairs, seating at least twenty-five shark suits. I recognized the back of Bad Habit's head, staring at the PowerPoint presentation, attentive, relaxed and in no rush to conclude the meeting. In fact, he seemed like the calmest person in the room.

I stood in the middle of the narrow hallway.

Am I really so forgettable...so unimportant...that he could stay in this meeting?

Seated at the head of the table was an older white haired gentleman who was dressed in a well-tailored three-piece heather gray suit. He pointed at Bad Habit and the room burst with applause. Bad Habit nodded, modest with gratitude.

Whoa, he must be pretty important here. Why didn't he ever tell me that?

Suddenly, the pregnancy fog lifted and clarity hit. He was the breadwinner on our team, I was the dead weight and yet I was demanding that he step out of some important meeting just so I can give him his tuna fish sandwich on wheat. I didn't even know if he liked tuna. Michelle would NEVER make Barack leave a cabinet meeting just to pay her some attention. I was being a brat. A selfish, self-centered, over emotional brat.

Shit. And I'm in trouble.

Knowing he'd go ballistic if he saw me sneaking around, I slowly backed away like I was near the edge of a cliff. I caught a whiff of her Chanel No.5 before bumping right into her.

"What are you doing back here?"

Well, there's my chance to get out of here unscathed.

I turned to face her and gasped. Beyoncé Wannabe was much taller than I expected. Damn near an Amazon woman.

"Ummm...I just...well. I was just gonna drop this on his desk and I–"

"I TOLD you, you couldn't come back here. Now what about that didn't you understand?"

Whoa there.

Amazon Beyoncé Wannabe was pushing her luck. Yeah, I was wrong, but I was also tired, thirsty, and most of all hungry. Nothing would stop me from ripping her tracks out.

"I wasn't trying to intrude, but I—"

"I'm gonna call security," she threatened, raising her voice.

"Look, I said I was sorry. Now here, take his lunch and I'll just go."

"I'm not taking that!" she shrieked, her high pitch voice echoed through the glass walls, creating a scene. "I don't know who you are and obviously he doesn't either. You could be some crazy stalker."

She smiled, taking pleasure in abusing the girl who can't see her feet. Silent for a moment, I muster out a sinister laugh and my recent epiphany became a distant memory, blocked by a rising temper.

Here I am in this hot ass city I barely know, pregnant beyond belief by a man who doesn't even respect me enough to excuse himself from a meeting to acknowledge my presence as a human much less a woman carrying his children and now I have this raggedy heifer calling ME crazy.

Forget WWMD, what would NeNe do?

"Listen here bitch," I began in a low voice. "I am exercising every ounce of my patience trying to deal with your fucking ass. So yeah, you're right, you don't know me, but once I'm through with you, you'll remember me for the rest of your sorry ass life and I'll still be able to sleep at night."

Alien 1 kicked and I took it as a 'Go get her Mommy.' I slammed his lunch on the floor, preparing to break the heffa in two, when I caught a glimpse of the fishbowl. Our fight had caught the attention of the shark suits. Bad Habit turned around and locked eyes on me. His expression went from shock to raging anger in a matter of seconds.

Shit, I'm trouble.

He threw a couple of words at the other gentleman at the table, excusing himself then halfway ran to our position in the hallway. I was so focused on him that I tuned Amazon Bitch, who was busy screaming at me, out. Bad Habit jumped between us like referee.

"What the hell is going on here?" he gritted through his teeth, directed at me.

"This bi...chick claims she knows you," she snapped while her neck rolled.

"She does, but—"

He stopped short, noticing Mr. Gray Suit walking towards us.

"What's going on here? Is everything ok?"

"Everything's fine, Mr. Paul. Just a misunderstanding," Bad Habit said with a fake laugh that I only heard him use around Caucasians. He bent down and picked up the lunch that I had slammed onto the floor, glaring up at me.

Trouble, yep, deep trouble.

"Oh," Mr. Paul said, unconvinced as he gave me a once over. "And you are...?"

I opened my mouth to reply but Bad Habit stepped in.

"This is Alexandria."

He smiled, but there was no sign of recognition.

"Alexandria. Pleasure to meet you." He shook my hand, turning to Bad Habit. "Is this your girlfriend?"

"Ummm...something like that," he mumbled.

"Oh?"

I smiled, taking a cue from the awkwardness. "Likewise, I've heard so much about you," I lied, feeling Bad Habit's eyes burning a hole in my back.

Mr. Paul glanced down at my stomach. I almost knocked him over with when I turned towards him. "My, you are pretty far along there Alexandria. He never mentioned he was expecting."

I looked up at Bad Habit who stopped breathing.

He never mentioned I was pregnant?

"Oh, realllllllly? Well it was a bit of a shock," I said, faking a laugh, trying to shake the feeling that I had been punched in the gut a couple of times.

"Must have been hard for you, seeing how you just moved down here last week."

Bad Habit stiffened.

Last week? Oh that's interesting. Seeing how I've been held prisoner for the last THREE months!

"Really!" I said, my voice cracking at a peak. "Well actually I'm not very far along."

"I see. Well, is it a boy or a girl?"

"Not sure yet. It's hard to tell with multiples."

"Multiples! Wow, so you're having twins?"

"No. I'm actually having quadruplets."

His eyes bulged and his mouth hung open, the usual reaction. Gasps from onlookers echoed in the hall, including one from Victoria, who hadn't moved from her spot behind Bad Habit.

Take that you Amazon bitch!

"Unbelievable!" He turned to Bad Habit. "And they're yours?"

We both winced at the unintended insult. He nodded.

"Well, it's no wonder then that you're trying to—"

"It was all very sudden!" Bad Habit joked, cutting him off.

Weird, what's with him?

Mr. Paul nodded excitedly. "Oh, well, where are my manners? You shouldn't been standing in your condition. Please come in. The board members will get a kick out of you. Victoria, get her some water please. I know my wife was always thirsty when we had our daughter, Emily. I can't imagine how you're feeling."

Victoria scoffed as she stormed away, throwing Bad Habit a vicious glare. Meanwhile, I was stapled to the floor, unsure if I was allowed to move. In just a few short moments, I aired all of Bad

Habit's business for the entire office to hear. Hands down the worst thing I could have ever done to the king of vagueness. I glanced wearily at Bad Habit, waiting for approval. With a sigh, he touched the small of my back, pushing me along.

Well, maybe it's not that bad. Maybe I'm overreacting.

Hopeful, I smiled at him, but my loving gaze was met with piercing eyes.

Nope, still in trouble.

We followed Mr. Paul into the fishbowl filled with curious eyes following us. The entire office was staring. He introduced me to the room like I was his high school science fair project.

"Quadruplets! Amazing right? I've seen stuff like this on TV but never in person."

A delighted Mr. Paul sat me at the head of the table. Bad Habit moved to the corner, hands balled into fist in his pockets, jaw locked, breathing through his nose like a street fighter. Victoria walked in, scowled at him again before slamming a bottle of water down in front of me.

"Oh Victoria, get some cookies from the kitchen too," Mr. Paul said without bothering to glance at her. He touched my back. "You'll love them, I'm sure. My Nelly had a crazy sweet tooth when she was pregnant with Emily"

I smiled at his warm reception. It was the first time in months that someone was happy to see me. Everyone in the room, except for the expecting the parents, seemed genuinely ecstatic about my pregnancy. After months of questioning glares and speculations, who knew I would have to come to his place of employment with complete strangers to feel loved.

The board members' questions were endless.

"What's it like?"

"How far along are you?"

"Will you have your own reality show?"

"How are you going to handle all those babies?"

I lied through most of the questions since I hadn't put much thought into the afterlife and tried to involve Bad Habit in the conversation, but he became a man of little or no words. The meeting had taken an unexpected detour from his previous plans, and he was not happy about it.

"Well, I'm sure you want to get back home Alexandria." Mr. Paul said and turned to Bad Habit. "How about you head home early with your lovely girlfriend. No sense in you being stuffed up here with us old fogies."

Bad Habit sprung from the wall as if it burned him.

"Actually, there were a couple of details on the agenda I was hoping we could discuss and since the board members are only in town every so often I thought maybe—"

"Nonsense. Nothing can be that important. Besides, Alex looks exhausted and you can use a little R and R yourself before you really become busy. Don't worry, I've managed all these years without you, I'm sure I can make it through one meeting."

Ouch.

I didn't even look at Bad Habit knowing his inner workaholic was ready to slice my neck, but he remained poised.

"Well, Mr. Paul, with all due respect, there are a couple of vital points I wanted to address in today's presentation, some of grave importance to next year's budget. Also, there's still the matter of the

Robert, Bush, and Creighton contracts that need to be addressed today or we'll lose these potential high profile clients. I'll show Alex to my office where she could rest... comfortably. Then, I'll return and cover some quick bullet points."

Wow, nice recovery!

Mr. Paul nodded in agreement.

"Well my dear. I wish you well!"

Bad Habit walked over to help me out of my seat, his hand gripping my forearm in an Ike Turner-like manner. I winced and managed a fake smile as he yoked me out of the fishbowl.

We walked through the halls, eyes following our every step. I tried to stir up conversation, attempting to defuse the ticking time bomb that was Bad Habit.

"They were really nice."

He ignored me, his face like chocolate granite as he sped through the hall. I was practically jogging to keep up with him. He opened the last door at the end of the hallway and pushed me in, slamming it shut behind him.

His office was cold, bleak, and uninviting. A large L-shaped black desk sat in front of an immense window, a black leather sofa sat against the wall. The bookshelves sat cattycorner, dusty and lifeless, but what disturbed me most were the various sized unopened boxes scattered about the room.

"Are you moving or something?"

He didn't respond, instead he led me to the couch and threw me down like I was shit on his hands. He was able to lose his composure behind the frosted glass walls that differed from the rest of the office.

194 | Blu Daniels

"Stay put! I will deal with you later!"

I bit my lip to keep from responding and he walked out, slamming the door behind him.

Apparently, the walls are sound proof too.

Time ticked by and my eyes started to droop but I snapped them back open. I didn't want to be caught sleeping when he walked in. I needed to be on high alert, awake and prepared.

Moved here last week?

No one in his office knew of my existence or that of Aliens 1 through 4. Was I really that surprised? No, just bit disappointed.

My hand absentmindedly traced one of the cardboard boxes near my foot, the lid half opened. Curious, I peered inside. Underneath the forest of bubble wrap, something looked way too bright for Bad Habit's taste. He claimed his favorite colors are black and gray, matching his office motif and home precisely. Ripping off the packing tape, I dug around inside.

I'm already in trouble, what's the worst that could happen.

Inside the box, wrapped in bubble wrap, was a sky blue glass smiling teddy bear lamp. The teddy bear was holding a crystal rainbow, sitting on a puffy white cloud. It reminded me of the Care Bears I used to sleep with when I was a little girl. I glanced around the room at the other boxes, reading the shipping labels: Simply Baby Furniture.

I don't believe it.

My eyes roamed around the room, measuring the boxes, all from the same company. Instead of being happy, I was only envious. Bad Habit had unknowingly shined a light on my lack of maternal instincts.

I never even thought about a nursery. He's more prepared than I am.

I was reaching for another box when the door swung open and I jumped back. He glanced in my direction. Regardless of the impending doom I faced, I grinned too wide, almost painfully so. Here I was assuming he didn't care, that he didn't want kids, and all the while he had been planning and preparing. I wanted to jump in his arms, but the look on his face told me to stay put. He slammed the door and dropped some files onto his desk, along with the lunch I attempted to deliver, which, from the look of the paper bag, had taken a beating.

"Ummm...that's probably spoiled by now," I chuckled, but that did nothing to ease the tension.

He pinched the bridge of his nose, squeezed his eyes shut, and breathed deeply.

"What the fuck are you doing here?" he finally asked, exasperated.

He opened his stone cold eyes and stared from the edge of his desk. I remembered I had the right to remain silent and did so, feeling butterflies rather than jerks and kicks. The Aliens were scared of their Daddy as much as I am. His head jerked, expecting an answer.

"Well?"

"I...I just wanted to bring your lunch," I responded in a mousy voice.

"Lunch? Is that all?" He lets out a sinister chuckle. "You could've left it at the desk."

"Yes, that's true...but I also wanted to talk. And it wasn't very easy for me to get down here. I came to see you."

He huffed and walked around his desk.

"And this couldn't have waited until I got back home?"

Bad Habit cut me with a malicious stare before sitting at his computer. He was as uninterested in me being in his office as he was with me being in his home.

"Why didn't you tell them about me?"

"What's there to tell?"

"Well, a lot actually. What, were you just going to keep me a secret?" I laughed nervously, the idea seeming ridiculous, but he didn't respond. His fingers slammed on the keyboard, eyes transfixed on the computer screen.

"Wow. You did, didn't you," I mumbled. "So why did you bring me here? I could've been a secret from New York. Why did you bring me all the way down here to be locked up in your house? We agreed—"

"I didn't bring you anywhere!" he snapped, turning towards me. "You boarded an aircraft under you own free will, but what other choice did you have? You were broke, unemployed, living off your parents, and past the point of no return. What else were you going to do? I think you've done enough damage to us both."

His eyes darted to my swollen stomach, revolted.

"So yeah, I agreed it would be best if you came here, but I never said you were going to be my girlfriend. That I would NEVER agree to!"

The Aliens feel my heart shatter into a billion pieces and fall still, cold as snow. My hope, no matter how trivial, was gone. He said the exact words I feared. The bear shaped lamp, hidden in the box next to me was a distant memory. He never had any intentions on being in a relationship, even for the babies' sake. It was pity. Pity that I lost my job. Pity that I had no money or health insurance. Pity that I was living at home with my parents. So much pity that he chose to lock me in a house under his control while he continued his bachelor lifestyle. And to top it all off, he blamed me for everything.

I tried to find my happy place, the one I used to keep my composure, that Norman Rockwell painting of us sitting at the table, eating dinner with our kids, smiling and happy. But his words were acid on the canvas. The room started to spin and my eyes glazed with tears.

"I didn't get pregnant on purpose. This isn't my fault!"

My voice quivered. His nose twitched but he never once took his eyes off the screen.

"You don't give a damn about me, do you? You don't care at all."

He rolled his eyes. "Don't be so dramatic. You knew what this was, don't try to act new."

"I didn't get pregnant on my own. I'm no Virgin Mary, but you're definitely no damn saint! You had just as much to do with this as I did. It was—"

"A mistake!" he shouted, startling me. "A ridiculous mistake that I wish I never made with you! We only dealt with each other for a couple of months and now I have to deal with your incessant drama and insanity for the rest of my life!"

I did a double take before rewinding his last words.

Did he just say couple of months?

"You asshole. It wasn't just a couple of months! How dare you try to downgrade what we were!"

"Which was nothing. We were nothing. I—"

"I met you two years ago! Before I got pregnant. Before all of this! You act like it was just some one night stand."

"You're delusional. It hasn't been that long. I had a girlfriend two years ago—"

"And you cheated on her with ME! You were supposed to leave her for ME!"

Hearing myself say the words that I had kept buried deep within my subconscious was a blatant admission to my true sentiments. My grudge, my hatred towards him, the undeniable core of our problem. The memories of us were agonizingly strong in my mind. And the fact that he couldn't remember them just as accurately was an insult to every tear I shed over him.

His mouth was open as if he was about to say something but he snapped it shut with a heavy groan.

"This is a pointless argument. What difference does it make? The point is we weren't together and we're still not!"

I stood up, shaking with anger.

"You know what. I've tried to make this as easy as possible. I cook, I clean, I stay out of your way, and I'm there whenever you want to fuck. But still somehow that's not good enough because at the end of the day all I am is a burden. A mistake!"

The tears streamed down my stony face like water over rocks, soaking the front of my shirt. He sniffed the air a bit, avoiding my eyes before burying his face in his hands with another groan, his voice muffled with frustration.

"Jesus, Alexandria! What do you want from me?"

The room was thick and stuffy but not from the Atlanta heat. Without an ounce of energy left in me, I stood there long enough to realize what I wanted.

"Not a damn thing," I whispered and stormed out of his frosty glass house.

***

The day before I decided to run away was the first day I saw the spotting. A hectic pattern of blood stained my panties. Ignorance being bliss, I layered on some toilet paper and went to bed. I had enough problems to deal with.

Bad Habit walked in the house around midnight. I didn't acknowledge him and he didn't acknowledge me. He slipped into bed without uttering a word while I pretended to sleep, wishing he would say something. A word, an apology. Either one would have eased my suffering. But nothing affected him. He slept like a grizzly.

I watched the sun begin to peek through the venetian blinds. The images of the lunch I tried to deliver, the sharp look Victoria gave Bad Habit, the words he used, my hysterical drive home from his office, all fresh in my mind. The Aliens chose to back off. I guess they knew I was in enough pain and didn't want to add to it. His words sunk in deeper.

"You knew what this was from jump...I never was gonna make you my girlfriend...a couple of months...mistake."

Broken and defeated, I shuddered and squeezed my eyes tighter to keep the unwanted tears away. The alarm buzzed over my head and I ignored it. He stirred then moved in my direction, leaning over me to shut it off. I could feel his eyes gaze on me, checking if I was still breathing. Satisfied, he rose from his side of the bed and headed straight to the shower. I didn't move. My actions in pure defiance, a subtle protest, vowing the morning would be different.

I will not iron his clothes or tie his tie. I will not make his breakfast or his lunch. I will not stand at the door and force him to kiss me. I will stay in bed. I shall not be moved!

The shower turned off and the door creaked open. Realizing I mean business, he sighed and continued about his business, ironing his own clothes, fixing his own tie.

Downstairs, he bustled about the kitchen. The microwave dinged and the scent of strawberries lingered from his instant oatmeal.

Figures, he doesn't need me.

After a few minutes, the front door opened then slammed shut. Silence. He was gone. I relaxed and breathed deeply until I heard footsteps on the stairs and froze again.

Jesus! Who could've broken into the house that quick?

Bad Habit sighed at the door and I snapped my eyes back shut. He walked slowly around to my side of the bed and sat on the edge, peering over me while I played dead.

"I know you're awake," he said in a calm low voice. I refused to open my eyes, no matter how delicious he smelled next to me.

"I'll be in a meeting all day, but I should be home early. DON'T go anywhere."

He rose from the bed, walking out of the room in a very serial killer like manner with his heavy footsteps. When I heard the car back out of the driveway, I exhaled. It was amazing how intense he could make a room feel in a matter of moments.

I rolled over, feeling the shock of relief to my lower back.

Fantastic, another early morning in hell.

Everyone was on their way to work, building their careers, reveling in their lives without a care. I had nothing, not even hope, to comfort myself with. I was the perfect candidate for a depression commercial.

It was early, but I knew Kennedy would be up and I needed comic relief.

She answered the phone with zero enthusiasm. She seemed cold and distant, rather than my spunky, sarcastic better half.

"What's up with you? Why does it sound like someone killed your cat?"

"Oh, nothing. Except...but...well...ummm...there's been some talk. About you and Bad Habit."

"Talk? What kind of talk? What could people possibly be talking about in D.C.? Unless there's some hidden cameras I don't know about."

"You know, it's a small world, and Bad Habit still got people here."

"What've they been saying Kennedy?" I asked flatly. She was talking like someone had a gun to her head.

"Oh, you know," she said, trying to downplay it. "The normal stuff. How you turkey basted yourself to get pregnant then went bat shit crazy, started pretending to be his wife, attacked him with a ruler, pulled a gun out on his cousin, and stalked him at work."

"WHAT!" I screamed, scaring the piss out of Sasha. Ok, so maybe I had been leaving out certain gory details of my day-to-day experiences with Bad Habit, mostly out of shame. But if I had known he was going to make me out to be some kind of psychopath, I would've started a blog.

"He's...been talking."

"Wait a minute. Have you been talking to him?"

There was a heavy sigh that could only mean what I feared.

"Alex, he's just...worried about you, I guess. Trying to figure you out and I don't blame him. He's been trying to keep people—"

"People? What people? You ARE my people! Did he call my high school gym teacher too? What exactly did he say Kennedy?"

"He...told me what happened," she said, like she was talking to someone on a ledge rather than her best friend.

"And why does it sound like whatever he told you, you believe?"

"Well girl, I'mma keep it real with you, you haven't been acting yourself lately. Coming up with this crazy idea to make him love you. I know it's the hormones, but for real, if he doesn't want you by now he's never gonna want you. I think you should take heed of that. Maybe cut him some slack and focus on—"

"I thought you hated him! You're supposed to be on my side."

"I DO hate him. Shit, I hate the way he took advantage of you."

"What?"

"Alex, let's face it. You were really smart and successful but you were lonely. Bad Habit took advantage of that. You knew he had a girlfriend and that he was an asshole but you messed with him anyway 'cause it was better to have something than to have nothing at all, right? Even if that something is a piece of shit."

I almost dropped the phone. Stunned, I retaliated brutally.

"This coming from the chick who sleeps with married NBA players for a living?"

"Ouch, Mary Poppins. Well, guess we one and the same then, huh? You dug your own grave and now you want sympathy? You're a fool!"

"*Be with a fool or be alone and a fool...*"

"Are you jealous that I at least have someone or is that what you really think?"

"Ha! I rather be alone than be anyone's doormat. And the old Alex I knew felt the same. It just makes me wonder–"

"Makes you wonder what?"

She took a long sigh.

"If this whole pregnancy...really was an accident like you said."

"I...I have to go," I blurted in shock and hung up.

In fifteen years, I had never hung up on Kennedy. The world was spiraling out of control. My plan, no matter how absurd, was backfiring like shit in a spinning fan. I never felt so alone, so trapped, so desperate to flee. It was suffocating. Then, I remembered what my mother had said right before I left.

"*If you need to, you can always come home.*"

***

"I don't think that's a good idea."

My mother's words over the phone stupefied me.

"What? What do you mean?"

"It's too late now, sweetie," she said and I could hear her washing dishes in the sink, Dad watching baseball in the background.

"Too late for me to come to my OWN home?"

"No, it's too late for you to travel."

Dr. Turner warned me that I wouldn't be able to travel after four months. But he didn't mention anything about life or death traveling.

"Oh Mom, it'll be ok," I tried to convince her, words coming out scratchy and desperate. "I won't fly, I'll just—"

"What happened Alex? Is everything alright? Why are you in such a rush to come home all of a sudden?"

I didn't want to tell her the truth. That I was living a lie, trapped in a suburban Atlanta hellhole with nothing but my paranoid thoughts and four Aliens playing soccer with my internal organs. I decided to play the emotional pregnant Alex instead.

"Nothing...it's just that I really miss you. And I want to come home." I whipped up some classic fake tears with a soft sob.

"Awww Alex, you can't sweetie. You have to stay put. Who knows what could happen. I talked to your boyfriend last night. He said you were getting pretty big."

My mouth dropped to the floor, the wind knocked out of me.

Who else has he talked to? And how the hell is he getting everyone's number?

"And he says you haven't been taking your vitamins young lady!"

I was Mia Farrow in *Rosemary's Baby* and the devil had everyone fooled.

He has her in on the conspiracy. My own mother!

"Alex? Are you there?"

"Uh huh."

"Tell you what, I'll try to take off next Friday so I can come and see you. How does that sound?"

"Sounds great Mom," I gritted through my teeth, knowing I would see her way before then.

***

Dear Me,

Bad Habit is a dick, you were right. Leaving this hot ass hellhole at once.

Love,

General of the Great Escape

***

There was no fight mode, only flight. I had to get back to New York. But if I was going to go, I needed to act fast, before he could stop me. My mother was right. I was too pregnant to travel by air. It was humiliating enough being as large as Costco shopping cart, I didn't want to add to it by dropping a kid on the tarmac. The twelve-hour car ride would be twice as long given my poor sense of direction and constant bathroom needs. The only other option was the fifteen-hour train trip. The next one was scheduled to leave at six o'clock. I had no idea where the train station was and knew it would take me longer than the average person to find it so I quickly zipped up my bag of clothes and dragged it down the stairs. There was a sharp kick from Alien 3.

"It's ok, I know what I'm doing. You'd much rather be a New Yorker."

I walked over to the counter where I left the keys the night before. Gone. I checked the usual hiding spaces to no avail.

Bastard!

I turned the house upside down and my searching started to fade. It was three o'clock. Bad Habit would be home in a couple of hours.

Fine, I'll hotwire the car. Shouldn't be that hard. I'm a New Yorker. It's in my blood.

The oppressive heat strangled me. I waddled to the car with a wire hanger and a metal bat I found in the closet. I was fully prepared to take a swing at the window when I hit another roadblock. A bright red club lock clutched the steering wheel.

No. He. Didn't.

"Is everything ok?" A voice behind me asked. Startled, I spun around with the bat. Jill jumped back five feet.

Damn it! What in the hell does she want?

"Uhhh...yeah, everything's fine."

Her eyes were wide and nervous, yet her lips wore a fake smile.

"Are you sure you're supposed to be out in your condition? Your...boyfriend said you weren't feeling so hot and asked me to check on you."

AHHHHHHH!

"I'm. Fine," I groaned and leaned back against the car. She glanced down at the bat.

"Well, maybe I should take you back inside. You shouldn't be out in this heat no way. May go into premature labor or something. Come on now, I'll pour us some sweet tea."

Sweet tea did sound nice.

"Uhhh...now's not a good time."

She gave me another cautious once over.

"Well, why don't you give me that bat?"

"No...no thanks, I got it."

"Alex, please, just give me the bat. It's ok. I won't tell anyone. I know how it feels. It's just harder for men, you know, to remain faithful while you're pregnant. Everyone does it, but—"

Oh good Lord, I don't have time for this.

"I'm not bashing his car Jill," I snapped, though the thought did sound as nice as the sweet tea. "I just lost my keys and I need to get to the station..."

I froze. I had said too much, but her face only brightened.

"Oh! Atlantic Station, oh sure, some shopping. Well, don't worry, I'll take you."

***

I read the sign for Atlantic Station but was dumbfounded by the scene. There wasn't a train or track in sight. Nothing but restaurants, bars, and retail stores, like a high-class strip mall with complex parking. It wasn't a station at all.

"Uhhh...where are we?" I asked, climbing out Jill's minivan.

"Atlantic Station. You said you wanted to come here, right?" she asked puzzled at first but then distracted. "Oh, Ann Taylor is right up here. I know you can't really fit their stuff now, but do you mind if we stop by?"

Atlantic Station? Not Atlanta Station? Oh no.

It was four-thirty. Time was slipping and I needed a plan B, fast. We rode up the escalator from the underground parking lot, greeted by loud clinking glasses, silverware hitting porcelain plates, the smell of grilled beef, fresh pizza, and lattes.

"You know some girl time may be just the thing you need!"

We crossed through a mini courtyard park. Couples snuggled on benches and kids rolled in the grass patch surrounded by mini kiosks. The heat was like a fat midget on my shoulders, slowing me down. I dragged my feet behind her, looking in every direction. People stared, watching, like they knew me. My belly was a big scarlet letter in the town square.

"This place is real real nice. They got a Target, a Dillard's, but I just LOVE Ann Taylor, don't you? Oh and then…"

Maybe they DO know me. Maybe they know Bad Habit.

It all seemed too perfect, staged, and unrealistic. My hands started to sweat.

"They had that fancy circus here 'bout a year ago and…"

A kid runs into my stomach and falls back on his butt like I was a moon bounce.

"Woopsy daisy," Jill said, helping him on his feet. The town square came to a full stop and stare.

Jesus, I'm a sideshow act!

"Henry takes me here sometimes on date night. It's real real fancy and…"

I was sweating bullets now, my heart racing, all eyes locked on my deformed gut.

They know! They've got to know. I've got to get out of here!

4:35.

In a frantic search for an escape, especially from Ann Taylor, I spun in a circle, armpits soaked and spotted a movie theatre across the courtyard.

"Actually, I wanted to catch a flick," I said brightly as the plan solidified in my mind. "Plus I really have to use the bathroom. How about you shop for a bit while I go use the little girl's room and check movie times. Then I'll meet you in a few. Sound good?"

She seemed suspicious but nodded in response.

"Great! See you in a bit." I didn't even wait for a response before speed waddling over to the theatre. Inside, I hid in the shadows, relieved by the air conditioning. Jill walked into Ann Taylor and I waited five minutes to be sure she was fully engrossed in her shopping before whipping out my Crackberry.

***

Wonder how long it'll take her to realize I'm gone?

When I arrived at the correct station, I handed the cab driver the last of my cash with an extra tip if he'd help remove me from the back seat.

How did I manage to get bigger overnight?

By the time I purchased my ticket and found the track, it was five-thirty. Just enough time to find a comfortable four-seater next to a bathroom. Like a fugitive, I glanced over my shoulder every ten seconds, ignoring the curious stares from the other passengers. My Crackberry buzzed in my purse. Bad Habit's name flashed across the screen.

Why is he calling my cell phone? Why wasn't he calling the house phone? He knows!

I combed down my hair, threw on my D&G sunglasses, and opened a newspaper in front of my stomach in an ill attempt at a disguise. I was so anxious for the train to leave, enough to burst out of my seat and drive the damn thing myself.

5:45.

The conductor listed the stops over the loud speaker as the engine purred beneath us. I stared out at the platform, hoping I wouldn't see Bad Habit running after the train like Larenz Tate in *Love Jones*, fearing he'd be able to stop a locomotive and drag me back.

And that's when I saw her.

Victoria the Amazon Bitch was walking down the platform, rolling a suitcase behind her, ticket in hand.

No.

She stepped up to the Grandpa looking conductor in front of my train car and I stopped breathing. They exchanged a few words. I couldn't hear their convo, but I was positive she was on the hunt for me. Another conductor shouted over the loud system.

"Attention ladies and gentleman, this is the Amtrak train to..."

The old conductor on the platform nodded and flirted with Victoria. She tossed her weave a little, gave him a man-eater smile, and handed over her ticket.

She can't be on my train! She can't be.

Blood surged in my knees, forcing me to stand in a panic. I wasn't sure what to do first. There was no way to get off the train without her seeing me. They were too close to the exit. I thought about maybe kicking her unconscious and then running. But run where? There was nowhere to hide from Bad Habit. I was trapped.

5:57.

The old conductor shakes his head. He hands back her ticket and points in the opposite direction. Victoria laughs apologetically.

She has the wrong train! Thank GOD!

She waves, walking off. The conductor waves back, watching her ass shake. I collapsed in my seat. Minutes later the train slowly crept away from station.

Safe. For now.

The phone rang again and I shut it off, right before passing out.

***

Maybe it was exhaustion or my lack of sleep from the night before, but I slept ten hours straight, the most I had in months. Stiff as a board, my back ached as I limped into the bathroom. Peeing like a racehorse, I ignored the spotting, layered my panties with more tissue, and checked myself out in the mirror. My skin was an unhealthy shade of ash, my eyes red and sunken. You could literally see the entire bone structure of my face. My morning sickness returned in full force right after I damaged Bad Habit's truck. I couldn't keep down a meal and lost weight in all the wrong places. Everything about me screamed the Grim Reaper's pregnant wife-to-be.

I tried to ignore the voices in my head telling me this was a bad idea. Kennedy was right, about almost everything. Because I was starved for it, I clung onto the one guy that paid me the slightest ounce of attention, then let him treat me like crap. I pretended I was happy being his side chick, just like I was pretending to be happy being his housewife.

Nothing had changed. I was still alone and a bigger fool.

But I wasn't delusional. We may have been operating under different systems of thinking, but one truth remained. There was something between us, a chemistry that couldn't be explained.

But is it enough?

The train pulled into New York Penn Station and I turned my phone back on. Voicemail full, twenty-five new text messages. I could pretty much guess who they were from. A text popped up.

WHERE R U?

I'm where I need to be.

***

"Yo, I just can't get over how big you got Al," my cousin Tyler said as we drove up the West Side Highway, on the way to my parent's house. Tyler was easy going and had more kids than I would eventually give birth to. He agreed to give me a ride after I begged him to keep it a secret, wanting to surprise my mother. I rolled down the window and let the Hudson River breeze hit me, catching the faint scent of street meat off the Halal trucks. My shoulders and back muscles eased, just the smell of New York made me dizzy with happiness and the cool air was a relief compared to the blaze I left in Atlanta.

What was I thinking giving all this up for the south and a fleeting idea on love?

"Wait 'til Auntie Viv see's you. She's gonna wild out! When's the last time you've been home?"

"Three long months ago," I said with a chuckle. It felt like it had been years. The sidewalks sparkled while the afternoon sun gleamed off the skyscrapers. There was little traffic and we made it back to my neighborhood in record time. We passed Ricky's and Larry was standing in front. I actually missed him.

Tyler turned down my familiar street and I'd never been so happy to see my three-bedroom shack. I was ready to run into the safety and comfort of my parent's arms.

I'll tell them what really happened. My mother will give Bad Habit the worst tongue lashing of his life. Dad will call some of his peoples and have him dragged outside. I'll never have to deal with him again!

But one would say it was the calm before the storm because as soon as we pulled into the driveway, panic returned.

"Hey, did your folks get a new car?"

He pulled alongside a burgundy Malibu. I read the Enterprise Rental sticker on the back windshield and slumped in defeat.

"No, Tyler. They did not."

Shit.

***

Hoping to use him as a shield against any impending attacks, I let Tyler walk in first. I was big, but he was ten times bigger with his broad shoulders and six-seven frame. The house was as I had left it, still smelling of buttered popcorn, allspice, and my mother's perfume. The familiar seasonings and spices welcomed me. There was no need to sound the alarm that I had arrived. Everyone was waiting in the living room, as still as a picture.

My mother stood in the middle of the living room, Dad on the couch, while my brother leaned on the doorframe leading to the kitchen, where my aunts sat at the counter.

And then, of course, there was Bad Habit, sitting on the love seat, with his back to the door, hunched over with his hands clasped together as if he was saying a silent prayer. He breathed in deep through his nose before the firestorm that is my mother began.

"WHERE HAVE YOU BEEN? YOU SCARED ME TO DEATH!"

I backed up behind Tyler, fearing he wouldn't be enough to hold her. He stood stunned.

"What's going on?" he asked, looking back at me. "What's with her?"

Chris chimed in with his usual smug manner.

"Alex flew the stork coop. She's been missing since yesterday."

Missing? Oh no.

I checked every face in the room, noticing the strain in their eyes. My mother looked like she had been wearing the same clothes for two days straight.

They were all worried...about me.

The Great Escape had turned into a made for TV movie on Lifetime about a missing pregnant woman.

"Did you know where she was this whole time?" My Aunt Viv shouted at Tyler, taking her place by my mother's side. "Jesus, Tyler! What's wrong with you?"

Tyler gave me a well-deserved side eye. I mouthed an apology that only he could see. No one deserved to feel the wrath of Aunt Viv.

"Nah, I didn't. I just picked her up from Penn Station—"

Uh oh.

The whole room, except for Bad Habit, flew into a frenzy.

"You took the TRAIN?"

"What were you thinking?"

"You could have been hurt! You know you can't travel in your condition!"

My dream homecoming was ruined. I really was Mia Farrow and everyone had taken sides with the devil. In their eyes I was no victim. I glanced at the back of Bad Habit's head. He was still sitting motionless. My mother noticed.

"And don't even look at him! He's been worried too."

Is she kidding? If Armageddon was tomorrow he wouldn't sweat it.

"He flew in late last night looking for you," she continued. "He had no idea where you were! We just came home from the police station. We had to file a missing persons report!"

He filed a report...for me?

Deep down, I knew my escape was only a temporary solution. Eventually, he would have figured out where I was headed. I only thought he'd call, from hundreds of miles away, giving me time to debrief and gain supporters. I never dreamed he would increase his frequent flyer miles on my behalf.

Bad Habit didn't budge, didn't even look at me.

Typical. He came up here to put on a show, like he does best. Pretending to care so he doesn't look like the bad guy.

It was the reminder I needed that I wasn't crazy or delusional. That he really was an asshole and that I hadn't made up the last few months. I folded my arms across my chest, sitting them on my stomach.

"Gee, I didn't know you actually cared," I hissed.

He may have them fooled but not me.

I was anxious for him to show his true colors, hoping he'd snap, lose his temper, just for a moment, so people could see the real Bad Habit. The one I'd dealt with for years. The one I have to live with for the rest of my life.

He dropped his head and chuckled to himself, a sinister snarl. Slowly, he rose to his feet, turning towards me. He did nothing but exhale a long tired sigh. His eyes strained and brimmed red.

Whoa. He really was worried...

I swallowed back the acid that I held on my tongue ready to spit at him. He stared at me as the room fell silent, stuffy with tense air. The others watched and waited for his reaction. He chuckled again, glancing over his shoulder at my mother.

"I'm going back to the station to retract the report," he announced, his voice low with utter disgust. "You'll need to come with me."

"Why! For what?"

"To prove that you're still alive. And that I didn't kill you."

I shivered at the word "kill," the idea seeming too possible. He walked towards me, eyes locked on my face, heat radiating off his body as he passed, leaving the door open for me to follow.

***

Dear Me,

Did I pat you on the back for yet another fantastic idea?

Love,

Rosemary and her four devil babies

***

Bad Habit dragged me to the station as proof that I was still breathing. The detectives questioned me and I responded like a poorly made robot. They raised a suspicious eyebrow at Bad Habit, who continued to hold his stone cold face, then let us go.

Back at the house, I sat slumped at the kitchen table, allowing my family to chastise me again. This was worse than the time I got caught trying to sneak back in the house after that epic house party my freshman year of high school. The hickey on my neck didn't help the situation.

Bad Habit stood in the corner watching, not contributing a single syllable. His eyes intense and sturdy, a lion locked on his prey.

Doesn't anyone else see this? You leave me alone for one second and the bastard's gonna kill me!

I feigned a stomach cramp and we agreed to finish the discussion in the morning. My mother helped me up to my room.

"I can't believe you would do something so stupid," she fussed, slipping a nightgown over my head. I smiled and held her tightly. I didn't care if she how mad she was, I was happy just being in her presence. She sighed and patted my head like a puppy.

I slept for all of four hours before waking up, struck by hunger pangs. The house was silent except for my heavy footsteps. I crept down the stairs and turned into living room, before coming to an abrupt halt.

Gah!

Bad Habit snored on the made up sofa bed, his face still wearing the same look of discomfort as earlier. Walking by him would be like walking next to the assumed dead Jason in *Friday the 13th* right before he grabs your leg while you try to escape. I shuffled in the opposite direction through the dining room towards the kitchen.

If I wasn't so mammoth, I'd swear I was going through early menopause. My skin could melt a couple of ice caps in Antarctica. I stuck my head in the open freezer door, the cold air a much-needed relief for my boiling body. I dug past the frozen leftovers until I found the vanilla bean ice cream I saw Chris eating earlier. I carried it over to the counter, retrieved the first gigantic spoon I could find and dug in. The sweet vanilla coating my tongue seemed to be my only victory of the day.

There was a faint rustling of sheets in the other room.

It's only a matter of time.

Like clockwork, Bad Habit appeared in the kitchen doorway in his basketball shorts and wife beater. I paused to look at his skinny chicken legs, feet hidden by his black dress socks. He stared at me through sleep-deprived eyes and for the first time in twenty-four hours, I wasn't scared of him. Instead, I sighed and dug into the drawer, holding a spoon out to him as a peace offering.

He shuffled over with a yawn, took the spoon and dug into the icy treat with me. We ate in heavy silence, stealing glances every so often. His beautiful chocolate face seemed less rigid, almost calm.

"I'm sorry...that I had you worried," I whispered between bites. It just felt like the right thing to say. He reflected for a moment, still avoiding my eyes.

"It's ok," he mumbled.

"You know, I really didn't think you would come after me."

He paused, looking up from the ice cream.

"So you thought I'd just let you come back to New York and not say anything?"

"Didn't seem to matter if I was here, there, or anywhere."

He sighed, shaking his head. We continued eating in silence. I had just stuffed a spoonful in my mouth when he blurted out what I never thought I'd hear.

"Ok, here is me apologizing," he said, begrudgingly. "I'm sorry for being a jackass. I shouldn't have spoken to you the way I did."

I slipped the spoon out slow, trying to hide the grin that was growing across my face. Bad Habit never apologized for anything.

Pigs must be flying somewhere.

"Alexandria I, admittedly, like control. I've taken calculated steps to make sure my life has some type of sequential order so I have power over everything. But you, you are the only thing I cannot control, no matter what I do. It frustrating...and intriguing, at the same time."

He seemed somewhat bemused yet entertained by this fact.

"Did you know I would run?"

He nodded, concentrating on the ice cream.

"I knew you would run, which is why I confiscated the keys. I just didn't conceive the lengths you would take to escape. I didn't think it was...that bad." He paused, still avoiding eye contact. "But perhaps the subsequent events of the last couple of days were intolerable. Still, it's no justification. I let my career and other's possible judgment dictate my actions towards you."

Even though we're the same age, there were times he really made me feel like a five year old. He was probably always this mature and proper, speaking perfect King's English from birth.

"How'd you know, really?"

"I came home early. Saw the car still there and the bag by the door, but no sign of you. I called Mrs. Konick, who was still looking for you. Then I called your mother to see when she'd last spoke to you. She said you mentioned you wanted to come home. So after I successfully searched every store and bathroom at ATLANTIC Station...and couldn't find you, I booked the last flight out. I never conceived a train until I opened up the computer and the last site you were on was Amtrak."

He laughed to himself.

"Once I landed, I checked with Penn Station. They told me your train had arrived, but there was still no sign of you. Your phone was off and no one at the station remembered seeing you." He exhaled, as if he was replaying the memory. "And that's when I started to get nervous."

He sniffed the air, trying to appear unaffected since he wasn't one to lose his cool in the midst of trouble.

"Missing person's report though?"

"If no one had seen you, in your condition, in the last twenty-four hours, something had to be wrong. I didn't want...to believe that."

He had a point. I didn't look like the average pregnant woman, more like those obese women you need a crane to hoist out of their own home. He chuckled. "By the way, I now see where you get your temper from. Your mom is indeed a force not to be reckoned with."

I smiled. My mother's temper was epic, a trait I undoubtedly inherited. I've seen her make customer service agents at Macy's cry because they didn't have her shoe size. And her rage was without the extra hormones pregnancy provided.

"You know, it's really hard being like this."

"Like what?"

"Fat."

He smirked. "I can't imagine."

"Well...you should try. Here, hold my stomach."

I stood in front of him, my back pressed against his chest and placed his hands under my belly.

"Ready?"

He nodded over my shoulder and I leaned forward, letting all my weight drop into his hands. He struggled to stand straight.

"Oh," he laughs, lips grazing my collarbone, sending shivers up my spine. "One of your kids just kicked."

"Our kids."

He straightened then let me go, staring down at my stomach.

"Right. Our kids."

"Ugh! Why do you do that?"

"Do what?"

"I say something about 'us' or 'our kids' and you get all...cold. You've never been Mr. Romanic or mushy but...damn, I can't be THAT bad."

He raised an eyebrow.

"Look, don't misinterpret my attitude as neglectful or callous. I've just been...very focused on the finished line."

"So focused you had time to sleep with Victoria?"

"I didn't sleep with her."

"Yeah right," I said, rolling my eyes.

"I'm serious. Yeah, we went out and flirted heavy. I guess because, like I said, I like having control. I missed having that capability and she was easy. But I never, ever slept with anyone else but you."

I don't know why, but that made some type of sense. In a crazy Bad Habit kind of way.

"And I wasn't drunk that night," he continued. "I meant what I said. I...like having sex with you."

He eyes burned into me and my heart did that silly flutter thing. His lips were calling me. I've wanted to kiss them since he walked into the room. My spoon scratched the bottom of the empty container, distracting me.

"So...what happens now?"

Even though we both said our respective apologies, I couldn't imagine going back to the way things were. He smirked and picked up the container.

"First, we need to get you some more ice cream."

***

Plans were set in motion before I even woke up. Bad Habit was returning to Atlanta. I was to stay at home for a week, then he would fly back to drive me down south. His explanation seemed legitimate, it was a chance for him to wrap up some deals at work without leaving me home alone all day.

My mother let her anger subside and took my extended stay as an opportunity to throw an impromptu baby shower. Since she's just as much of a tyrannical detail oriented planner as I am, she wasn't thrilled about having a last minute shower for her only daughter. But, nevertheless, she was happy.

"It'll be nice to have you home for this, rather than sending everything to you," she said after Bad Habit left for the airport.

Before he left, I could literally feel the tension between us start to dissolve. He even threw me a genuine smile. I hadn't seen one of those in months.

"OMG! You're alive!"

Kennedy flew through the door a few hours after Bad Habit left. Always the diva, she arrived as pretty as a Barbie doll with her flirty sky blue sundress and giant twenty-four carat gold hoop earrings.

"I drove up as soon as I heard. They said you were missing! I was about to kill that motherfucker!"

"Really?" I scoffed from the recliner in the living room. "I thought you two were besties now?"

She rolled her eyes.

"Ok. So you're bat shit crazy. Big deal! But you're not a turkey baster. And even if you were, I'd still love you."

She shrugged with a "will you forgive me" smile. Kennedy always puts up a good front. As much as she swears off babies and long-term commitments, I knew it was secretly something she wanted as much as I did. I smiled and hugged her.

"Shut up."

We laughed away our teary eyes.

"And girl! Your hair! We can't let you go looking like this to your party."

Nothing a good makeover can't cure, that's Kennedy's motto. A stylist by trade, she washed, cut, and straightened my hair, plastered my face, and buffed down those swollen things at the end of my legs that I used to call feet. Mom went out and bought a couple of cute dresses. Cute meaning they were bed sheets with bows wrapped around them. But I didn't complain. They were ten times more fashionable than my sweats. I was starting to feel like myself again.

For the rest of the week, I didn't lift a finger. My mother cooked every day, my father brought home new movies every night, and Chris updated my iPod. Being home made me conscious of just how drained I had been from trying to please Bad Habit. He called every so often to check on me and was scheduled to fly back the day of the baby shower, but I was doubtful.

Apologies are only Band-Aids on wounds, it takes time to heal and even longer to trust. And there was still the matter of that pink elephant sitting in the room with us in the shape of my growing abdomen. We had yet to talk about the babies or how we planned on dealing with them.

The following Saturday, dressed in a pink bed sheet with a red bow, I sat in a huge white wicker chair in the middle of the living room while my family and friends gathered around. Dozens of baby pink and blue balloons floated about, flowers spread on every table, and a large white sheet cake with little chocolate babies sat on the counter by the fruit punch. Some were there for the food and booze. Others were there just to get a peek of the freak show. Twins didn't run my family and I couldn't wrap my arms around my stomach and touch my fingertips.

Claire came with a stack of gifts from former co-workers, including one from Ralphie.

Kennedy, attending to her Godmother duties, helped host the party.

"Ok, it's time to open the presents!"

A mountain of presents towered to my left, doubles of everything.

Diaper genies, toys, clothes, bottles, baby wipes...who knew these kids would need all this stuff.

Mom had just passed me a slice of cake when the door opened. Tyler walked in, his wife and kids in tow. Behind them was Bad Habit. It had only been a week, but my heart hit my chest like static shock. He was dressed in loose fitting dark blue jeans, a hunter green Lacoste polo, and crisp sneakers, far from his usual uptight business attire. He stood by the door, smirking and nodded in approval at my new look, giving me a thumbs-up that only I could see. The way we stared was like we were devouring each other for the first time. Our own small private moment in the middle of a party, a few feet apart. I chuckled and tried to play it cool, but my coy blushing gave me away. Between him and the lavish attention from my family, it was the happiest I had been in months.

As the party came to a close Tyler and Bad Habit packed up the gifts in the trunk of his rented Jeep. My mother packed me in the passenger seat and held me through the open car window. I wasn't ready to let go.

"It's ok Alex, you'll be fine. You're in good hands," Mom beamed proudly, her eyes glassed with tears. "I'll try to come down in a couple of weeks. You should be alright until then, but please don't go running off and scaring me. Again!"

"Ok Mom, I promise."

It's amazing to have a mother that loves you no matter how many stupid mistakes you make. She raised the bar almost out of reach.

Kennedy stood next to her.

"Well, next time I see you heffa you'll be a mommy," she said, laughing.

Ice formed around my spine. I nodded wordlessly and hugged her.

A mommy?

She was right. In a couple of weeks I wouldn't be able to dodge the title any longer. I didn't think I deserved it after being so self-centered. I only thought of the little creatures when they bothered me.

Bad Habit shut the trunk, waving to the rest of my family standing in the driveway as he hopped in the car. Kennedy stuck her tongue out at me as she pulled Mom away. We said our finally goodbyes while Bad Habit drove off.

The road trip was ominous; we were driving back to hell...on purpose. Dread suffocated me with a pillow of unsettling silence between us. The hours passed like days, making me more and more anxious for the inevitable pain of whatever was going to happen now that we were alone again.

"Ummm...you cold?"

"Uh...no. I'm fine. Thanks."

He scrolled pointlessly through his phone.

"You, um, you need to use the bathroom again, or something?"

"No...I'm ok."

"O...kay."

Waiting for him to turn back into the Bad Habit I knew was like waiting for Dr. Jekyll to turn into Mr. Hyde. His phone saved us from the awkwardness.

"Hey man, what's up...yeah I'm on my way back from NY... I finished the amendments on your contract yesterday...What's that? Well considering it's a multi-million dollar deal, there are certain stipulations..."

Funny how men can carry on as normal but women were nothing but baby infused banter twenty-four seven. From his long-winded conversations, you would never know he was an expectant father. Right then I decided I needed to get my life back in order. I finished the business plan for my consulting business a week before I ran off and pitched it to Claire during the baby shower. She loved the idea, even promised to refer me to some of her clients. It would only be part-time, not enough money to move out on my own, but it was a start.

If Michelle can be an awesome mom and help run the world, so can I.

"Hey Dawn. Yep, I'm on my way back. What time is my meeting with Mr. Paul tomorrow? Well can you schedule a meeting with Jeff Roger's agent on Wednesday? Yeah and also pull up Mdot's contract. Yeah, his management now wants to add—oh really? That's great—then yeah I'll probably have this deal locked by Friday depending on the label..."

With doomsday fast approaching, you would think we would have loads to discuss. Heaps. Mountains. Seemed stupid to just talk about the weather or traffic like we were simple acquaintances, but there was no smooth way to bring up child rearing.

I tried to sleep but it was like resting on mattress filled with broken glass. Just waiting for something to cut me. I was unable to shake the feeling that I had made a mistake, that nothing would change, and that I should've stayed in New York.

Somewhere between North and South Carolina, I woke up from a nap just in time to hear the end of a conversation.

"I know it ain't her fault— I'm not about to be like Daddy." He glanced over, noticing I was awake. "Momma, I gotta go. Call you when I get in."

We pulled into the driveway around four in the morning and I cringed at the sight of the house. The throbbing of misery set in my chest.

Now I know how my cousins feel when they're sent back to prison.

Bad Habit yawned, his eyes barely open.

"I'll take the gifts out later, before I return the car in the morning," he mumbled.

I yawned in response and grabbed my purse, about to step out when he touched my arm.

"Wait for me," he mumbled and climbed out.

Whoa, is he's about to get the door for me?

He walked around and jerked open the door, holding his arms out as if to catch me. There had to be some reasonable explanation for the sudden chivalry.

"The truck is kind of high. I don't want you to fall."

"Oh."

He reached out his hand but instead of taking it, I slapped him with my purse. He stumbled back in shock and I snatched the keys out of his hands, jerking the door closed. I jumped into the driver's seat and sped out of the driveway, managing not to hit a single mailbox and headed straight towards the highway.

Ok, that didn't really happen. But I thought about it though.

I breathed in deep, like a captured runaway enjoying my last taste of freedom, sweet like wine and strawberries. Nothing much had change inside, although the house was fairly clean. Bad Habit was rather domesticated, even before I came along. He walked into the kitchen and I headed toward the stairs, knowing it would take me twice as long to ascend them. I gained another twenty pounds in the week I was away and walked like a hunchback in dire need of a pimp cane.

Real sexy.

I had just reached the top when he came running after me.

"Hold up!" He sprinted and jumped in front of the door.

What now?

Shaking his head, he pointed in the opposite direction.

"Wrong room, go in that one."

I took a long blink.

We're sleeping in separate rooms now?

"Oh," I said, trying not to sound devastated as my heart cracked like a mirror. I figured it was to make things clear between us, remembering there would never be an 'us'.

"Nah, not like that," he said catching wind of my feelings for once. "We're just switching rooms."

"WE are? Why?"

He opened the double doors, flicked the lights and I locked eyes with the glowing blue teddy bear lamp on top of a dresser. The bleak and bland color of the master bedroom was now a shade of smoky sky blue. There were four mahogany cribs against the wall, adjacent from two mahogany changing tables. A glossy white rocking chair sat in the corner, cradling a few small stuffed animals. The windows were dressed with sheer cream and blue curtains. Pictures of zoo animals adorned the walls. Underneath the window was a day bed with white linens.

"It's...it's a nursery," I gasped out.

"Well, this is the biggest bedroom in the house and you probably wouldn't want to run back and forth if we used the other rooms. All of our stuff is next door."

Dumbstruck, I stood in silence. One moment I was sitting in a twelve-hour drive, contemplating why I was with a man who barely uttered a grunt towards me. The next, I'm with another man who put together a dream nursery. My dream nursery.

"It's not done, but one of those kids is gonna be a boy, and I don't want him sitting in a powder puff pink room, sending him straight to queerville. Girls like blue... So..."

I wasn't listening to his tangent but I did hear him trail off, his eyes on me. I was too busy admiring his work, picturing myself holding one of my Aliens, rocking him in the chair, changing him on the table, sleeping on the daybed. I was actually picturing myself being a mother. I leaned against one of the double doors, the thought breathtaking. He leaned against the opposite door, tilting his head back as we stared at each other, motionless. Although his eyes sagged with exhaustion, a smirk of satisfaction crept on his lips. There was something about him in that moment that made me feel like mini firecrackers were set off on my skin.

Perhaps there is hope for us after all.

"I know we're 'not together' but would it been wrong of me to ask you to spend your last ounce of energy and kiss me right now?"

His head jerked up from the door. I had his attention.

"I'm not asking you to hold my hand in public, or even spoon me in bed. But if you could kiss me...right now...like you mean it...it would really help complete this ridiculously perfect moment," I said, smiling hopeful with a shrug.

His eyes searched my face, deliberating. Hesitantly, he pushed himself off the door and stepped towards me. Bracing for rejection, I had held my breath before he cupped his hands around my face and stared into my eyes. I forgot the way he could make my bones melt into jelly. I leaned back against the wall to support myself as he slowly dipped his lips toward mine. Deeper and deeper. I closed my eyes and sucked in his scent, smelling like rain, musk, and lust.

I need to find a way to bottle up his pheromones and sell them on the black market. Chicks wouldn't stand a chance.

His hands wringed into to my hair and I reached for his neck, pulling him closer. He pinned me to the door and we became lost in each other. And just as I began to wonder, why we didn't do this more often, his head jerked away.

"Ahh!" he said with a slight chuckle and I didn't have to ask why. He felt what I had. Alien 1 did not like the close proximity of his father to his mother.

"Wow, already cockblockers and they're not even born yet."

Seven Months

The one night I slept for more than two hours, impressive since insomnia was my new best friend, was the same night we were robbed...for real this time.

"ALEXANDRIA!"

Bad Habit shook my shoulders so hard my head banged against the headboard. I woke up, hung over with sleep.

"What the...I...huh?"

He was straddled over me, knees digging into the bed. This was a familiar position, but not with him still dressed in his suit and tie. His face was stoic but his eyes were wide, matching the way he screamed my name, searching my face.

"Shit," he gasped then yoked me up like a doll into an embrace that left little room to breathe. His arms were so tight around my back that I heard my spine crack. Something cold and metal pressed against my skin.

"Thank God," he murmured in my hair. "Are you ok?"

He was pinning my arms in the tightest bear hug imaginable.

We don't hug.

"Ummm...yeah?"

He let go and jerked me back to get a better look at my face.

"Did they hurt you?"

"They?"

"Someone broke into the house."

I blinked a couple of times, as if my eyes had anything to do with my hearing or comprehension and tried to focus, shaking off the grogginess.

"Wait...what happened? What time is it?"

He turned on the light and I squinted away, the glow burning my face. This was the worst way to be woken up. He was the king of torture.

"It's eleven thirty. Sorry I was late. I couldn't get out of this last meeting. Someone broke into the house but you're fine."

Did he just say he was sorry?

"I'm dreaming," I said, pulling away, expecting him to turn into Freddy Kruger. Bad Habit had a face I didn't recognize, a face of panic, worry, and stress. He stood up, placing his gun on the nightstand. I eyed it, realizing he was serious and that he had just hugged me with a gun in his hand. Two words describe our relationship now: Thug love.

"I'm surprised you didn't hear anything. There's glass everywhere."

"I guess...I was tired..."

But then I heard the glass, like someone's boots crunching over potatoes chips. I gripped Bad Habit's arm, a whimper escaping my lips.

"Police! Is everyone alright in here?" A man's voice called from downstairs.

"We're up here! Be right down!" Bad Habit called back. He reached below the bed, putting the gun away. In my half sleep state, I threw caution to the wind.

"What does some highly civilized lawyer like yourself need a gun for?"

He thought for a moment, face twisting into a painful guilty expression.

"I wasn't...always this 'civilized'. I mean...everyone has a past."

He looked at me like he was waiting for forgiveness. I didn't respond. I didn't want to know anymore.

Great, I'm sleeping with the enemy.

"You stay here and don't move. I'll be right back."

His voice wasn't overly concerned or patronizing. He was back to his calm self, however, less cold and formal. He turned at the door.

"You sure you ok? You want some water?"

"Water?"

Who is this guy?

"I'll bring some up."

When he was gone, I struggled out of bed to the bathroom with Sasha at my feet, her nose up my butt. By the time I brushed my teeth and climbed back into bed, Bad Habit returned with a glass of ice water and two police officers.

A tall dark, balding officer spoke from the doorway. "Evening ma'am. I'm Officer Powell. This is Officer Mitchell. First things first, are you okay?"

"I'm fine." And it was true. I was fine, calm considering the danger I just slept through. Bad Habit's demeanor was rubbing off on me, in a good way. He stood next to me, offering the water.

"Your husband told us what happened. I know you're on bed rest and I hate to trouble to ya but we had a couple of questions."

I sipped my water, waiting for Bad Habit to correct him but he just stood there. An entire thirty seconds of frozen silence went by. The officers glanced at each other then back at me.

"Ma'am?"

"Oh, right. Sorry. Go ahead."

They asked a few basic questions, learning I wasn't much help since I was dead to the world, then asked if I wanted to go down to the hospital to get checked out. I declined, fearing they'd use any excuse to try to keep me there.

"Well it looks like y'all were lucky," Office Mitchell said, while scribbling in his note pad. "Just got some damage to the back door. The only thing they got off with is a laptop and a radio. Think your dog scared them off."

Sasha was sitting next to me with her tongue hanging out her massive head, tail wagging, thudding against the nightstand. I couldn't help but smirk at the big goof ball.

"Could've been much worse," Officer Powell added.

All three men looked at me pointedly, thinking the same thought. I pulled the cover closer to my chest.

Baby stealers!

"Thanks officers," Bad Habit said. "I'll see you out."

"Alrighty. We'll have the report ready for you first thing in the morning and an extra patrol car come around the area. Sure they were just some first timers, probably some kids that don't know no better."

"Well in any case, I'm having a new alarmed installed tomorrow."

They tipped their hats and walked down the stairs.

"Aye Joe, ain't we been here a while back?"

"Oh yeah! That's the naked lady in the kitchen. She's the one who made them sandwiches…"

Bad Habit turned at the door with a relieved smile.

"I'll be right back," he sighed and followed the officers.

I smiled, relieved but more than that, I was happy. It's not every day that Bad Habit is nurturing, even overprotective of me. And it was the first time someone called him my 'husband' and he didn't cut off their tongue with switchblade. I rubbed my stomach, giggling.

Then one thought disintegrated my glee.

My business plan was on that laptop.

***

"So doc, is this Lamaze class thingy even necessary? We know I'm going to have a C-section, right? Why do I have to go to school when I'm just going to kick back and let you do all the work?"

Dr. Turner laughed as he took off his latex gloves. He had just finished an ultrasound in which Bad Habit was partly present for, even though he was standing right beside me, fidgeting the entire time. Under our new agreement, he promised he would come to my next check-up and was all but willing until we walked into the office. His mutating demeanor during the examination went from perplexed to enchanted, pleased to baffled all in a matter of a few short moments as he stared at the monitor. It was impossible to guess what he was thinking.

"Well, it's not so much the Lamaze class as the childbirth and parenting prep classes you need. My job is easy compared to the one you two will be doing for the rest of your lives."

Bad Habit and I both tensed up.

Geez, Doc, don't remind me.

The SpongeBob nurse walked in and gazed at Bad Habit like he was an egg McMuffin. He noticed, but didn't pay her any mind and focused on the doctor.

"So we should sign up for one right away then," Bad Habit confirmed.

"Yes, in fact, there's a terrific one I recommend to all my patients. It's called 'Multiple Blessings' and it's a crash course on everything you'll need to know, dealing with multiples. It's a bit late notice, but there's one tonight if you're interested. I can make a couple of calls and squeeze you in."

"Yes, that'll be great, thank you."

"Tonight?" I whined.

But American Idol comes on tonight! TV is my only sanity.

"Well Alex, to be honest you really should've taken the full course months ago when I recommended it."

Bad Habit threw me an angry glare.

Gee Doc, thanks for throwing me under the bus.

"Well, I've taken care of babies before! I'm sure I can manage."

Even though I've been fired from every babysitting job I've ever had.

Dr. Turner chuckled while he scribbled on his note pad. "And it looks like you haven't been staying off your feet like I told you to either."

"Sure I have!"

Except for that one little trip to New York, but who's counting that.

Bad Habit shook his head like a disappointed father.

"What else should she be doing that I don't know about?"

Dr. Turner put away his pad and took off his glasses.

"Well, I hate to tell you this, but I'm going to have to insist on strict bed rest, possibly under hospital care. There is some effacing, we can't risk anymore."

Hospital? Noooooooooooo!

"Whoa, whoa, wait a minute. Doc, please, I swear, I'll stay off my feet. But can I at least do it from home? Pleeeeeeeaaaaaazzzzze!"

He glanced at Bad Habit with a smirk.

"Has she been taking her vitamins?"

Bad Habit rolled his eyes.

"Marginally."

Frustrated, Dr. Turner set down his clipboard.

"Alex, you NEED to start taking care of yourself. This is serious. You've been hanging on by a string here but we're in the final quarter of this game."

I hung my head like I'd been sent to the dummy corner. "Okay."

"I'll let you stay home, but you'll need supervision," he warned before turning to Bad Habit. "She can't be at home ALONE."

Bad Habit nodded in agreement.

"Don't worry, she won't. I have an idea."

An idea? Uh oh.

***

Bad Habit and I sat in the back of the classroom like a couple of renegade high school students. It did seem like detention. Dr.

Turner neglected to mention the course was four hours long and I had the attention span of a crack baby.

Bad Habit nudged my arm, warning me to pay attention to the dry voice talking in the front of the class. The room was full of expectant mothers who didn't look anywhere near my size. In fact, I was sure we had the wrong room if it wasn't for the obnoxious "Multiple Blessings!" sign at the door, letting the whole world know our business. When I limped in the other women looked at me like I was Godzilla, faces crumbling in horror as they seized their husbands' arms.

That's right, be afraid, you're gonna look like this too!

After a brief introduction and tour of the neonatal unit, we returned to the classroom to watch a film on C-section deliveries and discuss the process. The other parents took diligent notes in their five subject notebooks like they were preparing for a biology mid-term. I crunched on Cheetos.

The movie was graphic, but no different from any other medical show I'd seen on TLC. Just a wailing wrinkled infant covered in bloody mucus attached to a long peapod looking cord being pulled out of a ripped open stomach. Suddenly, the husband sitting in front of us slumped over and fell out of his seat, fainting face first to the floor.

"Jack!" his expectant wife screamed, shaking him.

"Oh boy," our instructor, Nurse Beth, said calmly before rushing over. She tickled his nose with smelling salts. A few seconds later he awakened startled, his face a bright shade of green. She chuckled and patted him on the back.

"Don't worry, there's one in every class."

Bad Habit and I snickered at the same time then smiled at each other. For once, we were on the same mocking team.

After taking Jack to the recovery room, Nurse Beth returned with a cart of props. She was an older woman, about the size of a midget with a blunt black bob and a spunky drill sergeant attitude.

"Ok ladies and gentleman. That was eventful. Now, on to the hard part." She pointed to a shelf in the corner of the room filled with life sized baby dolls dressed in pink and blue onesies. "Fathers, go to the shelf and pick up your children. Remember to pick up the same number of children you are expecting and if you know the sex, that'd be good too."

The expectant fathers scurried over to the shelves, their wives happily looking on. Bad Habit sauntered over like he was too cool for baby school. They skipped back with their dolls and the class observed one another. Most couples had two, two had three. Some had sets of all girls, others all boys. They talked amongst themselves like they were gossiping about prom. But the room hushed as Bad Habit sauntered back with four dolls. Two boys and two girls. He smirked as he sat down beside me. The entire room stared back at our table.

"Two boys and two girls, aye?" I asked under my breath. We had no clue what we were expecting.

"Might as well since we're only two short of the Brady Bunch."

We snickered again.

Wow! This is way more fun than American Idol.

"Okay ladies and gentleman," Nurse Beth said, eyeing us. "Let's begin with some basic care."

It was at that point that the class started to go downhill. Well, for me at least.

Diaper skills, C+. Burping, C-. Feeding, D+. All around motherliness, D-.

Bad Habit on the other hand was an A+ student, diligent and focused during the demonstrations. Performing the tasks with swift ease.

Our babies will never have a diaper rash as long as he's around.

I was struggling with my "son's" diaper when he came over to help me.

"No, see, it's like this," he instructed as he taped the doll up. It was hard not to pout.

Is there anything he's NOT good at?

My mood went from lighthearted to sulky in a matter of minutes. I was failing at being a mother to a bunch of Cabbage Patch Kids. There was huge spotlight on my ill performance.

"Okay ladies and gentleman, good work. Now, let's put away our children."

Bad Habit scooped up the dolls and took them to the shelf. He stopped to chat with the other fathers in the corner.

I returned the bottles and remaining diapers, disheartened. Nurse Beth gave me a comforting smile.

"Don't worry dear. You'll get the hang of it in no time."

Her attempt to reassure me that I wasn't a complete failure (even though I was sure she'd point social services in my direction once we left) only made me feel lower. The grim reality was I didn't know how to care for a baby, which topped off my lack of maternal instincts. I waddled to my seat, passing the other mothers who had gathered in a small circle to compare notes.

"Oh no, I'm breast feeding, it's the only way."

"Oh me too! It's natural and much healthier."

"There's just way too many chemicals in formula. They want our babies hooked on that stuff like alcoholics!"

"We're also making our own baby food with organic fruits and vegetables."

"I have some terrific recipes! Sometimes, I mix peas and kale with a little tofu for dinner. Thomas loves it."

"Oh, that's a wonderful idea!"

"Absolutely."

I hope Bad Habit knows if I ever sound like them to promptly shoot me between the eyes.

Bad Habit was still caught up in conversation when one of the Stepford wives started talking to me.

"Hi, I'm sorry, I don't believe I caught your name," their leader, a freckle-faced blonde hippie interrupted my view.

That's because I never gave it to you.

"Alex," I mumbled.

"Oh of course, Alex, duh! I'm so forgetful, must be the hormones. I'm Maggie by the way," she said with a cheerful laugh. She was slender, toned, and her clothes looked like they were made of hemp. Her tan skin had a natural healthy glow, like she was from St. Thomas instead of hot ass Atlanta. I immediately didn't like her.

"So you're having quadruplets? That's wonderful! I'm having twins."

I stared at her puny stomach, trying to hold my composure.

Twins? She looks like she just ate a couple of burgers.

"Oh, that's...nice."

"Anyway, we're doing a natural birth with a midwife in the hospital," she carried on with the others. I assumed she just wanted my undivided attention and had no other interest but having the spotlight on her.

"I've got this terrific doula. She was recommended by one of the other pregnant mommies in my Bikram yoga class. We're going for a hike this weekend."

This skinny pregnant bitch is making me look bad.

Eager as ever to leave, I glanced back over at Bad Habit. He was still chatting, rolling his sleeves up to his forearms and I know it was unintentional, but the way he licked his lips almost made me drool. It was hard to tell whether it was my hormones or if actual feelings that made me so enamored, but he could look downright mouth-wateringly sexy at times.

"Is your life partner as excited as you are?" Maggie said, noticing my attention drifting away from her. I caught her raising an eyebrow at my ring-less finger and crossed my arms.

"Thrilled," I mumbled. Her eyes widened as she finally processed my mood.

"Uh oh! I see someone's a bit crabby today," she said in a squeaky baby voice, glancing at her fellow giggling Stepford sisters. "You should try some of my lavender oil. It really helps to relieve stress and anxiety."

Did this heffa just compare me to a bottom feeder?

"Also, you also really shouldn't be drinking that stuff," she continued, pointing to Bad Habit's fruit punch sitting on the table next to me. "It's really bad for the baby. You should really try to drink one hundred percent juice, if any juice at all. Try prune juice, it'll help with your constipation. And your mood."

No. She. Didn't.

I opened my mouth and Bad Habit swooped in, muffling my screams with his hand.

"Hi ladies, thanks for keeping her company," he said, charming them with his seductive voice.

They gasped at his intoxicating smile, simultaneously glancing at their respective husbands, still mingling in the corner.

"Oh it's fine," Maggie said with a giggle and lightly touched his arm. "I was just giving your life partner here some motherly tips. But I'm sure you have everything under control."

'Under control'? Is this skinny pregnant bitch hitting on MY man?

I opened my mouth and he slapped it closed again, holding me back from lunging at her neck.

"Why thank you. Well, we better get going. We've had a pretty long day. Pleasure meeting you lovely ladies!"

He gave a neighborly wave, reversing us back towards the door.

"No, thank you! A pleasure indeed! Hope to see you soon. Oh and take care Alex. Remember, one hundred percent!"

If Bad Habit wasn't pinning my arms back, I would have shoved the bottle down her throat. He whipped me around, dragging me by the hand out of the classroom right before I screamed out a couple of obscenities and stunned the hospital to silence.

"Relax," he said as we walked through the hall. "She seemed nice. What's the problem? She just gave you some motherly tips." A mischievous grin spread across his face and he ran away from my swinging fist.

"Yeah, well she only got two of those little monsters. I got four. I'd be a tree hugging Susie homemaker too if I was her!"

He grabbed my forearm before I got to the door.

"Hey. Wait here a minute, I'll bring the car around."

I nodded with a yawn and slumped into a waiting room chair while he walked out, just a frantic woman with long greasy brown hair, pulled into a sloppy ponytail, struggling to juggle a screaming baby and several bags rushed in. Her skin was dewy pale, eyes blood shot like she hadn't slept in days.

"It's ok Patty, it's ok," she cooed to the child. The baby's face was as red her strawberry blonde hair. The woman bounced the child on her hip with one arm, while digging through her purse with the other. She pulled out a pacifier and stuck it in her gummy mouth. The baby stopped crying just enough to throw the pacifier by my feet, as if she was insulted by it.

"Patty!"

I attempted to pick it up but it disappeared under my enormous stomach.

"No, no, no! I got it!" the lady said, rushing over. She bent down and her bag slipped off her shoulders. Papers and diapers scattered, bottles rolled.

At least it wasn't the baby.

As she knelt down in her heather gray pencil skirt and white oxford while trying to balance the baby on her hip, her other purse fell, its contents scattering in the opposite direction. It was a sorry sight.

"I'm so sorry. I wish I could help you but—"

"No, no. It's ok. I know how it feels not to be able to see your feet. Sit right there! Patty just isn't feeling so good. I don't know what's wrong. Gosh!"

She stopped for a moment to exhale, tears building in her eyes. She was the epitome of an overwhelmed working mother. I scanned the waiting room, hoping that someone who didn't have my handicap would come to her rescue, but between the teenager with a knife sticking out of his thigh and the old lady coughing up mucus, pickings were slim.

The baby wailed then stopped to stare at me. It was like having a staring contest with Sasha. She drew me in until I blinked.

"Ummmm...do you want me to hold the baby?"

I had no idea what possessed me to offer but woman's face instantly lit up.

"Oh yes, PLEASE!"

"Oh, wait I—"

She passed Patty like she was a sack of potatoes and I held her up by her torso, arms extended away from me like she was the spoiled leftovers you find in the back of the fridge.

Jesus, what have I done!

"Oh THANK YOU! You have no idea how much this means to me," she said, crawling on her hands and knees, picking up the contents from her bags.

"Um...yeah?"

"I'm Stacey. That's Patty."

Patty whimpered, her feet curling and dangling in the air. Skin so hot under my hands, she could give third degree burns. Her big blue eyes stared pleadingly at her mother.

"Um...I'm Alex," I cringed.

"I just got off work and came straight from day care. Patty got an awful fever. It's been going around."

Fever? Eek!

I was in no position to be holding a contagious germ-festering human. But she was so helpless, I couldn't just put her down on the linoleum.

"I, um—"

"Then I gotta hear crap from my boss for leaving an hour early..."

Stacy looked up and did a double take, the contents of her bag in her hands. "Ha! What in the world are you doing?"

"I'm...holding the baby."

She pushed her long bangs out her face, glanced at my stomach then back at me with a sympathetic smile.

"You never held a baby before?"

Feeling defensive, I pulled Patty an inch closer.

"Well...sort of."

"Oh it's easy," she said, sitting next to me. "Just curve your arm like this, like you're carrying a football, support the head. Then take your other arm and hold the bottom."

I followed Stacey's instructions, guiding Patty into the nook of my arm. She curled into me, her butt sitting on my stomach.

"Like this?"

"You got it! You're a natural."

She rubbed my stomach. Normally I'd be offended by strangers doing that, but considering I had her child in my hands, I let it slide.

"You hear that little one, Mommy is a natural," she giggled to my stomach.

Patty stared up at me, exhausted from crying. She had cute chubby knees and elbows, long lashes, and a little potbelly wrapped in a pink one piece. Kids never make me gushy, but it was hard to resist this one. She was rather adorable, sweet, and docile, like the Gerber baby. It must suck feeling so sick and the one person you want in the world can't hold you cause she's too busy working for a douche bag that won't let her out an hour early.

"Awww...poor baby," I whispered, pushing the sweaty curls off her forehead. She was burning up. Did Stacey know how to give her an ice bath, like my mother used to do when we were little to break the fever? Or how to mix that nasty liquid Tylenol with oatmeal to make it taste good? Patty's cheeks were soaked with sweat and tears while she gnawed on her own hand. I grabbed a tissue out of my bag and dried off her chubby rosy cheeks.

What a sweet baby. Letting a complete stranger, who just scored a D in parenting class, hold and soothe her like a pro.

"She's really pretty," I said, rocking her softly, watching her eyes struggle to keep open. Stacey turned and frowned.

"She? Patty's a boy!"

I stared back at her then looked down at Patty's pink jumper.

Uh oh.

Just in time, Bad Habit strolled over out of nowhere with a smile.

"Here, let me help you with that."

He kneeled next to Stacey, picking up the last few items under the seats then offered his hand and help her off the floor.

"Oh, thank you!"

"No problem."

Stacey finished repacking her bags, situating herself in the chair next to me.

"Your wife is awesome. This was such a big help. And so natural! She'll be a great mom."

I looked back down at Patty, waiting for Bad Habit to swoop in with his "she's not my wife" decree but instead, he was silent. From the corner of my eye, he nodded in agreement.

"Alex, mind if you hold Patty for a few more minutes while I check in?"

"Not at all," I said, suddenly confident.

"Thanks!"

She dumped her bags and rushed over to the counter, papers and insurance card in her hand, and I noticed she didn't have a ring.

Where the hell is Patty's father? Why is Stacey struggling alone with a sick baby and in serious need of a wash and trim?

Then it hit me. Bad Habit was jerk but he could be far worse.

Shit, that could be me.

Bad Habit stood back with a mischievous grin, shoving his hands in his pockets.

"What?"

He shrugged, nodding at my hands.

"That's a good look on you."

There was a glimmer of pride in his eyes. I looked back down at Patty, the boy, caressing his back with the strange desire to hum him a lullaby.

"Really? You think so?

He nodded, approvingly. "Yeah."

I grinned, cheeks burning like Patty's, wondering what Bad Habit was seeing. Maybe he was seeing what I was feeling, that I wasn't a total failure after all. That I was holding a baby and I actually liked it.

This isn't so bad. I could do this.

But Patty wasn't smiling. He frowned, his face turned another shade of red and his lips tensed up. Suddenly, he hiccupped and hurled white puke straight up like a volcano, smacking me in the face, catching the corner of my mouth. It reeked of curdled milk and spoiled rice.

"Patty!" Stacey screamed and rushed over.

Bad Habit stood frozen, mouth gaping. Trembling in disgust, I muttered the words through clenched teeth to keep anything from falling into my mouth.

"Get. Your. Unisex baby. Away from me. Now."

***

Dear Me,

Typically, when one says they 'have an idea' it's for the betterment of all parties involved. But that's for people who don't have a Bad Habit.

Love,

In Deep Shit

***

Her name was Mrs. Earwood. Her vibe, completely ambiguous. With her short, curvy body and forced chestnut hair that sat on the tops of her shoulders, she moved with a type of familiar grace. She had an air to her that reminded me of one of those strong women from the south, like a Sojourner Truth or Harriet Tubman. Every outfit seemed to be tailored to her body, nothing short of pristine. In the kitchen, she flipped eggs and bacon with a natural ease. In fact, it seemed like the entire house was at her command in a matter of minutes, achieving what I could barely do in months. Even her damn pancakes tasted better than mine and we were using the same mix.

Did I also mention she's Bad Habit's mother?

The brilliant idea Bad Habit concocted was twenty-four hour surveillance by the one person he trusted most. Even though I was a zombie with sciatica, I did not like the idea of a full time babysitter nor any type of subtle competition. I ranted and broke several plates to demonstrate my true feelings on the matter. But nothing could stop Bad Habit from sending her a roundtrip ticket from Boston to Atlanta and she wasted no time making sure I was chained to my bed, according to the doctor's orders.

I was forbidden to leave the second floor, leaving my pseudo mother-in-law in charge of my care. Sasha instantly became her new shadow.

Once again, faithful bitch to the end.

When Bad Habit and I first started dating, I had dreams of the day I'd meet his mother, his best friend. The only person he talked to every single day. I imagined she would accept me in her loving arms just like she did with his ex. I pictured us talking over the phone, planning trips to Boston, spending weekends shopping and gushing over Bad Habit. I'd spend holidays and birthdays with his family. She and my mother would become best friends, combining efforts to pressure us into marriage, linking our families together forever in a loving bond.

But the only bond Bad Habit and I created was an unwelcome fluke forcing us into a nightmarish circumstance. Not exactly the ideal time to get to know someone.

"Here we are dear."

Mrs. Earwood walked into the bedroom carrying a tray with a plate of cheese eggs, turkey bacon, wheat toast, and a glass of fresh squeeze orange juice. I sat up in bed, searching past her for Bad Habit. Her congeniality was surreal. It made me skeptical. She acted as if she had known me for years when I expected the extreme cold shoulder. After all, I was the home wrecking harlot who entrapped her son, stealing his proverbial future, making her an unexpected grandmother.

Ok, so I was terrified of her.

"He left for work already," she said, noticing my edginess.

"Oh."

He didn't even say goodbye.

"He's busy dear. Had some meeting he had to go to or something."

"Sure, right."

Do you know your son at all?

Her mere presence made me lose my appetite. She smiled as she broke my plus sized vitamins in half and set them on the napkin.

"Thank you," I said obediently.

"You're quite welcome dear."

As she turned, I wrapped the pills up, ready to throw them in my previous hiding place when I noticed her plopped in the recliner.

Uhhh...can I help you?

She dropped the soft wicker basket hidden under her arm, took out knitting needles and a bright roll of canary yellow yarn. She smiled, in a *Mommy Dearest* sort of way, her hands working over the yarn, fingers making mini nooses. I gulped and poked at my eggs, checking for rat poison.

"I'm making the babies some little hats, for the winter. Eat your eggs before they get cold dear."

Feigning a smile, I forced myself to chew on the tasty eggs. She was quiet, but it was a loaded type of silence, just like Bad Habit.

What lies has he told this woman about me?

She would have been the perfect ally if I didn't think she was trying to off me.

The television was still on from the night before. I pretended to watch, needing a buffer to cut the tension in the room. Something to keep myself from feeling like a caged animal with a haughty zookeeper. The yarn was actually a very pretty shade of yellow. I was looking forward to dressing my kids just like Michelle dresses her daughters. We'll be the most stylish family in history. Perhaps I'll have all girls, all super models. We'd rule at "Mommy and Me" pageants.

"Oh, I didn't know you knew Spanish dear."

I focused, realizing we were watching a one of those over dramatic Spanish soap operas. A big-breasted Latina and an

Antonio Banderas look-a-like were breathing into each other's mouth.

"Oh. Yeah...um...trying to learn."

She chuckled, shaking her head while focusing on her knitting but I could still feel her watching me.

Good grief, how do I get rid of her?

Finishing breakfast, I pushed the tray out of my way, readying myself for the bathroom run.

"Do you need some help dear?"

"No, no. I'm fine."

"You sure now?"

"Yep, I'm ok."

It took incredible amount of forethought and planning to get out of bed and like a stubborn ass, I refused to accept assistance. It sucked being dependent on the one woman whose opinion could make or break my future with Bad Habit.

The sex scene on the telenovela was becoming a tad too graphic to watch with my baby's daddy's mommy, but I couldn't find the remote. My Crackberry echoed from downstairs.

"Is that your phone dear? I'll go get it."

Once she was out of sight, I frantically kicked around my sheets until I hit something hard at the end of the bed. The remote was by my feet, light years away in my condition.

Shit.

As she walked up the stairs, I let the loud passionate scene play on, my eyes transfixed, pretending it didn't faze me.

"Sorry dear I missed the call, but someone named...Bad Habit called?"

Oh boy.

"Oh yeah, ha, that's my cousin. He's so silly. I'll call him back later."

The ringing house phone interrupts us. She heads towards the cordless on the nightstand and I scrambled to grab it before her.

"I've got it!" I shrieked, startling her. She, rightfully, stared at me like I was nuts.

"Hello!"

"Why didn't you answer your phone?" Bad Habit snapped.

Mrs. Earwood stood next to me, her eyes as intense as her son's.

Now I know who he inherited that fun feature from.

Feeling like a patient in a psych ward under orderly supervision, I winced a smile.

"Oh yeah, sorry. Must have slipped my mind," I said, with a nervous chuckle.

"Huh? Alexandria, what are you talking about?"

"Oh, really, ok. That's great! Can't wait."

"You're not making any sense. Who are you talking to?"

"Well, okay. Tell Aunt Viv I said hello. Talk to you later. Bye!"

I hung up with an innocent smile.

"My cousin. He's so...crazy."

Her eyes narrowed and sweat built on my neck. I didn't dare exhale. She returned to her seat as Sasha ran in carrying one of her remaining toys that hadn't been torn to shreds.

"Well hello there Miss Sasha! Have you come to visit your mommy? Look, she's right there!" She pointed and Sasha followed her finger. She trotted over, sniffed my arm, then trotted away, uninterested. Mrs. Earwood laughed and patted her head.

"Well, so much for that."

"Don't mind her. That dog is crazy."

"She's adorable. But he only got her to keep you company."

"Me? Oh no, your son was the only one who wanted that beast, not me."

"Oh, but he got her for you dear. He said you were in the house all day by yourself and needed some company."

Wait a second. Sasha was for me? What the what!

"I thought it was a wonderful idea. Give you a little...you know, practice."

I looked down at Sasha's toy, the expensive one I bought online that Bad Habit was pissed about and it all made sense.

"And I hope you like the nursery. I helped pick out the furniture. He said blue was your favorite color."

I smiled to the point where my cheeks hurt.

Wow. He remembered that?

"So, have you decided on any names yet?"

Shit, names? They're leaving me responsible for names?

"Ummm...no, not yet. Still deciding."

What if I screw up and give a kid some name that'll become notorious, like Katrina, Monica, or God forbid Patty.

"Really?" She smirked. "So you have some names in mind?"

Wow, she can read my mind! Just like Bad Habit. Creepy.

I liked the names Chloe, Marc, or Jacob. McQueen may be a bit too obvious. But I didn't tell her that. Instead, I said, "Well, I would like to name them after family members...maybe."

"Oh well, that's wonderful. I'm sure he'll love it if you name one of them after his sisters or brother."

Sisters or brother? Umm...what are their names again?

Mrs. Earwood went on sharing her family history, Bad Habit being a focal point. Like any proud mother, in her eyes, he was perfect. She obviously didn't know him like I did and that truth was almost rewarding. I had a one up on Mommy Dearest.

He's a mama's boy. Go figure.

"Well, you definitely know your son," I said with a yawn, settling back. It was time for my afternoon nap.

Mrs. Earwood nodded without looking up.

"It looks like you still have a lot to learn, dear."

Whoa...

The female Bad Habit caught me off guard with her belittling sharp tongue. I sat back up and winced a smile.

No way I can fall asleep after that.

***

The dream was so vivid.

I was sitting on a coral reef like the Little Mermaid in the depths of the ocean, mesmerized by the magical sea life around me. Crabs walked by and waved, tropical fish danced, and whales hummed a melody. Even the sharks were in a cheerful mood, as if there was no problem with me being in their world. Everything was perfect, not a seaweed out of place. Then, just when I thought we were about to break into a Disney musical number, four little goldfish swam up to me, frantic. They swirled around and I tried to hold them, but they kept slipping out of my arms. I couldn't understand why they weren't as happy as the rest of us.

Suddenly, the sea turned crimson and ferocious, like a tornado. The water was ice cold but somehow I was sweating. My body ached like I had the flu.

We need to hide, to take cover!

I scrambled to reach for the goldfish. I was desperate to save them although I wasn't sure why. A violent cramp made me buckle over in debilitating pain. But I kept reaching for the fish while my lungs struggled. I was drowning. I was dying. But why?

The earth began to quake and the reef shook. The ferocious current ripped through seawater and swept the four goldfish away. I screamed as they disappeared into blackness and water rushed into my mouth. My eyes shot open and I took my first deep breath on land.

Panting hysterically, the familiar cream ceiling stared back at me and the back of Bad Habit's head faced me.

How did he sleep through all that?

Covered in sweat, it took a second to regain my bearings until the stomach cramps returned, but this time I wasn't under the sea. It could only mean one thing.

Damn, I'm getting my period.

I had my menstrual cycle a few times a year and the pain never made me miss it. My cramps could wake me from the dead. I rubbed my side.

Ok, I'll need some Midol, my heating pad, my fat jeans, oh I wonder if I have any tampons left...

I shook off the grogginess with a gasp.

No, I don't have any tampons because I shouldn't have any tampons...because I shouldn't be having cramps because I am pregnant!

Another cramp struck and I held my protruding stomach, trying to detach it from my body. This was far worse than regular cramps. It was like every organ was being twisted out of my belly button. Terrified, I exhaled short bouts of air, trying not to freak until I felt something wet between my legs.

Did I just pee on myself?

I sat up on my elbows, shaking Bad Habit vehemently. He stirred with an angry groan.

"Ughhhh...what?"

"Something's wrong. We need to go to the hospital."

He turned. "Are you serious?"

I nodded, scared into silence. He jumped up, running across the room and turned on the light as I kicked the sheets off me, reaching my hand out for him. He turned and froze, his mouth dropping wide in horror, staring at my stomach.

Or below it...

"What? What is it?"

I stretched to get a better look, finally seeing the blood drenched sheets between my legs.

And then I blacked out.

Eight Months

Dear Me,
    I haven't written to you in a while because I've been tied down to this bed for weeks and I am pretty positive I have bedsores. I also found out that I can't pee straight. The nurses don't seem too happy changing my sheets every time I miss the bedpan. In short, I've been diagnosed with something called placenta accreta. Google it, cause I have no idea what the hell is going on. Thus, I'm writing this from my deathbed.

    I've asked that bastard for days to bring you to the hospital. He keeps forgetting, so I'm pretty sure he's been nosing around this journal. If that's the case, let me make it clear. I hate Bad Habit (if you're reading this, yes I'm talking about you) and his super sperm for doing this to me as I now look like Jabba the Hutt.

    May the force be with you,
    Princess Alex

***

The bed rest order was now a permanent heart-wrenching sentence, which I didn't fight. The surgery was moved up, making the babies over ten weeks premature. What little I knew about children, I knew that much was bad.

"It's the only way to save them. They don't have enough room to grow," Dr. Turner tried to explain.

Being ever so eloquent, I objected to the idea and responded like a mature adult.

"This is stupid!"

After spending months letting my body deform so they could grow, I'd be damned if they come out with just a minuscule chance of survival or webbed feet!

I wasn't allowed to move so I kicked my legs every so often to make sure they were still there since I couldn't see past my enormous midsection. My warped appearance didn't help my feeble confidence. Neither did the sticky film of grime covering my body (that only I could see) since I wasn't allowed to bathe myself.

Bad Habit showed up to the hospital twice a day in no more than five-minute intervals. Once to drop off his mother and another to pick her up, never meeting my glare. He supplied me with countless magazines, books, and DVDs then would mumble something about work, before heading out the door again. As if he was doing me a favor, bringing me mindless junk. They were mere distractions to his absence.

Mrs. Earwood tried to make excuses for his behavior.

"It's been very hard for him, seeing you like this, dear. He hasn't been able to sleep in your room at all," she said. "Plus, he got a bad fear of hospitals. Ever since his Granddaddy died he avoids them like the plague. But, don't tell him I told you that."

Bullshit.

Unfortunately for them, 'Operation Distract Alex' was no longer working and I was headed into full-fledged cabin fever. It would have been more appropriate to lock me up in an asylum with padded walls than the cotton candy pink maternity ward.

I'm a fucked up science experiment, a government conspiracy. This was no miracle, no miraculous conception. They probably implanted these eggs in me. As soon as these babies hatch, I'll be obliterated. They'll say I died during childbirth, but really I'm just a casualty in the bigger picture.

I soon stopped eating the food Mrs. Earwood tried to insist upon me. *Probably poisoned.* There wasn't a phone in the room and Bad Habit kept forgetting my Crackberry charger, giving me more reasons to be suspicious.

"How are you feeling today?" Mrs. Earwood asked cautiously as she moved through the room, opening the blinds, setting her purse on her chair.

How the hell do you think I'm feeling!

"The same," I mumbled.

The Aliens were pretty quiet. Probably high off the amount of drugs they were pumping in me.

"Well, you're in the paper again today," she said cheerfully, waving a newspaper.

"Great," I snarled and read the headline: 'Woman on Birth Control Becomes Pregnant with Quadruplets!' It was better than the *US Weekly* headlines. Some called me a miracle, a message from God, the next Virgin Mary. Others called me an abomination, a fraud, a poster child for abstinence. Pro-lifers and pro-choicers were having a field day.

I'll be used in teen sex talks for generations. My grandchildren will learn about me in health class.

It was another article on my background. Since I was also an unmarried heathen, gossip spread like an STD. Bad Habit took the no comment route on the status of our relationship. No one believed I used birth control and the paparazzi were on the hunt to find the mystery doctor that gave me the in vitro treatment. Dr. Feel Good was one of the doctors under scrutiny. I saw his picture in the paper, he was still looking as fine as ever, even in bad press.

PEOPLE Magazine paid Derrick for an exclusive interview, in which Bad Habit came out looking like a hero, the saint who saved my poor, lost, irresponsible soul for the sake of his unborn children. Like always, when a girl has casual sex, she's the whore. When a guy has casual sex, he's just being a guy. Women sent flowers to my room addressed to him with their phone numbers.

Like he needs another invitation for pussy.

Besides Bad Habit's invitations for sexual favors, gifts also started to pour in from all over, proving that being a freak had it's advantages. We were offered a two-year supply of diapers, baby formula, and an endorsement deal from *PARENTING Magazine*. I received letters of encouragement from mothers of sextuplets, quintuplets, and octuplets. They were the only ones who really understood my frustration with being handcuffed to a hospital bed.

"Good morning, Missus...I mean Miss. Stone."

One of the infant residents walked in, greeting me with a nervous smile.

Probably heard of the tray I threw at the last resident who couldn't find one of the bright blue veins in my transparent arm. Dr. Turner knew better than to send some juvenile in with a needle.

"What's so freaking good about it," I grumbled.

"Morning!" Mrs. Earwood replied loud enough to distract the doctor from my sharp tongue.

"My name is Dr. Meyers. I...just want to check the baby's heart rate, if you don't mind."

I rolled my eyes and waved her on. She proceeded to hook up the monitors in silence. I waited for her to fumble so I had an excuse to throw another tantrum, until the twinkling of her four-carat diamond engagement ring blinded me. It was princess cut with a platinum band.

The same ring I wanted.

To be young with a brilliant career and a man who loves you, to have your whole life ahead of you with endless possibilities. A life I would kill for. Every dream I had melted into nonexistence, like ice cream left in the back of a hot car. Meanwhile, her regal titles would identify her accomplishments for eternity. She would always be known as Dr. Meyers or Mrs. so and so. My only title seemed trivial in comparison. The title of Mom, a title only few people would know yet never received proper recognition for. A title I wasn't eager for. I would never be Director of, President of, CEO of, or award winning Alexandria Stone. Just Mom. I swallowed the envy and held back tears as a short but striking cramp ripped through me.

"Owww."

Dr. Meyers froze, eye wide in terror.

"Did I hurt you?"

"No, no, it's just—owwww!"

The pain came in hot angry waves, catching everyone in the room off guard.

"What the hell was—owwwww!"

The monitors shrieked in a frenzy. I gulped the air and let out an uncontrollable ear-piercing scream.

"Oh my God!" Panicking, Dr. Meyers ran into the hallway. "Help! I need help in here, now!"

Two seconds later, the cavalry rushed in behind her.

"Wait, what is this? Contractions? Am I in labor? Owwwwww! Why is this hurting?"

They talked gibberish as they worked over me. My head was heavy and my own heartbeat was a conga in my ear. My arms and legs went numb as the room became dreamlike. The same way I felt when I passed out in front of Bad Habit. I'll never forget the look on his face.

Damn, well, see you in a few hours.

My eyes blurred right before the room faded to black.

***

A familiar scent tickled my nose like smelling salt.

Bad Habit.

My eyes fluttered opened and Mrs. Earwood's voice boomed over the beeping monitors.

"She's coming around! Alex? Alex, dear, can you hear me?"

The whole hospital can hear you.

I was lying flat, which was unusual since they tried to keep me in a slight upright position to help with my circulation. Without looking down, I grazed my nervous fingers against my stomach then sighed. I was still Jabba the Hutt.

Bad Habit was standing next to his mother, watching me, a huge question mark on his face. I glanced past them out the window into blackness.

How long have I've been out?

My hospital gown had been changed; there were new monitors and IV drips surrounding me, the needles pinched my skin. A nurse I hadn't noticed before was scribbling on a clipboard, checking my vitals. She had blue spiky hair, thick make-up, and crooked baby doll eyelashes.

You'd think this hospital was a hair show.

"What happened?" I asked her, voice raspy and weak.

She was young, couldn't have been more than twenty. She opened her mouth then hesitated and turned to Bad Habit instead.

"I'll...just go get the doctor."

She turned on her heels and Mrs. Earwood followed her into the hall. The ominous vibe was more pronounced by the silence. I tried not to jump to conclusions, but I couldn't shake my trembling nerves.

Something's wrong. Really wrong.

Bad Habit moved closer, choking the bed rail.

"What happened?" I repeated, a tad more forceful than before. He didn't respond. He stood motionless, hovering, staring down at me like a towering tyrant. I hated the powerless feeling. I needed to prepare myself, to take some type of control of the situation.

"Sit me up." It was all I could think of.

He went to the side of the bed and grabbed the remote to elevate it. I didn't take my eyes off of him, hoping at some point his face would provide answers.

Dr. Turner walked in, along with his team. The look of sheer disappointment over their faces was a billboard that they didn't have good news.

"Alex," Dr. Turner started. No one could meet my stare.

This is bad. Really bad.

"Alex, there seemed to have been some complications...and—"

"In English Doc," I said curtly. We were past the anticlimactic stage. It was time to pull the trigger. He sighed and met my glare.

"We believe one of the infant's heart has stopped beating. I'm very sorry."

***

I once read an article on a speech Obama gave, mentioning how at three months old his daughter had meningitis and could've died. It was the most terrifying moment of his life, he said. It didn't mention how Michelle felt, how she reacted. So how are you supposed to feel? How are you supposed to react to something like this?

After they broke the news, Mrs. Earwood began to cry while I sat there, frozen and emotionless. Dr. Turner planned to expedite the surgery, giving the remaining babies and myself the best possible chance of survival, but none of his words processed. I was too dumbfounded by my unacceptable response, trying to understand the reasoning behind my lack of tears and the loss of sensation in my entire body. Every part of my body felt numb.

Is this what shock feels like?

Dr. Turner went over the procedure and left the room, ordering the nurses to give us space. We stayed up the entire night in silence. Bad Habit sat in a chair next to me, in deep thought. I stared down at my portly stomach like it was made out of glass, grasping it with both hands, trying to turn my twenty-twenty vision into my own ultrasound. I wondered what the other babies were thinking or if

268 | Blu Daniels

they knew. I had never experienced real loss. I'd never even been to a funeral.

To be surrounded by death so early in life...

In my heart I knew it was Alien 3. It explained why things were so quiet. After all, he was the little troublemaker. I had pictured him being in the NFL, given the way he punted every organ he came in contact with. He would've bought me a new house, a new car, and new Louis Vuitton luggage set. But now, he was silent.

The sun began to beam through the blinds, the start of another day in hell. There was a commotion in the hallway as the staff rushed to prepare for surgery. I meticulously counted the pale blue dots on my hospital gown, unconscious of my surroundings. Like a defensive mechanism, I was trying to find some order or some way to micromanage the situation. It didn't feel right just sitting still. I needed to plan, schedule, and execute. I needed to be in 'Alex' mode.

Shouldn't someone be calling a funeral home or something? Do they even make caskets his size?

And then, numbness subsided, the sensation was like a delayed reaction to a gunshot wound. Sheer, unadulterated, incomprehensible agony. It wasn't just some alien that died in my stomach. It was a human. It was a baby. A real live baby. It was MY baby.

And it was my fault.

My mind raced back to images of myself, running around Atlantic Station, cooking on swollen feet, cleaning with toxic chemicals, hitting my stomach against the steering wheel in Bad Habit's car. The food I didn't eat, the vitamins I didn't take, the help I refused, the spotting. I didn't listen to a single ounce of Dr.

Turner's advice. I was so preoccupied with my own wants, I never thought of the danger I was putting the babies in. The daring risks I was taking with their lives. Horror melted into me as my eyes held tears like puddles on brown concrete.

Mrs. Earwood got up and walked to Bad Habit.

"I'm...I'm going to get a cup of coffee before they start. Do you want anything?"

Bad Habit slowly stretched up from his seat, shaking his head. Both unaware of my new emotional condition. She touched his shoulder and pulled him into a hug.

"It's gonna be ok, son. They're gonna be alright."

Wait a minute, why is she comforting HIM?

No one was here to comfort me. No friends, no family, not even a nurse. Just Bad Habit and his mother, comforting each other, like they were the ones in pain. A concept I couldn't fathom since neither one of them were strapped to my bed. Their embrace was insulting.

He's not the one carrying a dead baby, I am!

I was alone again, a reoccurring theme with Bad Habit, aching at the loss of my child. A feeling so indescribable I could barely breathe. My child, the innocent victim in our twisted game. No one wins, everyone loses, and my child lost the most by losing his life.

Bad Habit's eyes flickered in my direction as a storm brewed inside me. It wasn't just a storm. It was a tempest of memories and painful regrets. All the times I should have said no and meant it. All the promises he made. All the lies he told.

Wait, this isn't my fault at all.

I gasped and Mrs. Earwood jumped.

"Alex? Dear, are you ok? Do you need anything?"

Steam rose to my throat as the blood boiled in my stomach. Alien 3, my baby, my child, was dead. And Bad Habit was being comforted.

Bad Habit raised a knowing eyebrow, recognizing the fury that was brewing. He quickly turned his mother towards the door, towards safety.

"She's ok Ma. I'll stay with her," he insisted. "Go get yourself some coffee."

Mrs. Earwood hesitated but nodded in agreement. Tears clouded my vision as she continued towards the door, almost in slow motion.

She can't leave me alone. Not with him.

"No," I whispered and they both froze at the first words I had spoken in over twelve hours. Bad Habit stood anxious. His mere presence was repulsing.

"Get. Out."

Bemused, he shook his head as if to get the wax out his ears. "What?"

"Get. Out. Get out of here. Now," I said, pronouncing each syllable, like the girl from *The Exorcist*. Probably looked more like her too.

Mrs. Earwood sensed the tension and rushed to my side, attempting to defuse the situation.

"Dear, you don't mean that. You're just upset."

I didn't take my eyes off of him as every word that I had been holding back came out of me with conviction.

"This is your fault. All your fault. I hope you're happy."

"Happy?" he said incredulously stepping back from the bed like it was on fire.

"Yes, happy. He's dead. My child is dead. The child you didn't even want to begin with. And he knew that. Everyone knew that you didn't want them as much as you didn't want me. You NEVER wanted me. I was never good enough, no matter what I did."

"Alex, maybe you should lie back down dear," Mrs. Earwood tried again, pulling gently at my elbow.

"You should've been there. For me, for our children. Instead, you were fucking around with that bitch, going out every night, and working ALL THE TIME. And I was at home, alone ALL THE TIME!" The tears started to gush as my voice cracked. "This would have never happened if you actually tried to take care of me, of us. So I didn't kill him. You killed him!"

"Nobody killed anyone Alex! Now stop it, you need to calm down," Mrs. Earwood begged.

"I hate you. I've always hated you. You want to talk about mistakes? YOU were a mistake. And so long as I'm alive, you will never EVER touch MY babies. Get out."

"Alexandria I think you better—"

"Get out. Get out! Get out! This is all your fault you selfish, arrogant, miserable, son of a bitch! GET OUT!"

I pushed his mother off, grabbed the closest object to me, and threw it at him with my last bit of energy. The vase of purple and gold wild flowers shattered on the floor inches from his feet. He stood in silence, fists clenched as he pulled his gaze away to eye the shattered glass surrounding him. He swallowed and the entire bone structure of his face moved like earthworms under soft soil. He was itching to strike me.

The nurses rushed in, brushing past him. They held me down while I wailed and fought.

"Ohhhh Goddd...my baby. He killed my baby! My baby!"

The violent hoarse sobs ripped through me while another doctor rushed in the room with a sedative. Bad Habit flinched then stormed out. His mother chased after him. Right before the room turned black again.

***

Salt. That's what my lips tasted like. Sea salt from the endless ocean of tears. As my eyes opened, everything was as I left it before they were forced to knock me out. I was still stuck between the chalky pink walls and the irritating fragrance of rubbing alcohol.

It wasn't a dream. This really is happening.

I didn't bother to look around the room to see who was hovering by my bedside. I didn't care.

"Alex dear? How are you feeling?" Mrs. Earwood asked.

"Is he gone?"

She tensed up, like she was preparing to hold me down again.

"Yes."

I waited for the rush of relief to come with that piece of news but it didn't.

He's probably off wasting his money at one of those crusty strip clubs with girls that flip on the poles using only the cracks of their asses. I hope he catches gonorrhea and his dick falls off.

"Alex, honey, are you ok?"

I wasn't surprised to hear my mother's voice on the other side of my bed. She stroked my disheveled hair, but I didn't want her near me either. I didn't want to be a mother, a wife, or anything anymore. I was ready to end it all. Death, by a million paper cuts, if need be. There was nothing left to live for.

"Does it matter?"

"What do you mean?"

I rolled on to my back and caressed my stomach.

"Even if I was ok, even if I...we...make it through this, what happens then? I'm alone. I'm about to be a baby momma for a man who doesn't care about me. So what's the point?"

The future grandmothers glanced at each other, at a loss.

"I'm such an idiot. I should've never let it get this far. Abortion would have been better."

My mother gasped at the words I've never said aloud but had considered on numerous occasions.

"Alex, don't you ever say that! He's just as upset and—"

"Damn it Mom! You just believe anything he says! When are you going to see it? He doesn't care!" I screamed, grabbing the rail with a violent shake. She jumped back.

"I don't want him there with me. I don't want him in the operating room and I don't want him touching my babies."

"Alex, you don't mean that. He's going to be a father—"

"A father? You call him a father? If he was any type of father he would've been around! He wasn't. So don't you dare give him a title he doesn't deserve! You have no idea what I've been going through. What people have been saying about me! I'm NOT crazy! I didn't do this to myself!"

274 | Blu Daniels

Tears filled my eyes again. I wiped them off with the back of my hand.

My mother cast another worried glance at Mrs. Earwood.

"Has it...really been that bad?"

Mrs. Earwood, taken aback by the insults toward her precious son, clutched her pearls.

"Well...no one expected this. But it is what it is and he has dealt with it as best he could. He's been a determined wreck, really."

I groaned and slammed my head back on the pillow. Her blindness made me want to vomit.

"He just got the idea of what he had to do and stuck with it," she continued.

"What idea?" My mother asked.

"You know. About the money and being a full-time father and..."

We both stared blankly. Realization coated her face.

"Wait a minute. He didn't tell you, did he?"

"Tell me what?" It was more of a rhetorical question since I wasn't interested. In fact, I didn't even want her in the room since he was an extension of her.

She beamed, proud to share more of Bad Habit's hidden agenda.

"He's been pulling all these extra hours, extra deals, extra whatever so he can save money. From the day you told him you were pregnant till now he's been—"

"Oh I don't care about the money!" I screamed in frustration and this time they both jumped back from the bed. "I don't care if we were broke living in the box on a damn corner. At least I would've known he cared about me. Now, I'll be alone, taking care of four...I mean three...babies by myself!" I shuddered at the thought of Alien 3 still inside me.

"But see, that's what he didn't tell you. He saved up enough so he can be around after the babies are born, full-time. He's taking an entire year off. Already got the firm's approval and everything. He didn't want you to do this alone. That's why he's been working so hard, he wanted to make sure you guys had enough to get by."

My mouth dropped like it was expecting food.

An entire year off?

My mother held my hand with a grin, relieved. But I held my ground, refusing to fall for another trick.

"That...that doesn't make any...how can he be THAT much of an asshole and then out of nowhere...well, why didn't he just tell me?"

Mrs. Earwood shook her head with a knowing smile.

"I guess he was waiting for the right time."

Humph!

"Well, that still doesn't mean he cares about me."

"Dear, you should know by now, he's not one to talk about his feelings. He shows things in his own way."

A slight tingle of guilt rushed to my face and I stared at my stomach.

Me and my big overly dramatic mouth.

A nurse walked in with fresh hospital gowns and sensed the intensity of our conversation.

"Sorry to interrupt, but I have to prep her for surgery."

My motherly council stepped away from the bed to make room.

"Is anyone going into the operating room with you Ms. Stone?"

I gulped, torn by my stubbornness and pride. I said some awful things to him, things I didn't mean. But after everything I'd been through, it didn't seem fair that Bad Habit benefit from the fruits of my child labor. Yet, I didn't want to take the honor of seeing his children brought into the world away from him. The punishment seemed too severe; it would be something I could never take back.

But I didn't have a chance to decide. Bad Habit stormed into the room and marched to my bedside. He was pissed but contained, like he was focusing all his energy on not losing his temper. I flinched away as if he bucked at me.

"I'm going to be in that delivery room and I don't give a fuck what you think. You'll just have to deal with it," he said like he'd been practicing the statement for hours and then raised an eyebrow, daring me to say no.

My mother grumbled at his pompous declaration, but his smug aggressive swagger wasn't new to me. And to be honest, I didn't want to be alone. But instead of just lying down and taking it, I fought back. Because there was one thing I forgot in all this, something that had been missing for months. The most important lesson I learned from Michelle: self-respect.

And Michelle doesn't take shit from nobody!

"Don't talk to me like I'm the maid. I'm not your wife or your girlfriend, but I am the mother of your damn children! I don't just demand your respect, I've EARNED it. And if you can't manage that, then once I'm out of here, I will take MY children, move back to New York, get on welfare, and we'll be communicating through lawyers and supervised visits because I'd rather do all that than be with you any other way. You have no control of any of this but I will respect your position. So lose your fucking ego and act right! Do I make myself clear?"

His tense face loosened, almost shocked, but he took a deep breath and nodded.

"Ok."

The room was frozen around us, waiting for his next move.

With a long exhale, he nodded and turned to the puzzled nurse.

"What do I need to do?"

***

I watched enough medical dramas to know what the inside of an operating room looked like but it didn't relieve the stress of actually being on the table. The room was a cold refrigerator with a spotlight that shined over my stretched out belly. There were crowds of nameless masked faces surrounding me, busy preparing. Once Dr. Turner pulled them out, each baby would have a dedicated team of doctors and nurses running each kid through cleaning and checkout like a car wash. A large sheet draped beneath my neck like a tent, blocking my view of the operation gore. As promised, I couldn't feel anything past my chest.

This delivery is gonna be a piece of cake! I bet that skinny pregnant bitch from parenting class is screaming for an epidural now!

Bad Habit stood motionless in his smock. He slipped his hands into his pockets, rocking back on his heels, his eyes measuring every person and object in the room with intense scrutiny. I touched his arm and he turned to me.

"I know this isn't the best time to talk about this, but...if anything happens to me..."

His eyes darted away, lips making a tense line.

"If...anything...just make sure they know who I am. Make sure they're happy. Ok?"

He nodded, still avoiding eye contact.

"And, if I do make it out of here...I want to see him first. No one else. You got it?"

We locked eyes and for the briefest of moments, we were communicating on another level. We were finally on the same page, only two years too late. He nodded again in agreement.

"One more thing, if I shit on myself, that story lives and dies in this room."

"What?"

"Nothing. Now, hold my hand and tell me everything they're doing to me," I said with a grin. He didn't protest and took my hand willingly. We never held hands before. It was a closeness that was as comforting as the medicines they were drugging me with.

"Ok, we're ready," Dr. Turner said and began directing his staff.

"He's slicing you open," Bad Habit whispered. I exhaled, trying not to picture the scar that would remain.

I'll never wear a bikini again. Goodbye my lovely two piece copper Juicy swimsuit with matching sarong. We had a good run.

Bad Habit leaned over the tent to take a better look.

"Man, you're even nastier on the inside."

"You're only saying that because I'm incapacitated. Just wait till I jump off this table."

I couldn't quite see past his mask, but I was sure there was a genuine smile there.

"Ok guys, here we go," Dr. Turner yelled. "Baby number one, a healthy girl!"

The room cheered as he held her up over the tent. I only saw part of her shriveled little body before they rushed her over to a cleanup station.

We watched them come out, one by one, Bad Habit clutching my hand the entire time.

"Wow, look at them," he gasped.

Suddenly, the cheering settled to a low murmur.

They must be taking him out.

I snapped my eyes shut but not in time to miss his little blue hand.

"Wait...hold on." Dr. Turner's voice became serious. Jumbled voices surrounded me.

"Doctor, her pressure is..."

"Baby number four has a..."

"I...I think she is..." Dr. Turner screamed.

Then, there was a gush and a splatter, like a bucket of water was dumped on the floor. The room fell into a silent shock. The doctors stared at each other, eyes bulging which confirmed my greatest fear.

I crapped on myself.

"Oh my GOD!" I shrieked, willing my body to move. Dr. Turner snapped out of his trance and barked orders. The room flew into a frenzy.

"Oh shit!" Bad Habit said under his breath, the color draining out of his face. A nurse slid a stool under him.

"This is so embarrassing," I cried while a strange dizziness made the room spin. "You can't tell ANYONE!"

"What?"

"Ohhhh...you'll never look at me the same again!"

Bad Habit sucked his teeth.

"You didn't shit on yourself you idiot!" he snapped. "That was bl..."

"Damn it!" Dr. Turner snapped. "Bleeding in the...I need suction..."

Wait, what's going on?

"Dr. Turner, her pressure is—"

"Starting compressions! Call surgery! We're bringing him up!"

Him? Surgery? Which one needs surgery?

My pulse was in my ear. The room spun like the scrambler ride at Coney Island. Bad Habit turned to Dr. Turner, his face perplexed.

"Dr. Turner, why is she breathing like that?"

"Alex?" I heard Dr. Turner's voice through the crowd of blue scrubs. "Alex, you need to stay calm, ok?"

Why is the room getting dark? What is this, mood lighting?

"Get me surgery, NOW!"

"How is she doing?"

Bad Habit squeezed my hand but I couldn't squeeze back.

"Alex, are you ok?"

Hey, he called me Alex! Wait, I can't speak, what's going on?

"Alex?" Bad Habit demanded. "What's wrong with her?"

My eyes rolled back. The frantic voices in the room were distant, like echoes under water.

"She's in d-fib!"

"I need to stop the bleeding or we'll never..."

"Pressure is down..."

Uh oh. This can't be good.

"Ok people, she's crashing, let's move, move, MOVE! Alex, how you doing, talk to me! Alex—"

"Heart rate is..."

"Alex!" Bad Habit demanded.

And then there was silence.

***

I'm dead. Wow. I missed that white light I was supposed to walk towards didn't I? Damn it! Can I get anything right?

No harps, no clouds, no wings, and no endless buffet of ice cream. Death wasn't as relaxing as I thought it was going to be. I expected spa like conditions. Instead, it was black and freezing cold. I figured I'd be telling this story from the grave. Seemed fitting.

Death was what I asked for yet it didn't feel rewarding. I felt cheated. Life didn't flash before my eyes and the sense of restlessness wouldn't leave me.

It'll be fine. I'll just haunt Bad Habit forever. The ultimate revenge!

Out of deathly boredom, I tried creating my own montage. Bad Habit's smile was my first thought, breakfast with my parents was my second, Spring Break with my girls was my third. But then, out of nowhere, there was a flash of a small hand. It was just a hand, but it resonated with me more than any other memory. A baby's hand...

Wait a minute, that's MY baby's hand!

I realized I could feel my heart beating, heavy like it weighed five thousand tons.

I'm not supposed to be dead! Wake up stupid! Wake up!

I strained, ordering every part of my body to move. Toes first, then fingers. The larger limbs would have to wait. My ears felt like they were stuffed with cotton, but I could hear the muffled sound of my name. With one last grueling push, I gasped out loud. The air burned my dry throat.

"Alex?"

Was that Bad Habit?

Willing myself to move was more challenging than fighting death. I opened my heavy lids and focused on the blur in front of me. After a few blinks, his handsome face came into focus. He was almost unrecognizable. He looked...old, like he had aged several years over night. Judging from the scruffiness of his usual baby soft face, a couple of days had passed. The lone fluorescent light over my head accentuated the changes.

"Alex?"

Looking for my tongue, I gurgled out a strange sound. He smiled, relieved, and leaned in closer to brush a strand of hair behind my ear.

"Hey," he whispered. His mischievous grin reminded me of the first time we kissed, how adoringly he stared at me. How I couldn't imagine being more beautiful in someone else's eyes. My body defrosted and I squeezed my legs together to combat the throbbing.

Of course that would be the first feeling I would regain.

"You called me Alex," I croaked out, becoming fully aware of the amount of pain I was in. Every breath aggravated parts of my body I didn't know existed.

He chuckled and placed a finger over my lips.

"Don't try to talk."

Besides the bedside light, the room was a black backdrop. Date and time uncertain. The smell of lilacs and lilies tickled my nose. We were surrounded by lush flowers and bright 'It's a Boy/It's a Girl' balloons.

I'd love a mirror right now. Well...on second thought, maybe not.

I tapped my fingers against my hollow stomach. An empty spaceship, no more Aliens.

But where are they?

Pain was replaced by anxiety. Not having them inside me yet not knowing where they were ensured terror. I had a vague memory of what had happened, but since the last eight months felt like a dream, reality was not certain.

The most perplexing issue was not knowing just how many children I actually had.

Was it three or four?

"You're...ok. You're back in your room." Bad Habit seemed calm, which was slightly reassuring. "You suffered a hemorrhage and they had to operate. They had to...well...you suffered a lot of damage...down there. So they had to...well, you've been out for a couple of days."

Bad Habit was never one to be at a loss for words and his eyes never held so much pity. I lifted my limp arm and placed it over his trembling hand.

The loss of blood, the mini coma, the pain...

This was no simple surgery. A simple surgery wouldn't make me feel so...empty. I smiled and nodded, giving him a chance to change the subject. I didn't want to mourn for the loss of my uterus, that wasn't as important as my baby.

"Where is he?"

Bad Habit smiled. "I'll have them bring him in."

He spun around and jogged out the room. I closed my eyes and tried not to imagine myself holding a stillborn. Promising myself I would only remember him when he was alive and kicking in my stomach. I turned and noticed an unopened card on the nightstand next to a Gucci bag with a large purple bow wrapped around it. The exact one I wanted. I reached for the card and tore it open.

***

Dearest Alex,

I hope this letter finds you well. My apologies for the belated baby shower gift. Seems that many women had a busy winter this year and found themselves in a similar predicament to yours. Of course, not to your extremes. I've been following your story on the news and I must agree, you are a national headline.

Though I may not have been there to witness your day to day struggles, through it all I believe you handled your situation with sacrifice, grace, humility, and humor. Don't ever forget that those are all the outstanding qualities of a good Mother. The ones I saw in you from day one. You are a risk, but you deserve the highest of rewards. And when you look into the eyes of your children, you will receive it. Let me know if you need anything, I'm just a phone call away.

Best,

Ellen

***

There was nothing to do but smile.

The door opened and I held my breath. Bad Habit came rushing in followed by the blue haired nurse pushing an incubator that was hooked up to several monitors. I met her grinning sticky glossed lips with a frown.

Since when do they hold stillborn babies in incubators?

Bad Habit stood behind the incubator as the nurse pushed it closer to my bed. I stared inside the plastic box and tried to make sense of what I was seeing through a wall of tears. Inside the case, I watched a tiny baby's chest inhale and exhale short bouts of air. A long tube was attached to the perfect petite nose on his cute wrinkled face.

"Oh my God!"

"Say hello to your son," the nurse beamed as an unexpected sob burst from my lips. Bad Habit sat on the edge of the bed, peering inside the incubator.

"I named him Alexander, or Alex for short. I figured you wouldn't mind."

He stuck his hand in one of the openings, careful not to touch the wires, gently gliding his fingers on Alex's tiny leg. After studying his movements, I followed, reaching my hand in with his, noticing the bandages and stitches on his little chest.

"I...I...just don't believe it." I brushed his arm. Alex flinched and I giggled at his little movements. It was like playing with a new toy on Christmas morning, something you'd never thought you'd get. I felt like Tiny Tim.

God bless us. All of us!

"I told him I promised that he would be the first person you saw."

It was almost confusing to be so happy to see someone I never met before. Little Alex was like a defibrillator to my heart. Every ounce of pain was replaced with sweet joy. I glanced at Bad Habit. He was so proud he was glowing, almost sparkling.

"Thank you."

He tipped his head as if to say 'all in a days work' but looked like he hadn't slept in days. Yawning, he turned to the nurse behind us.

"Do you think there's enough room on here for the both of us?"

She nodded and stepped out of the way. Bad Habit carefully slid himself onto the bed next to me. It couldn't have been very comfortable, with the limited space, but he didn't seem to care. He eased his head next to mine and wrapped his arm around me, a move that would normally get my immediate attention, but my eyes never left Alex. His supple skin was like warm Play-Doh. He looked so fragile, I was almost afraid to touch him.

"Hi Alex," I whispered. "I've waited a long time to meet you. Such a troublemaker, I knew you were a boy."

Alex continued to sleep, his tiny fist clinched.

"You were the ringleader, always kicking and punching. Can't say that I blame you. I wasn't doing everything I was supposed to."

Bad Habit chuckled over my shoulder and softly rubbed my arm.

"I named him after you because he came back to life after everyone thought he was gone."

His breath tickled the back of my neck and I turned to face him, our noses centimeters apart. We hadn't slept in the same bed in weeks. The nerves in my body began to tingle, sparking back to life, the high was what I needed. Unaware of my withdrawal, I realized could never quit my bad habit cold turkey.

He sighed, trying to shake a thought away. "You scared me, you know that?"

Apparently, the thought of losing me to death resonated with him more than anything else we had lived through.

I let a small smile leak. "Sorry."

"Don't let it happen again," he warned wryly.

"I'll see what I can do."

Eight Weeks Later

Dear Me,

I know this is TMI, but I'm writing this to you from the toilet while taking a dump! One of the many I have taken without the assistance of laxatives or prune juice. I haven't had gas in weeks and I'm at least 10,000 pounds lighter. But in exchange for these small freedoms I've become the prize-winning cow on this farm. I churn out milk for these leeches every twenty to thirty minutes. One of my boobs is actually bigger than the other. I keep it hidden behind these beige orthopedic bras that I thought I wouldn't have to wear until I was way in my sixties, shopping for neon windbreaker suits at JC Penney.

After we were discharged some random women offered to donate some of their breast milk to our cause. I, respectfully, declined. Seemed too much like sharing a toothbrush.

Did I mention there are four of them? All four, accounted for. Aliens 1, 2, and 4 came out like clockwork. Alien 3's heart was so weak that they actually performed open- heart surgery while I lay dying on the table. Oh yeah, guess I also didn't mention I almost bled to death.

Funny thing is I still don't feel like a mom. What I feel is nothing more than exhaustion. I've been waiting for that burst of motherly joy, like an epiphany, but all I feel when I look into their cribs is dread. They are a loud, needy, greedy bunch. So I've taken more of a business approach to dealing with them. My project management skills have kicked into full combat mode. I setup my schedule board in the kitchen, color-coded by kid, and assigned individuals to their respective duties: Director of Diaper Enforcement, Chief of Gastrointestinal Eruption, Head of Bottle Reinforcement, and so on.

I, Chef Left Breast, am allowed two-hour increments of sleep during each feeding cycle since there's no given time when all the leeches are sleeping in unison. Bad Habit follows my schedule precisely and doesn't dare complain. He's been quiet, actually. Guess he's realized we're not playing with dolls anymore. Well, got to run, think I've sprung a leak.

Over and Out,

General Alex a.k.a. Maggie Moo

***

Lil' Alex was tucked in one arm sleeping while I folded laundry with the other. My arm was like his permanent cradle so Bad Habit gave him the nickname Little Football. After almost losing him, I was afraid to ever let him go.

Mrs. Earwood and my mother stayed with us for the first few weeks and we sure as hell needed the help. It was a fulltime, demanding job. Harder than any job I've ever had. Although they were a tiny, fragile, wrinkled bunch of little mole rats, their lungs were fully developed and they proved it every chance they could. They were screaming banshees and had the uncanny ability to reach octaves I thought no human could possess. We were finally falling into a comfortable routine, and the Golden Girls were packing to head back home.

Bad Habit emerged from his office after hanging up from a call.

"Who was that?" Mrs. Earwood said. She was sitting on the daybed in the nursery, burping Alien 2. I almost dropped Alex. I never had the audacity to ask Bad Habit who he was on the phone with.

"That was my boss. He invited us to the company Christmas party down at the Twelve Hotel, offered us a room. I told him I appreciated the gesture but couldn't possibly accept. He understood."

"But why not?"

"Yeah, why not?" My mother chimed in from the rocking chair while feeding Alien 1. "You two could go. The kids are sleeping longer now. It'll give you a chance to get away and have a night to yourselves before we leave next week."

Bad Habit shook his head, unconvinced.

"Thanks but there's absolutely no way you two can handle this on your own."

My mother scoffed as Mrs. Earwood let out a chuckle.

"Boy, I have raised seven children besides you. I think I can handle it."

"And if it gets too much, which I doubt it will," my mother added. "We'll just call for backup."

Bad Habit glanced in my direction and I pretended not to be enthralled in their conversation, not daring to contribute to the instigation. That would only make him say no that much faster. He sighed in defeat and held his arms out towards me.

"What?"

"Pass me the ball. I know you take longer to get ready."

Beaming, I damn near threw Alex across the room and ran into the bathroom.

Finally, a real night out!

Fearing he'd change his mind and I would miss my one opportunity to escape baby central, the chance for a night without being a pregnant freak show, I moved like a cartoon character. I beat my hair into submission, shaved, plucked, and buffed in ten minutes flat.

I hadn't worn make-up in so long that my mascara had dried out and my lip-gloss evaporated to dust. I mixed in some water, plastered my face, and tinted my pallid cheeks. My room had turned into the hectic backstage scene of a fashion show. I raced around, tripping over dirty baby clothes, spit up napkins, and Sasha, cursing at the fact that every pair of panty hose I owned had a run in them. I pumped my last bit of milk and stuffed myself into a full body corset. The purple satin couture dress was two sizes too big when I first found it at a Vivienne Westwood sample sale, but I was determined to have it in my collection. Now, I was ecstatic I never got the chance to have it tailored. It concealed my ugly post baby bulge perfectly. I threw some clothes into an overnight bag, squeezed into a beautiful pair of gold Jimmy Choos, and stumbled down the stairs.

"I'm ready! I'm ready!"

Bad Habit stood by the door, smirking, and I knew he heard my frantic production. I attempted to play it cool as he gave me a once over. His cranberry button down shirt and charcoal pants complemented his milk chocolate complexion. He opened the door and ushered me out with an approving nod, never knowing the tingling sensation I get when he's chivalrous.

***

"Why look at the happy couple!" Mr. Paul greeted us at the elaborate entrance of the hotel lobby. "You two look so refreshed. Why, you don't look like you had a baby at all young lady."

I love this old man!

"It's called bounce back," Bad Habit said, wrapping his arm around my waist, smiling proudly.

Puzzled, Mr. Paul nodded in agreement.

"Oh, right. Well, go on in, have a wonderful time."

The ballroom was sparkling with Christmas decorations, dazzling plum and ruby red lights, infused with the sweet smell of cinnamon and pinecones. Large round dining tables draped in crisp snow-white tablecloths with mini Christmas tree centerpieces surrounded the parquet dance floor. We took our seats and mingled with other couples while being served roast lamb, baby potatoes, and sautéed spinach, our glasses topped with champagne. There was an open bar next to the DJ who was spinning music that anyone, even people without rhythm, could dance to. I noticed Victoria and her new lace front wig eyeing us from across the room and smiled.

And take that Amazon Bitch!

The night was glorious. It was wonderful to be out in plain sight, not hidden in the house like the Hunch Back of Notre Dame, and among adults who weren't my elders or medical caregivers. Most importantly, people were so drunk that no one thought to ask about my mini tribe at home or my bizarre pregnancy. For one night, I could forget all that had happened and just be Alex. Best of all, Bad Habit never left my side. He was the life of the party. Joking, laughing, and schmoozing with his fellow colleagues. They all loved him, basking in his witty personality, a side of him I don't see often.

The DJ put on a slow song and couples began to drift towards the dance floor. I turned to pour myself another glass of champagne and Bad Habit grabbed my hand.

"Come on," he said, standing up. I locked myself to the chair, waiting for the punch line to his joke.

"Are you serious?"

He smiled and led the way to the glitzy dance floor. The balls of my feet were screaming but I couldn't...no, wouldn't, refuse his offer to dance. He stopped in the middle of the floor and pulled me close, holding the small of my back. Gushing, I almost self-imploded.

"Wow. This is...different," I said as we twirled around.

"Hmmm...how so?"

"Well, we've never really danced before."

"What are you talking about? We've been to the club."

"Drunk twerking and grinding doesn't count."

"I guess you're right. That's a first," he said, smiling wryly as he moved my arms around to his neck, our noses almost touching. He whispered in my ear.

"So...Alex...tell me something I don't know about you."

I shivered at his orgasmic voice.

"Well, what do you want to know?"

He shrugged. "I don't know. Anything."

"Well that's a hard question. Sometimes, I feel like you don't really know me at all, so I don't know where to begin."

He sighed and I held my breath.

Did I just ruin our moment? Me and my big mouth!

"I guess I feel the same way."

We swayed in silence before he changed topics.

"When you first saw me, what did you think?"

I was stunned by the question at first, but I quickly came up with a suitable answer.

"I thought you were, sort of full of yourself. I never expected you to be...well...kind of cool, I guess."

He smiled. "I get that a lot."

"Can I ask you a question?"

He stared at me in silence, waiting.

"Did you ever see yourself...with me...honestly?"

He rolled his eyes. "Does it matter?"

"That wasn't an answer."

"Well, I didn't see all this. How could I? I'm not a psychic you know."

"I don't mean now. I mean before the babies. Before I even got pregnant."

He breathed in and avoided my eyes.

"No. I didn't."

"Oh," I said, trying to play it cool. When it comes to Bad Habit, you really shouldn't ask questions you don't really want to know the answer to.

"What I mean is, at the time, I had a girlfriend..."

I groaned in disgust at the mention of "She Who Shall Not Be Named."

"I know that, you don't have to remind me. We both knew what we were doing. Don't try to act innocent now."

"But when I broke up with Rachel, you immediately wanted to be the substitute. There was no clear interpretation of what we were from the beginning and you wanted to take our situation into a whole different dynamic. I wasn't ready for another relationship. I wanted to get to know you but you wanted to spend every free moment together. And it wasn't like I had an exorbitant amount of time to give. I was working full time, going to school–"

"Ugh, you don't have to list off your credentials again. I know but–"

"The point is if I wanted to spend time with my friends, or just relax by myself, you would have this attitude of record proportions. I never expected you to have such a temper and I was stressed out enough. We weren't in a relationship. I didn't have to accept your nagging. So I shut down, threw up this huge shield, and didn't let you get too close."

I dropped my eyes, realizing he had a point. But he also had a knack for Jedi mind tricks. This unique way of reversing blame and making you question your sanity.

"You say you weren't ready for a relationship," I said with a measured voice, reminding myself not to lose my temper in front of his coworkers. "But you seemed pretty damn ready to have me regardless. If I tried to spend time with you, it was because we spent so little time together. You were always using your busy life as an excuse, but you had time for what you wanted to have time for. And somehow, you always had time to have sex, but never had time for a date. Do you realize that tonight, right now, is the first time we've ever been on a date? A real date!"

He scoffed as I continued.

"I felt like a ho the entire time I was with you. What kind of girl knowingly sleeps with someone else's boyfriend? You don't know how hard that was for me. To push aside my morals, all for the chance to be with you."

"Well, I can't help the way you feel."

"For starters, you could've at least tried to make me feel like I was some type of priority in your life or at least a friend. Even now, I know nothing about you. Your damn coworkers get more of your real personality than I do."

"And how can you say with unwavering certainty I'm not being the real me around you? Do you honestly know the real me? Have you taken a moment to think about that? Seems like the 'me' you know is the 'me' you made up in your own head."

Damn, another point! This is not how I wanted this convo to go.

"I never thought you were my ho and I never intentionally tried to treat you as such. I said I wasn't ready for a relationship, not that I never would be. But you wanted me groveling at your feet like you're a damn princess, and that's not me. Granted, I'm not the most expressive dude in the world, but you were unable to practice one shred of patience. So I shut down. Didn't want to be bothered."

I locked eyes with him. The song changed but we continued dancing.

"Well, if you didn't want to be bothered, then why did you still want to have sex?"

"Seriously, do you have to ask? Or do you really have no idea how addicting your pussy is?"

His hand gripped my waist tighter as he stared at my bottom lip.

Whoa!

"Well...if my patience was the problem then I only acted that way because you shut down. It was like you didn't care if I was there or not. You have no idea how much that hurt me. I never felt so...unwanted. And confused. So you didn't want to sweat me, fine. But did you have to treat like a smut?"

"How so? Did I throw money on the bed after we were done?"

"No but you didn't TRY either. This relationship has always been an eighty twenty ratio. You let me go above and beyond for you. You were always late, you constantly stood me up, and you never..."

My rant was cut short by his angry groan.

"What good is this conversation if it's happened in the past? It is what it is and I can't go back and change it."

I chuckled, hearing him say his mother's favorite phrase.

"Ah, there you go. When you know you're wrong you change the subject."

"No, this is just not a conversation worth having at this juncture."

"Then I guess we'll agree to disagree. It doesn't matter anyway, it's not like you actually cared about me then."

He rolled his eyes.

"Right, I just move in and shack up with any old girl."

I sighed and gazed around the near empty dance floor. The song had changed again but Bad Habit hadn't loosened his hold on me, even in the midst of our argument, though I was ready to throw him out the nearest window. I glanced around at the other couples, wondering if anyone was having a conversation such as ours.

"So what happens now?"

The root of our problem, our unsaid grudge against each other, was our inability to agree on what had happened in the past. All I wanted him to do was admit he hurt me. Admit that he was wrong for the way he treated me. But what difference would that confirmation, that admittance, really make? It would never change the past or the future. Our pig-headedness, finger pointing, and pride stunted our potential growth.

"What do you want to happen?"

"I don't know, really," I sighed, as we stared at everything but each other. "Can I ask another question?"

He groaned. "Go ahead."

"When you first saw me, what did you think?"

He focused on my face and stroked my back with a smile.

"I thought...wow, she's something. I've seen a lot of girls, but you...I couldn't keep my eyes off you. I wanted you from day one."

I laughed knowing he wasn't one for a lot of mushy talk.

"And when they were...reviving you...all I kept thinking was...what other goofy dork is going to make me smile every day like you do?"

I playfully punched him in the arm and he smirked, pretending I injured him. We stared at each other, both satisfied the tension had faded.

"Still, I could have treated you better though. I should have."

I gave him an 'it's ok' smile. "Maybe we should start over. You know, by being friends."

"I think it's a little late for that, don't you?"

"Why?"

"Well, it's kind of crazy saying 'Sooo, friend, how does it feel being the mother of my children?'"

My head snapped back. It wasn't until he proposed it that I remembered I had a rack of kids at home waiting for my boobs.

"Oh, right. Well...I don't know. It really doesn't feel any different. I feel lighter, ten times more exhausted. But I guess I was waiting for this magical moment when it would hit me, you know, like the 'ah ha' moment. It just hasn't yet. And I'm kind of worried it never will."

Bad Habit gave me a sympathetic nod. The four kids at home just didn't resonate with me. It didn't feel like they were mine. I just felt like I was the nanny who breastfed.

"So, how does it feel being a dad?"

"Man, its incredible! When they look at me...I can't describe it. They're absolutely perfect. I never imagined how amazing they would be."

He sighed with a huge smile and I envied his admiration, feeling the bliss radiate off his body.

"We need to get along more. For the babies' sake and plus...I don't want to hate you anymore."

He nodded. "Ditto."

The slow song ended. The DJ threw on the Village People. Bad Habit and I stared at each other.

"So what do you want to do now?" I asked. He wasn't the type to break out into the Y-M-C-A with the rest of them.

"I was thinking we could put this room key to good use." He grinned, flashing a hotel key card. I gulped and my body went rigid. We hadn't had sex in months. Virgins were braver than I was at that moment.

"I...I don't think I'm ready."

"It's been more than six weeks, you'll be fine."

Of course the bastard knows nothing about pregnancy but knows when a girl is able to have sex again.

"I...thought we were going to start off as friends," I said, backing away from him. He caught my hand.

"And I told you we were more than that."

"Ok. So what are we?"

"We're parents who have the night off." He laughed, intertwining our fingers.

"Real cute," I said with an unwilling smile. "And what will we be tomorrow?"

He shrugged as he pulled me off the dance floor towards the door.

"We shall see."

***

We rode the elevator up to the tenth floor in silence. I followed him to our room, my every step dragging. Goosebumps riddled my skin. He opened the door to a plush suite with warm decorative lighting and hung the 'do not disturb' sign on the knob before locking us in. A lush fruit basket and a bottle of wine sat on the table. I walked into the enormous bedroom and plopped down on the king size mattress like a robot, kicking off my heels. My knees were shaking; I clasped my sweaty hands over them.

Why am I so nervous? It's just Bad Habit.

He shuffled around in the other room, opening the mini bar, pouring something into a glass. Every sound seemed to be followed by an eerie pause. I tried to remember how it felt making love to him without the enormous roadblock in the shape of my belly between us. But it was a distant memory and it scared me shitless. Everything was different now. We were no longer just Alex and Bad Habit.

In fact, he wasn't a bad habit at all. He was as simple and necessary as breathing.

He walked in and his eyes widened for a fraction of a second before he passed me a glass. I clasped both hands around it and shot it back. The vodka burned down my throat, but I needed it to soothe my trembling nerves. I fell back on the billowy comforter, hoping it would help the blood rushing feeling in my head. He joined me on the bed and turned off the bedroom light. The room was pitch black besides the orange glow of the city, twinkling through the sheer curtains.

I reached for his hand just as he reached for mine. We sat in silence, just listening to each other's breathing. Then suddenly with one quick move, he rolled on top of me. I gasped, teeth still chattering. He stared at me, caressing my cheek with the back of his hand. There was something different about him. His eyes weren't as harsh, cold, or lustful. They were more smothering and adoring. I gulped.

"Relax, Alex," he chuckled, pushing away my frozen hands that were locked on my chest.

"I...ummm...think"

He ignored my stammering and kissed me, his thick lips moist and warm. The shock was an immediate relief to my nerves. We were lost in each other, struggling with each other's clothes, not bothering with foreplay. Buck-naked with my legs spread apart, I took a deep breath to ready myself. My joints tense and stiff, like I woke up from a long nap. He continued to kiss me, taking his time to touch every part of my body, like a blind man reacquainting himself with his surroundings. But the more he kissed, the more it felt like stalling. I pulled away from his last kiss and stared at him, his eyes a bit wider than usual.

Wow, he's nervous too.

I smiled at that realization and took matters into my own hands, literally. With a newfound courage, I eased him inside of me. He moaned, staring into my eyes, hoping for reassurance.

"Let's just take this slow, ok?"

He nodded in agreement and slid in further, holding back with much effort. But it wasn't long before he found himself and his cockiness returned. He wound his waist, digging deeper into me then pulled out a little before diving back in, groaning. He thrust until I thought the bed would break beneath us. I screamed his name, digging my nails into his flesh hoping I'd break the skin.

I wasn't a virgin again but I was definitely out of practice. He was wordless, unusual for our romps. My hair matted to my sweaty face. I tried to ease away from him, feeling he was too much for my new body to handle. He wrapped his arm around my waist and pulled me on top of his lap.

"Where are you going? Don't run from me."

I gasped, my moans quickening and he pulled at my hair, kissing my neck. I was tightening, twitching, ready to cum and buried my head into his shoulder. He grabbed my face, raising it to his.

"Look at me," he said, his face dripping with sweat. "I want to see you."

And there, in that moment, is when I fell in love with my baby's daddy. If it was ever a question before, it had been answered. He wasn't perfect, he was no Prince Charming, and he wasn't always good for me either. But he was the one, plain and simple. We stared, burning each other with our eyes, and I released so hard it felt like seizure. He came not far behind. We collapsed on the bed, catching our breath as the aftershocks rippled through us. My muscles were pudding contained by hot skin.

"Did it hurt?" he asked a few minutes later from the other side of the bed.

"No," I answered, happily. I felt amazing, almost as good as the first time.

He chuckled. "Wanna do it again?"

"Absolutely."

***

Dear Me,

Now, without further ado, may I present the starting line up!

Alien 1: Bethany a.k.a. Beth a.k.a Daddy's Girl

Alien 2: Aiden a.k.a. A.I a.k.a. Little Cockblocker.

Alien 3: Alexander a.k.a. Alex a.k.a. Little Football

Alien 4: Brandi a.k.a. B a.k.a. Head Bitch in Charge

Love,

Mom-In-Chief (JUST like Michelle!)

***

"We're out."

"Of what?"

"Everything."

Bad Habit stood staring into the fridge, combing past bottles and empty orange juice containers. Since the Golden Girls left, Bad Habit and I had been in full swing baby mode. But who knew the loss of four hands would be so detrimental to the team. The house looked like it had been turned upside down and shaken and it had only been four days.

"Fuck!"

"Now what?"

"We're out of Alex's medication too."

He held out the empty bottle and I froze. Alex's heart condition required a twice a day supplement in his formula as well as extra feedings to keep him at a healthy weight. I clutched him tightly, curled in my arm.

"I thought you called in the prescription!"

"I did," he said, sighing in defeat. "Four days ago. I never got a chance to pick it up."

Brandi and Aiden were asleep upstairs in the nursery under close baby monitor surveillance. Bethany was curled up in Bad Habit's arms while we stood in the kitchen, dumbstruck. I paced around, trying not to panic.

"Well, maybe we should call your cousin or—"

He gave me a cynical look and I stopped short.

Definitely a bad idea. He'll sell the meds on the block.

Bad Habit rocked Beth before giving himself a resolving nod. I could almost see the light bulb click above his head.

Uh oh.

"Oh no! Tell me you're not seriously thinking what I think you're thinking."

He kissed the top of Bethany's head before placing her in a basinet on the table.

"I'll be gone for an hour tops. I'll pick up some groceries and Alex's medication."

"Whoa! You can't leave me here by myself!"

He grabbed the keys off the counter and headed towards the door. Horrified, I followed with Sasha at my feet.

"The kids will be asleep for at least another forty minutes. I'll be in and out by then."

"This is insane! You can't leave me!"

"Calm down or you'll wake them," he warned in a hushed voice.

"But I can't handle this by myself!"

"You got any better ideas?"

I tried to think, but my mind wouldn't cooperate. I was too distracted by the possibility of him leaving. He swung the door open, letting in the crisp New Year's Eve air. The afternoon sun burst into the room. I covered Alex with his blanket.

"I promise. I'll be right back." He slipped into his jacket and I shuddered at the familiar phrase.

I'll be right back'? Oh God, he'll be gone for hours!

"You always say that and it's always a lie!" I blurted out in desperation, my voice cracking.

Bad Habit doubled back and held my face between his hands.

"Alexandria, you can handle this. If I didn't believe this I would never be able to leave," he said, like a teacher speaking to a student. With a momentary pause, he kissed Alex and raced out the door. "Besides, Sasha will help you."

"Yeah, if she doesn't eat them first!"

After watching him back out of the driveway, I closed the door and leaned against it, staring into the looming house.

"Ok. It's ok. Just relax. Breathe." I wheezed up air. "He'll be back."

Sasha stood in the hallway, giving me her famous blank stare, her tail wagging until her whole body turned towards a noise coming from the kitchen.

The kitchen! Oh no, Bethany.

I sprinted with Alex, Sasha happily following, assuming we're playing a game. Rushing to the table, I was momentarily confused to find Bethany still sleeping in her basinet. But the baby monitor crackled from the battlefield. I double-checked the schedule board. It was time for Aiden's feeding. If I didn't pump him with milk soon his wails would call for reinforcements. Carefully, I place Alex in the basinet with Bethany, preparing to heat a readymade bottle. I opened the microwave and set it for thirty seconds. Alex and Beth started to stretch and stir. They both were about to wake up. I rocked the basinet, hoping to delay the inevitable. Aiden's cries still crackled through the monitor, growing louder.

Damn, this is the longest thirty seconds in history.

I glanced at the microwave and gasped. I had set the timer for thirty minutes not thirty seconds. The milk was a steaming foam latte.

"Shit!"

I ran to back to the microwave and I grabbed the bottle. It slipped, scalding my hand and dropped into an empty steel pot on the stovetop. Then, almost in slow motion, the pot tipped over, crashing onto the marble floor with an ear-piercing echo.

Oh. Shit.

Five seconds later, the screams began. Wailing from upstairs and down, laced with fear at the unknown terrifying noise that woke them from their slumber. Sasha, confused and baleful, started to bark. Overwhelmed, my eyes began to water and I crouched into a ball on the floor, wheezing, holding my knees to my chest. The moment of doom was upon me. The walls of the kitchen were caving in. What little sense I had left tried to talk myself out of a breakdown.

Calm down Alex. Relax. It's ok.

I didn't want to be unfit mother. After all, I hatched out four kids, under insurmountable odds and lived through it. How could I not believe in myself? Bad Habit believed in me. In the end, it boiled down to one thing.

What would Michelle do? No, what would Alex do?

I jumped up, wiping my tears and prepared for battle. A plan resolved in my mind as I went into work crisis mode. I grabbed Sasha by the collar and dragged her out to the backyard. I put four bottles into the microwave and set it for exactly thirty seconds. Scooping up the basinet, I whisked Alex and Bethany up the stairs into the nursery. The four infants cried like an out of tune choir. I was nervous, yet worked like a calm machine.

I checked their diapers before putting them in their cribs, propping each baby up on pillows then ran back to the kitchen to retrieve bottles, testing them to make sure they weren't scalding. When I returned to the nursery, I adjusted a bottle for each baby but they continued to scream.

Jeez, you'd swear I was feeding them cod liver oil and chitlins.

Racking my brain, I tried to find an alternative solution.

What am I missing? What didn't I do? Police will be here any moment to take me away!

And then I had a genius idea.

A chapter in one of the baby books I had read months earlier popped into my head. They needed something familiar to calm them. Something they experienced while still inside me.

I raced into my bedroom and turned on the television, maxing the volume so it could be heard through the walls. An episode of *Law and Order* was on, something I watched ad nauseam while I was pregnant. I raced back to the nursery, and gently picked up each screaming infant. I never held all four of them at once before. Securing them in my arms, I carried them over to the daybed like a waitress with an armful of orders.

Don't drop them. Don't drop them. Don't drop them...

Their bodies were tense and furious. I curled them into my lap, propping the bottles up again to their mouths and waited. Between the sound of my rapid heart beating and the television muffled by the dividing wall calmed them down and one by one, they began to simmer. Their cries dwindled to low murmurs and then drifted into a peaceful slumber, suckling over their bottles.

OMG! I can't believe it worked!

I took a deep exhale of relief, amazed by my own brilliance. The sun was starting to set, sending beams of golden light into the room, warming us on the bed, almost like a halo around them. Aiden grabbed my finger with his tiny hand, holding it tighter than an ill fitted ring.

And then, like someone had opened a window, cool air filled my lungs.

"Wow," I whispered, unable to tear my eyes away from them. They were breathtaking. They didn't look like pruned up moles, angry milk leeches, or even aliens. They were rather angelic, remarkable, and I never noticed before, but they were the absolute perfect blend of Bad Habit and me with their toffee colored faces.

"Wow." It was all I could muster. The wondrous creatures, the ones I'd been terrified of and dreaded for months, were nothing short of perfect. I kissed his hand as my heart exploded.

"Perfect."

"Alex!" I heard Bad Habit call my name from downstairs in a panic, figuring he saw the mess in the kitchen and Sasha chained up outside.

A moment later, he came sprinting into the room like he was expecting a crime scene. He stopped short, noticing us on the bed.

"Whoa," he whispered. "They're all sleeping."

I nodded and kissed their heads gently, inhaling their fresh baby soft skin. They smelled wondrously new, like spring with a hint of baby powder.

My new favorite smell.

"I...bought you some ice cream. Strawberry," he said and raised the bags that were still in his hands.

"No thanks," I said, not bothering to look at him.

I have something much sweeter.

Surprised, his eyebrow arched as he watched me, but he could've been on another planet for all I cared. I had just fallen in love with my own children. An irrevocable, indescribable, ineffable kind of love. One that erased all my previous thoughts, feelings, and misconceptions. Nothing else mattered except them.

Even if I'll never wear a bikini again and could literally use my extra sagging belly skin as a picnic blanket.

Bad Habit, feeling the peace of the moment, set the bags down and took off his jacket and shoes. He climbed into the bed with us, wrapped his arm around my waist, and placed his chin over my shoulder, staring with me at their pure exquisiteness. He marveled at them the same way I did. Something we could both agree on, for once.

Who says happy endings have to be perfect?

"Braxton?" I whispered without thinking.

Bad Habit smirked. "Yes?"

I chuckled and shook the thought away with a satisfied sigh.

"Nothing. Just felt like saying your name."

Braxton smiled and held me tighter.

***

Dear Alex,

Stop leaving your journal around. And you need to work on your spelling.

Best,

Braxton a.k.a. Bad Habit

Acknowledgements

I'd like to thank God for blessing me with this incredible life and sending me signs when I absolutely needed them. Thanks to my parents for always supporting my weirdness, even though I hope you never read this book. Thanks to my Brother for being the infant I was able to raise. Thanks to the Grandparents, Godparents, and Aunts who raised me. Thanks to my mentors Tayari Jones and Marie Brown for soothing my anxious writer nerves and answering my annoying emails. Thanks to my editor Tee, you can make a book bleed but your notes are hilarious!

Shout out Santagati for being the best ex ever! Shout out my fake Trini and crazy writer sister Raquel, I am in awe of you. Shout out to Malik 16, Indigo, and Keiry Joy, Tara, and Jihaad for being my family. Shout out to my ROC Girls, Nicole J, Nicole W, Tiffany T, Tiffany S, Simone and Adana for being my sisters. I'm so glad I went to Howard U. Shout out my crazy clique, Eb, Aura, Shanelle, Jess, J Mo, Starr, and Monee for always including me, even when I'm too busy writing to join. Shout out the Ladies, Crystal, Lyneka, T. Nicole, Sue for BK summers and s'mores. Big ups to Brooklyn, the Write in BK Fam, and all those who come to my Christmas parties. Shout out to my dog child Oscar for forgoing walks so Mommy can finish her morning pages.

And shout out to Bad Habit for being the inspiration...and the lesson.

About The Author

Blu Daniels is a TV professional by day, novelist by night, awkward black girl 24/7. A Howard University graduate and Brooklyn native, she is a lover of naps, cookie dough, and beaches. She currently resides in BK with her adorable chihuahua, Oscar, working on her next two novels.

Follow her on twitter @BluDaniels

Learn more at:

http://bludaniels.blogspot.com

http://writeinbk.com

Excerpt from *BAD HABIT*
Coming Fall 2014

"**N**o! And you can't make me!"

"Alexandria, for the last time, get out the damn car!"

"No!" she shouted, sounding more like a snot nosed bratty toddler than the mother of four. I held the door open while she glued herself to the seat, crossing her arms in ridiculous protest. She wouldn't even look at me.

"Alexandria...Get. Out. The. Car. Right. Now," I hissed, gripping the door. There was a slight hesitation in her eyes. After a few moments frozen like a statue, she slowly came back to life. Unbuckling her seat belt, she stormed out the car with a huff, slammed the door shut and stumbled before catching herself, glancing to see if I noticed.

Always the graceful one.

We were parked outside the Atlanta Superior Courthouse on a blistering hot afternoon. The sun was just starting to set on my patience. The patience I reserved for days I had to deal with the stubborn bitch. I rubbed my throbbing temple that only beats

318 | Blu Daniels

around her. Every gray hair I have on my body in my young age, I hold Alex personally responsible for.

"I can't believe you're making me do this," she growled under her breath. "Look at me, I look a mess!"

She had on loose fitting jeans, a stained stretched out v-neck top, and the crusty sneakers she wore when running errands, which we just completed. Her face was void of makeup and her long, rich, black hair was pulled back in a sloppy bun. I shrugged, pretending not to care. Actually, I didn't care.

"We have to. Now, let's go."

I headed towards the main stairs, fully expecting her to follow but found myself walking alone.

Damn this woman!

She avoids my glare, holding her stubborn pout as I charged back. But the way she jumped and her widening eyes said it all. She was scared, as she should have been. She was wasting my time with her headstrong bullshit.

"What is it now Alexandria?"

She shook her head, fuming.

"No dress. No reception. No cake. No wedding. No RING!"

I loosened the tie stifling my neck and I kept a level tone. Yelling wouldn't get me anywhere, especially with her.

Hustlers Commandment # 6: Never raise your voice. The loudest one in the room is the dumbest.

"Well we won't be able to afford any of that if I continue paying your medicals bills out of pocket."

"This is fucking nuts! I won't do it and you can't make me," she screamed, stomping her foot down, drawing attention to her ludicrous tantrum. I rolled my eyes and glanced down at my watch. It was five thirty.

He'll be leaving soon.

"Fine," I grumbled.

"Fine," she snapped, narrowing her eyes at me as opened the car door.

Not so fast!

With one swift move, I seized her forearm, spin her around, and throw her over my shoulder, cave man style.

"Ahhh...put me down you bastard!"

She kicked and wiggled but it was like one of the kids trying to fight their way out of my hold. I marched up the stairs of the courthouse with little effort. A year ago, this feat would have been impossible. They said Alexandria weighed close to two hundred pounds during her last trimester. But she lost most of the baby weight within six months without even trying. Being responsible for four infants, you tend to forget to feed yourself in the process.

"Braxton put me down! I'm not fucking playing!" she screamed, bucking like an untamed horse, hitting my back with the palms of her hands as we entered the building.

I carried her wailing body through the halls until locating the office in question. Knocking quickly, I let myself in and just as I suspected, Judge Dennis was hanging his up his robe, about to leave for the weekend.

"Braxton? What a surprise!" he said, eyeing Alexandria curiously. "What brings you by?"

Judge Richard Dennis was a close family friend that I had known for years and had been instrumental in my career advancement. He wrote an outstanding recommendation letter for Law School and spoke to Mr. Paul at the Etose Firm about my capabilities. He was a role model and my most trusted mentor.

"Help! He's kidnapped me!"

"Judge, you think you can marry us?" I asked, skipping the pleasantries.

He frowned, taking another look at Alex, still violently wiggling over my shoulder.

"Ummm... right now?"

"Yes, right now if you don't mind?"

He hesitated, glancing at his blonde court clerk, Helen, sitting at her mahogany desk in the corner. She crossed her arms, annoyed by our sudden presence.

"Uhhh...and you think your...uhhh...friend here wants to?

"NO!" Alex screamed.

"Yes, she wants to," I corrected.

"Really," he laughed. "Well, usually you carry your bride over the threshold after the wedding."

"Cold feet. Trust me, she's ready."

He took another glance at Helen before letting out an uneasy chuckle and shrugged.

"Alright. Let me just get my book. Helen, would you pull up the forms please?"

He disappeared into his chambers as the juvenile clerk rolled her blue eyes at me. My unexpected visit was keeping her working longer than she intended. Her tits looked good as hell though. Ignoring the hostility, I walked over to the leather sofa next near the window and threw Alex down like a sack of potatoes.

"Owww!" she screamed, fumbling to get her bearings. She stared up at me with her dark, gorgeous chocolate eyes, infuriated.

"Listen, we have to do this now or your insurance is going to double on Monday and Dr. Keegan isn't exactly the cheapest doctor on the block."

"Oh, so you're forcing me to marry you just so you can save some money? Be damned if you did it for love!"

I grinned. These type of outbursts used to irate me to the point of insanity. But now, they're entertaining, in fact, rather comical. Seeing her fist clenched up, cheeks puffed, and eyes wild like ferocious puppy.

"Look, let's just do this now so we have the proper paper work and we'll worry about the big production shenanigans later. Alright?"

And exactly how I presumed, her eyes eased up. She liked that idea, but would never concede to that fact.

"Fine," she barked. "But I don't like you. Not one bit!"

"That's fine," I said with a nonchalant shrug, just as Judge Dennis stepped out of his office.

"Ok, lets...uh...get started. Helen, would you stand as a witness?"

I yoked Alex up to her feet and she unwillingly stood with her arms crossed. Judge Dennis ran through the procedure as she continued to sulk, sucking her teeth at every other word. She glanced at her watch, tapping her foot on the carpet, as if we were holding her up from nothing. I wanted to shake the shit out of her.

"Do you, Braxton Earwood, take Alexandria Stone to be your lawfully wedded wife?"

"I do," I said, staring down at her scrunched up face as she rolled her eyes in response.

"And do you," Judge Dennis started cautiously. "Alexandria Stone, take Braxton to be your lawfully wedded husband?"

The entire room paused in suspense. Alex gazed around, rocking on her heels, humming. Fucking humming!

Like a damn child, I swear!

"Alexandria," I growled.

She sucked her teeth and checked her nails. Judge Dennis threw me a nervous glance.

"Alexandria!"

"Aight! Yeah, yeah, yeah, whateva. I do," she snapped in her thick New York accent.

Judge Brown raised an eyebrow but continued.

"Then by the power invested in me and the State of Georgia I now pronounce you husband and wife. You may now...uh...kiss your bride."

"Gah," she snorted and I grinned, only because I accomplished the last item on my things to do list for the day.

#10 Marry Alexandria.

I stepped towards her, cupping her pouty face. Her once stormy eyes softened in my gaze. There was always something about her eyes that made it hard to focus at times. They held a thousand emotions, none of which she was able to hide very well, although she tries. But my dick gets hard every time I look into them. She gulped and stared up at me, right before I tongued her down, clutching her closer to me, erasing all of her pent up tension.

She's too easy.

With a nip of her bottom lip, I let go and steadied her before she lost her balance. Her eyes lit up, face shocked. She knows I hate public displays of affection, but it was necessary for the moment. She mouthed a 'whoa,' eyes crossing slightly.

After we signed the necessary paper work and paid the fee, Helen made copies of our license and walked it down to the state office for filing. Alex stood by the door, quiet and somber, probably daydreaming, as she often did. She had a tendency to get lost in her own world.

"Thanks Judge. Forgive me for the last minute request. I owe you one," I said, shaking his hand. Alex snarled and walked out.

"It's quite alright Braxton," he said, bewildered from the last thirty minutes spent in his office. "Let's schedule lunch sometime next month. I want to talk you about something."

"Sure. Will do, sir," I said and followed a sullen Alex out the courthouse.

The sun was set and the sky was an array of blues. A few orange streetlights illuminated the empty parking lot. As we strolled back to the car, I reviewed our marriage license for the third time, just to ensure she signed it properly, using her real name, and not a fictitious one. She did seem that childish. I planned to fax it to my insurance company as soon as we reached home. Alex was still pretty quiet. She stared at the ground with slumped, defeated shoulders.

"Well, that was easy," I said cheerfully, knowing my demeanor would drive her insane.

"I hate you," she mumbled, stomping her feet.

"Yeah, I know, and that's fine, MRS. Earwood!"

Her head shot up at the sound of her new name.

"Yuck," she seethed and bolted ahead of me. And at that very moment, something about the way her ass moved in her jeans, how her shoulders arched back, and the sight of her back of her long neck, made me want her. Bad.

Just as we reached the car, I skipped ahead of her to open the door. The back door.

"What is this? Now you're driving Ms. Daisy?"

I smiled. "Just get in."

Confused, she hesitated for a moment before climbing into the truck. I followed, pushing her along the cream leather seats before closing the door behind me.

"What are you doing?" she snapped but I was focused on her lips. Thick, pouty pink, and tasty. I gripped her waist and pulled her towards me. Her stiff body froze at my touch as I kissed the spot on her neck, right below her ear.

"What are you doing?" she repeated, her voice softening as she weakly tried to squirm away.

"It's our honeymoon," I replied, muffled as I kissed the back of her neck. She smelled like oranges and baby powder. Her body started to melt. I was tackling her defenses.

"Really? In the back of the car? Gee, how romantic."

She chuckled as if she thought I was joking, but I wasn't. I pulled her on top of me, eased up her shirt, and slid a hand around her breast. She squirmed but I locked my other hand around the back of her neck, holding her still. She let out a small moan.

Not talking shit now, huh?

A quickie was all I needed.

I laid her down across the seat and ripped off her jeans as she pulled at mine, pushing them down to my ankles. I slammed on top of her and she didn't fight me. She opened up and I slide in quick, leveling myself with the door and back of the seat.

"Ohhh...Braxton...but we're in the...ohhhh...I–"

"Shut up."

I flipped her on her stomach and she pushed against the window. I slammed into her, grabbing a handful of her thick ass. My strokes were banging her into the car door. I liked her in this position.

Damn, she feels so good.

"Braxton...AH...Braxton," she screamed as the truck rocked.

Her bun unraveled, hair draping over her shoulder. I grabbed hold of her long ponytail and pulled back, whispering in her ear.

"You don't like it? Your new name?"

"No...no...I love it," she moaned as I bite her earlobe. The glass began to fog. I grabbed her shoulders and her back arched, her skin hot under my touch. Her pussy starts to throb around me and I rammed into her harder.

"You sure?"

"Yes...yes, I...oh oh oh...ah!"

"You gonna cum?"

She let out a pent up scream and deflated.

"Yeah, that's what I thought."

Shit this feels good.

My nut was coming so I yanked her hair, just for being such a ridiculous fucking person this afternoon, before finishing with a groan.

Good thing I put those tints on last week.

We collapsed and laid curled up in the back seat. All I kept thinking was that I was out of shape and needed to hit a gym. Shouldn't have taken that much out of me to make her cum. Alex snuggled up to my chest, dozed and sated. She always conked out after sex. I watched her chest rise and fall, shooting shorts bouts of air through her nose. As hard, stubborn, and down right bitchy she could be, she was utterly peaceful and beautiful when she slept.

I'll give her another five minutes.

It wasn't my first choice to marry Alex. Not that I presumed I would never get married someday, just never thought it would be her. From the moment we met, now five years ago, we've had more ups and downs than an average rap career. But our relationship has been far from average. Many asked if I regretted fucking her. After all, she was only a jump off, barely had a friends with benefits status. To say I used her is a bit strong, however not a complete falsehood. But I wasn't ready for fatherhood, nor the responsibilities that came long with it. Regardless, I don't believe in regret and I wasn't about to turn out like my Pops.

We still had forty-five minutes on the sitter clock but the kids were probably antsy. The length of their patience matched their mother's. My phone vibrated on the drivers seat. I glanced at Alex, hoping it doesn't wake her.

It's probably Tiffany. I'll call her back later when Alex's asleep. Hope the word won't spread too quickly that I'm no longer a free man.

Alex stirred, her childlike eyes opening. There were moments, days, even weeks where I was completely indifferent about her.

From the very beginning, she wasn't exactly my type yet somehow, she always seemed to surprise me. Her beauty captivated my attention and before long, I found myself feigning for her. She had me dick whipped like some pussy. A man of my caliber should not be so easily taken. But she had the determination of a fruit fly, buzzing in my face relentlessly. I don't deny that I didn't want her, that I treated her like shit, or that it was selfish to keep her dangling by a mere string of hope, but what she wanted was more than I was ready to give. And what she was willing to take away, I wasn't ready to let go of.

"Hi," she whispered, her gorgeous smile gleaming.

"Hi."

"How long have I've been out?"

"Couple of minutes."

She stretched with a yawn and scratched the tip of her nose like a baby. I resisted the urge to cuddle her to my chest and stay in the back seat of our car forever.

She's absolutely adorable.

"Is it time to go?"

She cocked her head to the side and frowned. Seconds passed by before I realized I was staring and shook out of my daydream to focus.

"Yeah, just about," I replied and sat up in the cramped backseat, passing her the clothes I tore off and pulled up my pants.

She sighed with a shrug while dressing.

"Oh well, I guess back to the real world."

"Yeah, I guess, MRS. Edgewood."

"Quit it! That's not my name," she balked, hooking her bra back together. I snickered and buckled my belt.

It's going to be fun teasing her about this.

I opened the door and stepped out to stretch my legs.

"HEY!" She screamed, covering her half naked body with her shirt. "I'm still getting dressed back here! What's wrong with you?"

I glanced around the empty parking lot.

"There's no one else here but us."

"Still, you never know."

"Oh I'm sure the paparazzi got some great footage of the car rocking," I teased and walked around to the driver's side door. She sucked her teeth and finished dressing, sliding out of the back seat, stumbling over her own feet. I laughed and she cut me a stare.

"I hate you," she mumbled, opening the passenger side door.

I shrugged and climbed into the car.

"That's fine. I love you," I said and proceeded to check my Blackberry for any missed messages. I was right. Tiffany had called and sent a text.

Hey Baby, What R U up 2?

I smiled, remembering the last time I saw her, wearing that royal blue halter dress showing every curve around her tiny waist.

The way she looked in that dress...that ass...those legs...damn.

I shook away the thought and turned the ignition. I was just about to pull off when I noticed the door ajar light and turned to Alex. She stood outside the car, eyes bulging, mouth gaped open.

"What the fuck's wrong with you? Get in the car, we have to go!"

Her head snapped as if she just woke up then scrambled into the car. She fumbled with the door, struggling with the seat belt like she had never used it before.

Shit, I really hope the kids don't inherit her goofiness.

She stopped fidgeting and dug her nails into the sides of her seat, breathing heavy as she stared out the windshield. Something had spooked her stupid.

"You ok?"

"Yeah, I'm fine," she croaked out. "I just...well...I...love you too."

Her face immediately turned red under her dark butterscotch skin as her eyes locked on the floor.

"Oh," I said, catching wind of her feeling. Right. We had never uttered those words to each other before. It surprised us both that I would be so spontaneous since I wasn't the type to speak without calculating my every word.

But...do I really love her?

We sat in silence, both contemplating the significance of the historic moment. Real talk, Alex was never the quintessential Mrs. Right. She was irritatingly annoying, impatient, and had the air of a spoiled brat with an adult's fuming temper. Yet, I couldn't picture my life without her. Looking past all her faults, bottom line was she an incredible mother to our children, something I valued highly. She was bright and witty, whether I'm laughing at her or with her and though I can't confirm the exact number of woman I've been with (I stopped counting after fifty) I was sure no other woman felt as good as her.

So maybe I do love her...in a sort of perverse way.

I never doubted she loved me but I had to admit, it was relieving to actually hear her vocalize it. I cleared my throat to break up the awkward silence.

"Come on, let's go see what your rugrats are up to," I said with a grin, putting the car in drive.

She bit her lower lip and nodded, smiling like she was about to explode with happiness. And as crazy as it sounds, I couldn't help but feel the same way.

Made in the USA
Middletown, DE
11 August 2015